# Blood Music

# Blood Music

**A NOVEL**

*Jessie Prichard Hunter*

TURTLE BAY BOOKS
A DIVISION OF RANDOM HOUSE·NEW YORK
1993

Library of Congress Cataloging-in-Publication Data
Hunter, Jessie Prichard.
Blood music: a novel/Jessie Prichard Hunter.—1st ed.
p.    cm.
ISBN 0-679-41824-5
I. Title.
PS3558.U4815B56      1992
813'.54—dc20                                          92-50495

Manufactured in the United States of America
on acid-free paper

2   4   6   8   9   7   5   3

First Edition

*To my mother, Lois Hartley*

# Blood Music

# 1

The air was very still. If you sang a "fa," say, in the key of A—that would be a D—if you sang a D it would simply hang there on the air, without an echo, for as long as it took to slide the knife in.

The young woman was kneeling in the grass with her back to the man, playing with a baby. The baby was just learning to walk. The man couldn't tell whether it was a boy baby or a girl baby. It would walk two or three steps and fall down, on its butt, on its knees. The young woman was laughing.

The man would play a game: If the woman turned around and saw him he would kill her. Not do what he usually did—not with the baby there—but just use the knife. If she didn't turn around he wouldn't kill her.

He looked at his watch. If it was a game there had to be rules; there had to be a time limit. The woman was playing with the baby about thirty feet away from the manicured hedge around the president's house. This was a secluded part of the campus, overlooking the river. A lot of students didn't even know about it. Even though it was one of those March days that are an early taste of spring to come, there weren't any young couples half-hidden in the grass or looking out at Manhattan across the river. Ten forty-eight. If the woman didn't turn around and see him in three minutes he wouldn't kill her.

The woman turned her head. He could see the slope of her cheekbone, her downturned mouth. Her face was calm but her mouth turned down anyway, she had a pout like somebody, some old black-and-white actress. She seemed to be listening. The knife handle was sweaty; he didn't like that. He couldn't afford to lose his grip.

The baby mewed like a cat and the woman turned away without seeing him. Blond hair. He'd always loved blond hair. An image rose in his mind: blond hair matted with blood. Long blond hair matted with blood.

The Circle Line tour boat was going by, sightseers on the river. Why had he thought of that? It seemed almost like a memory, but he had no such memory. Not of hair just that color. The memory seemed sepia-tinted. The woman was pointing at the Circle Line, showing it to the baby. The skyline of Manhattan shimmered like a mirage in the morning sun. Two minutes and forty seconds to go.

The baby was looking at something, it had picked up a rock. It looked at it as though it had never seen such a thing in its life. For some reason that struck the man as funny. He wiped the handle of the knife along his pants leg while he laughed silently, holding the blade carefully so he wouldn't cut himself. He couldn't bear the sight of his own blood.

Two minutes and fifteen seconds. The baby was sitting quietly, looking at its rock. The Circle Line was gone. The woman was looking out toward the water, at the sunlight shimmering on the water. He could image what she looked like full-face, the pouty mouth.

Bloody blond hair matted across an open mouth. He roused himself, he was dreaming under the warm sun. One minute and forty-two seconds. He saw the woman's back tense, a fine light shiver like a ripple across the coat of an animal. She knew somebody was watching her. It was funny how women knew. Stare at them long enough and they always know it, as if sight were a weapon, a burning beam.

The woman reached out and touched the baby, a light caress down its back. To make sure it was okay. One minute five seconds. The baby looked up and chortled: a butterfly. The woman's stiff back relaxed—a butterfly. Small and yellow, they were called cabbage butterflies. The Finnish say that if the first butterfly of the season is yellow that means it's going to be a good summer. He remembered that from books he'd read as a child, they were called the Moomintroll books. One minute even.

The butterfly fluttered above the baby's head. Maybe it was the white ones that were called cabbage butterflies. He didn't know what the yellow ones were called. Bette Davis. A mouth like Bette Davis's.

The baby was delighted. The man could see part of the woman's face again, the fine line of her nose, her mouth widening in a smile as she looked from the baby to the butterfly and back to the baby. He couldn't see what color her eyes were; he wondered what color her eyes were.

One blood-spattered blue eye, staring at the low ceiling. Forty-five seconds. The woman turned her head; she saw him. She had a pretty face.

The man tightened the muscles around his jaw: a smile. Her own smile was like the beat of a butterfly's wing, tenuous, afraid. Then broader, because she was with the baby and she expected indulgence. He bared his teeth. He hoped that was an indulgent smile. He would have liked to spring, like a leopard, to show her his true essence. To come at her like a bolt of clawed lightning out of the clear blue sky.

Her eyes were blue. He walked toward her; what would be the last thing that she saw? "Little bookus," she was saying to the baby. She had already forgotten him. "Little bookus." The leaves of the tree above her head, in a pattern against the sky, a white cloud. That would be the last thing.

He walked behind her and she didn't see the knife in his hand. It was so easy. He jerked her head back so fast she didn't have time to cry out, and he slit her throat. The green leaves, a white cloud.

The blood flew out in a perfect arc and he laughed aloud. The baby watched but made no sound. That was good. That had been a risk.

The woman gurgled, once. He felt it, like always, like love. There was blood in her blue eyes. Just that one small sound, a trapped cry, an unfinished note. He walked away without looking back. When he got a little way away he started to whistle.

The baby was looking at its mother. The butterfly had come back. The baby put out a tiny hand. The butterfly dipped for a moment to the blood at the woman's neck. The baby reached up to touch the butterfly; its hand was covered with blood. The baby laughed. The melody, hanging on the air without an echo, of Schubert's Quartetsatz.

# 2

Hoboken is haunted by its waterfront. Forty years ago the waterfront breathed like an anthill, it heaved and pulsated with working men. The boys went off to World War II from the Hoboken waterfront, and to its dirty grandeur they came home. Marlon Brando filmed *On the Waterfront* here, down by the Hudson River, by the Maxwell House plant. The Maxwell House sign is famous. It can be seen from across the water: GOOD TO THE LAST DROP.

Hoboken is without grace; it is a very friendly dog with mange. It is the proud hometown of Frank Sinatra. All the Italian restaurants (and there are many) boast little shrines to Frankie, walls full of pictures signed, "To my favorite chef." The two cappuccino cafés on Washington Street play Sinatra music all the time. Hoboken is made up largely of three- and four-story tenement row houses; there is always garbage in the street. West of Washington the streets have flowery names: Bloomfield, Garden, Park. Where the old Italians and young couples from across the river give way to Hispanics and Indians and blacks, where the one project is, the streets have presidents' names: Jefferson, Madison, Monroe.

The tiny parks are full of dog droppings. There are many, many children and new babies. For two weeks in April the short oval poplar trees bloom, and the town is almost pretty. White flowers cover the trees like a mist, and then they fall off and blow through the streets, collecting in milky puddles in the gutters.

The whole spread of the Manhattan skyline lies across the river from Hoboken, a gentle, taunting, undulating curve of beauty and success. Stevens Institute of Technology lies along a promontory above the river. Couples come to Castle Point Overlook on the weekends, often with baby carriages. They can see the World Trade Centers at Battery Park, and all the way south to the Verrazano Bridge, which shimmers like distant medieval battlements. From farther up the campus they can see north to the George Washington Bridge.

In spring, when the temperature sometimes goes to ninety, people come out of their apartments like prairie dogs; they head up to Stevens and lie on the grass in their bathing suits, watching tour boats from the Circle Line go by.

Many of the Stevens students live in dorms on campus or in the beautiful Victorian homes that line the streets directly around the grounds. These the college has converted into frat houses. There are great hundred-year-old stone houses with bedrooms enough for twelve children. There are stone towers, flights of stone steps up to front doors, stone lions guarding the front doors, bay windows. Inside there are fancy moldings on the living room ceilings, and big, overheavy chandeliers.

Zelly Wyche liked to go walking in that part of town, liked to look in the windows and think about other people's lives.

She and her husband, Pat, liked to take the baby up to the
Stevens campus on the weekends and look at the river. Zelly
had grown up on one of those streets, in her mother's house,
a great big rambling warren with five cherry trees in the
backyard.

One weekday morning in late April, Zelly was sitting at
the dining room table reading *The New York Times*. She
wished she were sitting at a table in a big, airy kitchen, looking out the windows at the fruit trees in the backyard. But
there was no table in the kitchen, and no window, and no
backyard. There wasn't even a dining room; the table was in
the living room, in front of the bookcases. Pat's books,
mostly. And she'd really rather be reading the *Post*; it was a
rag but it was more fun than the *Times*. Pat had the *Times*
delivered so Zelly could read it in the mornings the rare
moments she wasn't tending to the baby, but by afternoon
she usually gave in and bought the *Post*.

Today she would certainly buy the *Post*. WOMAN FOUND
DEAD IN THE WEST VILLAGE, read the *Times*. The *Post* would
have a screaming, satisfying headline: SLASHER STRIKES AGAIN!
That was the fifth one. One of the murders had actually
happened in Hoboken, fifteen minutes from the West Village
by the PATH train. Zelly was sure it was the same killer.

There had been five murders in four months: one in Hoboken, three in the Village, and one just below the Village, in
SoHo. The one in Hoboken wasn't the first, and it didn't
really seem to be the work of the same killer: the woman
wasn't raped. She was found knifed to death in broad daylight; her baby boy was found sitting next to her. The baby
had blood on it. The *Post* had had a field day with that; if the
baby hadn't had blood on it the *Post* would never have covered a murder in New Jersey.

The other four victims had been found with their throats

slit and their bodies repeatedly stabbed, raped right before or
right after they died. Even the *Post* was reticent on that point.
All but one of the women had been blond. Even the Hoboken
woman was blond. "Attractive," as though that were a pre-
requisite for getting yourself killed.

Zelly considered herself something of an expert on serial
killers. The Son of Sam killings had happened in New York
City in the seventies, when Zelly was twelve. That's what
started it for her. A postal worker in his twenties named
David Berkowitz called himself Son of Sam and shot girls
with long dark hair. Sometimes he couldn't see properly and
shot boys with long dark hair. He killed three people and left
one woman paralyzed and one man with a steel plate in his
head before the police caught him.

Zelly followed every detail of the Son of Sam case as it
developed. It wasn't every day that a serial killer operated
right across the river, with stories daily in the papers and
reports nightly on the television news. Son of Sam even sent
letters to Jimmy Breslin at the *Daily News,* vaguely poetic,
terrifying maunderings that Zelly spent hours trying to de-
code.

One night Zelly and her cousin went with his father to an
apartment building in Forest Hills where his father worked as
a doorman. They were going to pick up some things from an
apartment where somebody had died, a chair and some
books. Zelly waited in the car while her cousin and her uncle
went upstairs to get the stuff. Sitting alone in the car under
the streetlight, she realized that the street on which the car
was parked was the very same street where Son of Sam had
shot and killed a nineteen-year-old girl a month before. Zelly
didn't know how far away it had happened, two blocks or a
mile or three doors down. She got a comb out of her purse
and started to comb her long blond hair, thinking, sending a

message to Sam: It's blond, Sam, look if you're out there, this is blond hair, it's not dark at all, it's light. She was scared to death. Lots of girls cut or dyed their hair that summer.

From that time on, Zelly had found her avocation. The body in the wood, the vampire invisible among the daylight crowd, became her area of expertise, until by the time Pat met her she was a party-talk encyclopedia on the intricacies of the sociopath's desires, the psychopath's will.

When Zelly had begun her reading, serial killers had still been called mass murderers. Now mass murderers were people who killed a lot of other people all at once, the way that man did down in Texas, aiming his gun at random but shifting the muzzle away and firing whenever he caught sight of a woman out of the corner of his eye. Serial killers usually killed women or little boys or teenagers—almost never fully grown men—and generally they raped or mutilated their victims. Zelly knew all about it, Dean Corll down in Houston— she couldn't even think about that—John Wayne Gacy in Chicago, the Green River Killer in Seattle, still uncaught eleven years later.

Son of Sam wasn't like those; he was simple, elemental. He never touched the people he killed. But the West Village Slasher, as the papers were calling him, raped and he knifed. There hadn't been any mutilations in these killings; Zelly thought of Dean Corll even though she didn't want to. They found one victim with his penis gnawed almost in half; he was thirteen years old. When the Slasher killed he held the head back, exposing the jugular vein like an offering. And then he stabbed, eight wounds, five wounds, eighteen. Morton Street, Greenwich, the West Side Highway.

The first of the Slasher murders had occurred back in January. The woman had been twenty-two, of Riverside in the Bronx, and she was supposed to meet some friends at a surprisingly elegant Spanish restaurant down near the old docks on the icy, run-down riverfront. Her body was found one block over and two blocks in, next to a flight of iron steps leading down to a deserted basement in an otherwise occupied building; the steps were covered with debris—black plastic garbage bags and broken bottles and used condoms—and the frayed rope that hung across the entrance had been neatly cut. The woman's face was frozen in a puddle of shiny, blood-scummed water; the body had to be pried free with ice picks.

The second victim was found on Morton Street in late February, many blocks over and down, in an entirely safe part of the neighborhood. Her body lay naked inside the narrow vestibule of her apartment building, her hand clutching a set of bloody keys. Eighteen years old, and she'd arrived in the city less than a year ago to study art at Parsons. The papers love a murder like that one.

The third was the March murder on the Stevens campus. Few of the newspaper articles included this one in their lists of the killings. She'd been twenty-six, just two years younger than Zelly.

In the first week of April there was a killing in SoHo, just south of the West Village, in which the victim had had brown hair. She had been murdered the same way, raped and then knifed, and left half-clothed next to a construction Dumpster. She had been cut with particular ferocity. Thirty-four years old, older than the others. Not blond, not young enough. The papers had hesitated: she wasn't the Slasher's type. But Zelly had known immediately that she was a Slasher victim. And now Cheryl Nassent, only three weeks after the last killing, proving Zelly right; why would he kill again so soon, if not to make up for his mistake?

Zelly knew all the victims' names. The first was Belinda Boston, a beautiful name; she was the worst for Zelly, who could not get out of her mind the image she had seen on television, police workers bundled against the January cold, wielding long-handled ice picks and talking to one another as they worked. The second was Elizabeth Moscineska, a strange name, Zelly thought, for Nebraska. Rosalie Howard on the Stevens campus; then Linda Swados, damned by the press for dying too dark and too old, as though she had cheated a more deserving young blonde out of a particularly American death. Of course none of the women resembled the others in the least, their hair ranging from Midwestern corn-colored to ash. And plain brown for Linda. But to the killer they had probably all been the same woman.

Zelly read the article in the paper twice. In the other room the baby was sleeping. While she read Zelly unconsciously pulled at her bottom lip with her teeth. Pat kept telling her to try to stop but she couldn't; it was just nerves. Cheryl Nassent had been nineteen years old. She was found late last night on the West Side Highway by a passing motorist. Naked, her throat slashed. The police didn't think she'd died far from there. She was more poignant in life to Zelly than the others had been in death: there was something in the newspaper picture of Cheryl that reminded Zelly of herself, a certain shy bravado behind the there's-a-camera-pointed-at-me smile.

Cheryl had been out on the town with a bunch of friends. Everybody was high and it was such a night, seventy degrees at ten o'clock, the last week of April. Zelly had wanted to go out last night but her mother wasn't feeling well so she couldn't baby-sit, and then Pat had to work late anyway. He did electrical work, wiring. Wyche Electric. He didn't have a storefront yet, just the van and his tools, but he'd always wanted to start his own business and he could fix anything electrical; he could make wires sing. He'd begun the business back in November, about the same time the baby was born.

Zelly was terribly proud of him, making a go of it by himself, thirty-one years old and already making it with his own business. Still, she was getting tired of being so much alone.

Cheryl had gotten separated from the others somehow, going from one bar to another, everybody drunk and laughing all over the street. That was in the middle of the Village, at MacDougal and Bleecker, where all the tourists and the people from the boroughs went. Nobody knew how Cheryl got over to the West Village. Zelly thought that probably the police knew she hadn't been carried far after she died because of the way the blood settled. Pat thought she was morbid.

The baby stirred in her crib in the other room. Zelly didn't hear it but she felt it. In a minute the baby would start to cry. Zelly always knew, when the baby was still in her womb and it didn't move for a while she could make it move by thinking about it. Mary. Six months old now.

Zelly looked up from the paper. Her eyes were crystal blue, and her mouth was wide. She looked about eighteen. She looked every moment as though she were about to smile.

"Found naked at the side of the West Side Highway." Zelly could remember having stopped to talk to Rosalie Howard once, on the street outside Bel Gusto, where she went to buy cappuccino muffins, which she ate surreptitiously while Mary was napping. Zelly and Rosalie had talked about losing weight, about how hard it was to lose what you gained when you got pregnant. Rosalie had had a very big baby boy, and they'd talked about that, how much bigger the boys are and how much more they eat; Rosalie's boy was meaty, he looked like a tiny sumo wrestler. And Rosalie had told her about the mothers' group she wanted to start, just four or five neighborhood mothers and their babies getting together once or twice a week. "You lose touch, you know?" Rosalie'd said. "You start thinking that nobody else has ever had your problems." And Zelly had nodded a vigorous assent.

After that Zelly and Rosalie had smiled at each other whenever they met, pushing their strollers up and down Washington Street in the afternoon. Zelly always meant to stop and get to know her better. Now she was dead.

Mary was crying. Pat might come home for lunch; he almost never did but he might. And Zelly liked to have the house nice for him. He worked so hard. If she started now she could vacuum the living room and wipe down the kitchen and make a couple of sandwiches before lunchtime. She looked at Cheryl Nassent's smile and folded the paper and went to tend her baby.

# 3

John Nassent was pulling himself back together. He didn't really remember the funeral, and so far he hadn't gone back to see the grave. Two weeks. Cheryl was buried in Calvary Cemetery, an enormous city of the dead that stretched for half a mile on either side of the Long Island Expressway.

John kept expecting Cheryl to come down the stairs for breakfast in the mornings. His wife was gone, and now Cheryl was gone. John had been married for eight months. Molly hadn't liked Cheryl. She hadn't liked the way John and Cheryl could sit silently, for hours, reading or watching television or just looking out at the yard from the back porch; she had not been brought up in silence. John had no defense against her accusations that he and Cheryl seemed to communicate without words and to need nothing but each other's company. Molly said it made her feel like the other woman.

But John and Cheryl lived deep below the surface, where if

no light fell at least there was the assurance that no danger could penetrate either.

John had risen to the surface once, to love Molly, and then his silence had quenched her flame. She could not follow him, and she could not free him. He too had the capacity to burn, and burn ferociously, but so far neither love nor rage had much troubled his depths. When Molly left he had signed everything, paid for the lawyers, wished her well. He had not questioned her and he had not fought for her. But now his sister had been raped and murdered.

John came by his reticence by blood. When Cheryl was killed he could not believe it—literally could not—because it had already happened. When he was nine years old his mother had been found broken across the hood of a white Chevy Impala. She had been raped and then thrown off the roof of the twenty-four-story building where they lived in Fresh Meadows, Queens. Two boys did it, seventeen, eighteen years old. They dragged her up to the roof as she got in the elevator and nobody heard. John's father kept expecting her to come back from the movies around eleven. At eleven twenty-five the whole south side of the building heard a thud. John's family lived on the north side, on the seventh floor. They didn't hear the thud, and they didn't hear the screaming either. The papers made sure they found out about the screaming.

Cheryl had been six months old. She didn't remember her mother at all. She didn't remember the trial. How the two boys had planned the crime, everything but the victim, for months. How they waited at the elevator. How they dragged her up the last flight of steps, where the door to the roof was never locked, how for twenty-five minutes they raped her, how one of them had balked at the last minute at throwing her over the edge and the other one had said,

"The bitch is history, man, don't you want to hear it when she goes?"

John's father had heard it for the rest of his life. After the murder the family had moved a few miles away, to Bayside. They never spoke about his mother; his father almost never spoke at all. It was as though what he was listening to in his head were more compelling than any momentary reality. And John never knew, all his life he would wonder, was his father listening for the turn of the key in the door or was he listening for screams?

John's father had died a year ago. Liver cancer. John didn't know whether to be sad or happy. John knew that as a last tribute to his wife his father wanted a terrible death, but he had made sure his father was denied that. The last thing his father said was, "I won't have to listen to it anymore," but he was on morphine then and didn't know what he was saying. At the funeral neither John nor Cheryl had cried.

One night when John was seventeen a group of his friends went to somebody's apartment, the parents weren't home, and it was in the building in Fresh Meadows. On the nineteenth floor. After they'd been there awhile somebody said, hey, it's a nice night, let's go up on the roof. We can look at the stars. And John walked up the staircase where the rape and murder couldn't have happened but it did happen.

It was easy to get up to the roof. Nobody had ever locked the door. That hurt John, that nobody ever bothered to make sure the roof door was locked even after his mother was raped and murdered up there.

Everybody was high, and nobody knew about his mother. John wished he could remember her better. He looked around the roof under the crescent moon; he wondered which corner it had happened in. There were no stars. For some reason he was sure it must have happened in a corner. He drank a lot of beer. The moon got farther and farther away. He and his friends sat leaning against the low brick wall behind the door—was it here? If it were daylight would he see the faint stains of blood that eight years of weather had failed to erase? He drank and drank. He had read once when he was a little kid that the vibration of a sound never stops unless something stops it. If you bang on the side of a lamppost that hollow sound it makes will go on and on forever unless you lay your hand against the cold metal and kill the sound. John had always imagined that the sound just moved farther and farther out into space, forever. Were his mother's screams still echoing somewhere out in infinite space, in the dark, alone? What could he grasp to stop them?

The crescent moon was moving when John decided to take a walk along the edge of the wall. Dirty white cement, about a foot wide. He looked at the moon while he walked. Everybody thought it was hilarious. He spread out his arms and thought about flying. What would it feel like to fly? What had it felt like to fall? He used his arms as rudders against the sticky summer-night air, and he leaned way out over the edge of the wall. Like a bird flying. It was such a long way, there were toy cars and toy trees and a make-believe sidewalk down there. There was even a white car. He thought that if he fell the act of falling would be frozen forever, he would be falling forever, like a sound, above the toy trees and the toy cars and the make-believe sidewalk.

His girlfriend grabbed his ankle. He almost did fall then, he really thought he was going to fall. He never forgave himself the look on her face. He never told Cheryl.

Cheryl had grown up quiet in that quiet house. She was so

afraid of worrying her father that she barely let herself make friends; she was always in by nine. Cheryl was plain, the kind of plain that becomes beautiful once you fall in love with it, but nobody had ever fallen in love with it. Cheryl went to school, she came home. She volunteered with child burn victims once a week. She went to the movies alone. She saw *Raiders of the Lost Ark* eighteen times when it came out. John thought that that's what she thought she was, or hoped she could be: the professor who took off her glasses and changed her hat and all kinds of wonderful, exciting things would happen to her.

In the last year she'd gotten a low-level job at a travel agency and made some friends, loud people, the harmless kind of wild. She was thinking about joining the Peace Corps. Of taking all her love and dedication and quiet efficiency and capacity for wildness somewhere nobody knew her and just inventing herself there. John was proud of her, but he told her that he didn't want to think of how much he was going to miss her when she was gone.

He had helped his father change her diapers after his mother died. His father didn't know how to do it. John knew how; he had watched his mother. Cheryl laughed when he tickled her belly button when the diaper was off. She was never going to take off her glasses now, and no one was ever going to run his fingers through her long, thick, honey-blond hair.

John stood in a narrow place, above a great abyss. His father had fallen. John could fall or he could fight. His mind was very clear as he sat at the kitchen table looking out at the crab-apple trees in the backyard. His father had fallen. He would not fall. But to keep his balance he had to have a goal. He had to have something to grasp. If he didn't, he would hear Cheryl's voice until the day he died.

He would find the man who raped and murdered his sister. He would look into his face. He would silence forever the sounds that lingered behind that man's eyes, because only he had heard them, and only his death would silence them forever.

## 4

They were going to have company tonight. They had company so seldom, what with Pat's hours now, and the baby. Gail and Philip, friends of Zelly's from high school, and Greg and Lizzie; Pat and Greg had once been partners in a moving business, Two Men W/Van.

It was Zelly's idea to have them over, no reason except the May weather. She felt awfully isolated sometimes, with only the baby and the newspapers for company. And her mother. Zelly had nine brothers and sisters but they were scattered across the country and she'd been out of touch with most of them since the baby. That was her litany. Nothing was the same since the baby. Even her husband. He didn't touch her as often—but she tried not to think about that. He was so nice otherwise. And of course he was working so hard. That was another part of the litany: he was working so hard for her and the baby. Even in the honeymoon of their love they had not stayed awake till dawn; it didn't occur to her now to make love in the middle of the night when he came home. She even felt a small conventional guilt about making love at all with the baby in the house, and although she'd never said anything she sensed Pat knew.

But now his neglect of her was like a small, unidentified lump in her breast: she didn't know if it was going to get better or if it was malignant. Or if there could be a simple surgical procedure and then the lump would be gone.

She and Pat were cutting vegetables in the kitchen. Pat was good that way, he'd help out if you asked him to. Not if you didn't ask, but she didn't expect that. Nobody expected that. Zelly was trying a recipe from *Gourmet* magazine. Her mother had gotten a sample copy in the mail, and Zelly thought the Monterey Jack–jalepeño-cilantro raviolis looked awfully good. And they didn't seem too hard; most of the time when friends came over she made a pasta dish or chicken but she felt like trying something different.

Mary was playing with some pots on the floor at their feet. "In the park today the mothers were talking about that woman who was killed," Zelly said as she skinned cucumbers.

"What woman?"

"Up on Stevens campus two months ago. Somebody there knew her. She used to bring her baby to that park, you know? On Tenth Street."

"You didn't know her?"

"Not really. I met her once. I didn't go to that park. I was going to Church Square until two weeks ago. But I didn't like the mothers there. And last time this two-year-old kept coming up to Mary and trying to hit her."

"Was it a boy baby or a girl baby that woman had?"

"It was a boy. God, Pat, it was in the Jersey papers for a week."

"You know I don't read about things like that."

"I know. Just the baseball and the book reviews. There's a killer loose practically in our backyard, in case you're interested—"

"I'm not. The Yankee game is on tonight, you know."

"You told me six times. You and Greg are going to ruin my dinner by putting on the baseball, aren't you?"

"Not during dinner. You're going to ruin dinner by talking about this murder nonsense, aren't you?" But he was smiling. Mary did a drumroll on a pot and hit her hand and cried.

"You know it's the only thing anybody ever talks about these days," Zelly said as she scooped her up. "When Son of Sam was in New York in the seventies—"

"I know, I know. I was there. All the brown-haired girls wore kerchiefs or cut their hair, and nobody talked about anything else."

"Well, I can't tell our guests what to talk about!"

"But that's all you talk about yourself. Why couldn't I have married a girl who's into stamp collecting? Birdcalls? Coins?"

"Or at least the Yankees." Zelly laughed.

"At least." And he smacked her ass lightly. She was pleased he'd touched her; she leaned over, about to pat his rear in return. "I just can't believe," he went on, "that anybody would expend so much energy on such a silly topic."

Zelly's outstretched hand went stiffly to her side. He was just ragging her, like everybody else. Everyone teased her about her fascination with serial killers; they always had; when she saw her brothers and sisters at Thanksgiving or Christmas it amounted to a tribal ritual to tease her about it. Now she prickled defensively.

"Silly?" Mary had stopped crying and was back on the floor trying to stick a stalk of celery through the little metal handle on one of the pots. "Silly? When there's a pychopathic killer running around the streets—"

"I doubt very much that he's actually running around the streets at this moment."

"At this moment he's probably driving around. Serial killers spend a lot of time driving around their territory, fantasizing and reliving their crimes."

Mary was hitting Pat's pants leg over and over with her celery. "Here's somebody who spends all her time reliving her crimes," Pat said, kneeling to pick her up. She laughed delightedly and hit him in the face with the celery. "Maybe tonight after everybody leaves you and I can spend some time fantasizing."

"You make fun," Zelly said, "but it fascinates me." She felt a pang of unhappiness or anticipation. He talked like that—but usually he just talked. She wished she knew if he meant it. She wanted to say something back, something light and sexy. "I can't stop people from talking," she said instead.

"Well, I wish you could," Pat snapped suddenly, harshly, and the baby started to cry in his arms. "We shouldn't have even invited people over, this is going to ruin the whole—oh, take her. Honey, I'm just tired. I can't wait till everybody goes home and I have you all to myself."

"And the baseball all to yourself." But she was pleased.

"Of course. I love to think about baseball. Maybe later you can give me a reason to think about baseball. Here, I'll take her. What were you crying about, Mary-girl?

"I'm sorry I snapped at you, honey. I just want to relax tonight. I don't want to listen to a lot of amateur detectives go on about why the Slasher this and why the Slasher that and a lot of crap about his mother or something."

"There isn't always a problem with the mother. They almost never find out why they really do it."

"No more, okay? And he's not going to come over tonight and tell your dinner guests why, either."

"Oh, he isn't? And after I invited him specially."

"He'd love your hair."

"As long as you love my hair."

"I do. Anything more for me to peel? I feel like I'm on KP duty."

"Just the onions for the salad."

"I know something else I'd rather peel."

He joked too much; she didn't want to be disappointed later. She leaned up to kiss his cheek. "Later," she said. "Now we have to cook."

# 5

Mary had gone down like a lamb, and everybody had liked the raviolis. Zelly had never tried anything quite that ambitious before. Maybe she would subscribe to *Gourmet*. Now she was stacking plates, flinching every time a piece of china banged sharply against the deep porcelain sides of the sink. All through dinner she'd been afraid somebody would start talking about the Slasher and irritate Pat again but nobody had. She could hear voices in the living room. When she turned on the water it was too hot and she burned her hand. Then she was just washing the dishes.

Zelly had made coffee and now Greg and Pat would be waiting for the baseball game to start, and while they waited they would discuss the abstruse particulars of the game so dear to men. Lizzie and Gail would be talking about their jobs. When Zelly came back into the room they would talk about how they wanted to quit their jobs and do what Zelly was doing, staying home and taking care of a baby. Philip would probably be talking with the women.

When Zelly turned the water off the voices from the living room came on suddenly, as if she'd flicked a volume knob on too loud. "—afraid to go into the city," Gail was saying. Coming into the room Zelly looked over at Pat but he was looking determinedly into space.

"Just in time, Zelly!" cried Philip. "They're playing your song!"

"I was just saying that with these Slasher attacks it's getting so I'm afraid to go into the city at all," said Gail.

"I wouldn't worry," Pat said, "you're not his type."

"That's right," said Zelly. "He goes after women with blond hair."

"Like you, Zelda," said Pat, laughing.

"I hate it when you call me that. And I know like me. I don't even feel safe here in Hoboken."

Lizzie leaned over toward Zelly. "What's that nail polish?" she asked.

"Rosewood," Zelly answered, waggling her fingers. "From the QuickChek."

"You think that murder at Stevens was the same guy?" Philip asked.

"I told you, Zel, if you're worried just don't go up there," said Pat.

"That's easy for you to say," Gail said.

"I think the weird part is the staging," Zelly said. Pat was looking at her but she didn't pay any attention.

"What's staging?" asked Lizzie.

"Staging is when the killer leaves the body in such a way that not only is it certain to be found, but he's making a statement in the way the body is first seen."

"You mean like a tableau?"

"Exactly," said Zelly. Pat had wandered over to the television and stood leafing through *TV Guide*.

"The Green River Killer, in Seattle, once left a skull out by the side of the road to be found," she went on. "And he even brought some bones up to Oregon so the police would find them there and get confused about where the murders were being committed."

"You know, Perez is probably going to take a beating tonight," Pat said, and he and Greg became immediately oblivious to the conversation. Zelly was relieved; she was having a good time.

"So these killers aren't acting on any kind of impulse," said Philip.

" 'Cause I need some polish for my sister's wedding," Lizzie was saying to Gail. "I don't usually wear any but I'm a bridesmaid and she's insisting."

"Oh, no. That's a real misconception." Zelly was leaning forward, intent on her explanation. "It's not the moon or anything like that. The impulse to kill is irresistible—but it isn't blind. Serial killers inevitably kill a certain kind of victim—blondes, little boys, teenage girls, whatever. And they're completely aware of their actions."

"Your sister's getting married? Is it that broker guy she was seeing?"

"So it's not like Lon Chaney in the werewolf movies," Philip said.

"Lon Chaney, Jr.," said Pat. So he *was* paying attention.

"No, it's not. They have to kill, but they're completely in control within the boundaries of their mania. They usually kill about once every four weeks, and a lot of the time it really is around the full moon. But they plan—not every single crime, per se—they just plan to be ready to kill."

"He's not so bad," Lizzie said to Gail. "They've worked a lot of things out."

"I still want to know about the staging stuff," said Philip. "The Slasher just undresses the victims and leaves them right out in the street."

"Oh, gross," said Gail.

"That's an incredible risk," Greg said.

"It's a ritualistic thing," said Zelly. "Knowing that the body is going to be found is part of a ritual. But it is unusual to leave the bodies right out in the street."

"You women all love this kind of thing," Greg said.

"Now, don't tell me we all secretly dream of being victims," Lizzie bridled.

"What's the ritual part about, Zel?" asked Philip. Pat had stopped paying attention again. He leaned over and the television leapt to life, and the room was filled with the monotone of a sports announcer's voice; immediately it seemed as if they had been listening to it for hours.

"These killers are often very proud of what they do," said Zelly.

"I think with your coloring," Gail said to Lizzie, "you should wear something more orange."

"Proud?" asked Philip. "How could he be proud?"

"Well, remember this guy's a fruitcake," said Greg.

"That's so easy to say, isn't it?" Pat said suddenly. "The guy's a fruitcake. Maybe he's trying to create something, or to re-create something. Like performing a piece of music. Maybe what this guy's trying to say has to be said over and over, because he wants to present it perfectly." Zelly stiffened: he was making fun of her.

"But I really like that color," Lizzie said.

"But what is it he's trying to say?" Philip asked.

"Don't encourage him," Zelly said, but Pat was suddenly quite intent.

"Maybe he doesn't really know himself yet. Maybe that's why it's got to be done over and over again."

Greg laughed. "You make this sound like a piece of performance art, not a series of rape-murders."

"He must really hate women," said Gail.

"I think all men have contempt for women," Lizzie said.

"And fear," Zelly put in.

"Fear?" asked Pat. "What of? When you're so easy to kill."

"Oh, that's a charming thing to say," said Lizzie. "You said Rosewood, right?" picking up Zelly's fingers.

"I'll get you some," Zelly said.

"How would you kill a woman?" Pat asked Greg.

"Christ, that's a hell of a question," said Philip.

"Your husband is in a delightful mood tonight," Gail said to Zelly.

"He's just making fun of me," she said. She was biting her lip.

"How about you, Philip?"

"I can't answer a thing like that. I wouldn't kill anybody."

"Isn't it amazing the things men can say about women in polite company and get away with it?" Gail said. "One time this guy told me he didn't trust women because he could never trust anything that bleeds for five days every month and doesn't die."

"Christ," said Zelly.

"Please forgive us all," said Philip.

"A gun would be easiest," said Greg, "but throttling would probably be more interesting." Lizzie reached over and slapped his arm.

"Well, of course strangling has its points," said Pat, watch-

ing the game. "I might start with that. But there is a certain
elegance to using a knife. A certain appropriateness." Zelly
glared at him.

"It's all your fault, Zelly," said Philip. "Pat's been listening
to you too long. You read about this stuff long enough and
you start thinking about how to do it."

"Look," said Pat, Mattingly just hit a double. Come on,
Greg, stop encouraging my wife. Come watch the game."
The men withdrew to the sofa but Philip was obviously still
listening.

"Yeah, but how do you explain *my* husband?" Lizzie was
asking Gail.

"Usually it's assumed the mother had something to do
with it," Philip said from over on the sofa.

"You know, it's always the mother!" Gail burst out.
"You'd think fathers just simply didn't exist! I hate that, that
it's always got to be the woman's fault."

"It isn't, really—" Zelly began.

"I think men are in awe of what a woman is capable of,"
Gail went on. "We can perform a miracle, and men just can't
handle that."

"It sure didn't feel like a miracle when Mary was born,"
laughed Zelly.

"But it was," said Gail, and Zelly nodded.

"I think men are afraid of us," she said. "I think men resent
our power."

"And don't forget the power of the mother," said Philip.
He was leaning away from the game. Pat and Greg were
looking at the screen.

"The mother really is everything to a child," Philip went
on, "especially if she breastfeeds. Literally everything. I
think, at least when the baby is very small, no matter how
much the father helps out."

"Jesus, look at that," Pat said excitedly to Greg, "a man home. Philip, you're missing this."

"—and a boy child, in the normal course of gaining independence, has to get much further away from his mother than a girl child does. A girl is always like the mother—the mother is never fully 'other.' But a boy child at some point must accept the fact that the mother is 'other' in every way. And maybe some children, maybe if they've been damaged in some way—I'm not saying it's always the mother's fault, but maybe a child that's been terribly hurt has a lot more difficulty accepting the mother as 'other' without denying her entirely—and by extension denying all other women."

"Phil, you're deep," Pat said. "And you just missed two runs."

"I think all men deny women," Gail went on. "I think they deny us a fundamental existence, or the right to existence."

"I like women," Philip said pathetically, and they all laughed.

"Hey, Zelly," said Lizzie in the sudden small silence, "it's our turn. How would you kill a man?"

Gail laughed. "Oh, good," she said.

"Pat's right," said Zelly, "we're easier to kill than they are—easier for them, anyway. Women don't have as many alternatives. I guess I'd have to shoot him."

"You two were made for each other, you know that?" said Philip. Greg and Pat were watching a number of bikini-clad young women on the television dance around a beer truck.

"But the Slasher must really hate women an awful lot," Gail said again.

"He doesn't necessarily hate women," said Pat. "They're just there, you know?" Zelly wished he would just watch the TV.

"You mean he might hate men, or himself, or the government, it's just easier to take it out on women?"

"Well, there's the sexual thing with women. Women are everywhere. Unprotected."

"Remember those 'Why Ask Why' commercials from last year?" Gail asked Lizzie. "I hated those."

"Who knows what motivates the Slasher? For all we know he might think—"

"Oh, God, so did I. Whoever wrote those *really* hated women."

"—the moment of death is the moment of greatest love."

Gail and Lizzie were laughing.

"What did you say, Pat?" Zelly asked.

"Some such shit," said Pat.

"Holy fuck!" Greg burst out, "look at that fastball!"

"I thought they outlawed fastballs," Lizzie said.

"Spitballs," said Pat.

"The papers say he does it because of the full moon," Gail interjected.

"All crime goes up at the full moon," said Zelly. Pat was watching the game again. "But he killed Cheryl Nassent three weeks after he killed at the full moon, because that time he killed the wrong woman. He was looking for a blonde but he killed a brown-haired woman by mistake."

"He killed somebody by mistake?" asked Gail.

"You know what I mean. Her hair must have looked lighter under the streetlight."

"Was that her name, Cheryl?" Pat asked; now there was a man on a ski slope with a woman in a bikini on his lap.

"What kind of idiot would kill a woman by mistake?" laughed Greg.

"It's not funny," said Lizzie severely.

"I didn't mean—"

"When's the next full moon?" asked Philip.

"Tomorrow," said Pat. "Can't you leave that Slasher crap alone even for one night? Give it a rest, Zel, come watch the game."

# 6

Zelly had been a cashier behind the counter at a discount beauty store when she met Pat. She had gone to college but had not gotten a degree; she'd never been inclined to the practical; she loved English Lit courses but barely scraped by in her major, business and administration. She could not type, her fingers became toes. She had no business or, indeed, practical aspirations at all; she wanted a husband, she wanted a home of her own, she wanted to have a baby without really understanding what taking care of a baby entailed. She had no big dreams, no creation within bursting to emerge. She was waiting for something. In the cosmetics store at least the nail polish was free; it seemed as good a place as any to wait.

Pat came to the store several times, making transparently unnecessary purchases, before he asked her out. They went to the movies and they went to concerts, and he never took her dancing but he was unfailingly considerate, if cool, and his aspirations fell in with hers: the picket fence, the dog in the backyard, the tricycle on the sidewalk in front of the house, pot roast and pie smells wafting out the kitchen windows.

Pat had big dreams. To have his own business, to be his own man, a yearning for perfection and control. He wanted to hold his destiny in his hand. Her husband was a genial person with a ready wit and a sharp intelligence, but Zelly was aware of currents that ran far below his easy smile. He seemed calm but he was not calm. Pat had never seemed, even when he was courting her, to have only one face. He contained a mystery; it was the mystery that made Zelly love him. Her imagination lent him Brontëan depths.

Zelly's satisfaction with her life sprang from a solid grounding in the pleasures of normalcy; from the little Pat told her about his childhood she suspected his desire for normalcy sprang from something deep and unquenchable of which even he was largely unaware. What little he'd told her—his parents dead before he was six years old, an unsympathetic uncle and an aunt whom he seemed, obscurely, to hate—pointed to a lonely, fragmented past. Pat had grown up something of a loner, she thought, something of an outsider among the precocious sophistication of his generation, with its easy experimentation with sex and drugs. Zelly and the baby grounded Pat—he seemed to want to re-create in their marriage a sanctuary from a much earlier time.

Zelly had had boyfriends before she met Pat; she had been popular. But she'd never fallen in love. That was one of the things she was waiting for. And when she fell in love with Pat the strength of her feelings frightened her. She didn't know if he had any idea how much she loved him. She never pushed it on him, never strove to crack his own cool, indulgent facade. And she had been certain, until the birth of the baby, that she was met with an answering passion.

Zelly halfheartedly pulled a paper towel across the formica

kitchen counter. He would expect dinner to be waiting. Even when he got home after midnight he expected something to be sitting in the microwave. Well, there were a few raviolis left. The baby was sleeping in her crib and the whole apartment was spotlessly clean but still Zelly moved around, wiping this and that.

TV or a book? But she stood at the counter, looking out the window. There was a full moon tonight. May eighteenth. She had shown it to Mary when they went out for their afternoon walk; it hung pale in the pale day sky. The Slasher might strike again tonight.

There was a noise on the stairs outside. Footsteps, light but measured, coming up the stairs. Pat. They had made love last night, after everybody went home. What was that he'd said, something about the greatest love? At the time she'd thought it was weird—but there was his key in the lock. And he was whistling, his favorite piece of music. Zelly put the rag down and went to greet her husband. His favorite piece. Schubert's Quartetsatz.

# 7

Were there ever voices? He wasn't sure. A chorus of heavenly seraphim—and the everyday murmur of his wife's voice, the baby's crying, the irritated or supplicating voices of infrequent clients. When his hands were on electrical wires he felt grounded in a certain reality; a precise, mathematical reality of positive and negative.

There were two worlds, and he walked the tightrope between them uneasily. The sudden surge of light or power, the clean calm wires unentangled, circuits restored to their proper channels; these things cleansed him, and then he went into the chaos that waited outside.

There weren't really voices, but there was music. High and far away and all the time. Nobody else could hear it. It got louder slowly, over days and weeks. It used to be soft and far away always, but now it got louder; sometimes he recognized the music and sometimes he didn't. Beethoven and Chopin and Delius and Bach. Strange dissonances, the drum-

ming from *The Rite of Spring*. It underlay conversations, it
provided a counterpoint to sight. Lately when days and weeks
had passed the music began to overlay everything else; it
became images. Sometimes he said things and then was unaware of what he had said. Part of him was astonished that
anybody knew about the Slasher murders. Nobody else could
hear the music. And nobody else could see the image that
came into his mind more and more often now, unbidden: the
matted hair, the eye, the blood on the ceiling. Things he
could not remember ever having seen.

He drove and drove the dark streets. Sometimes he went to
the meat-packing district up above the West Village, where
the whores sucked him off. He didn't hear the music when
they took him in their mouths. He heard nothing; blessed
blackness descended and he was lost to himself. His wife had
tried to do it for him once. He had not let her—if she had not
been his wife he might have killed her. The good women of
his imagination did not do such things.

He had never been able to control his fantasies. The bloody
eye, the broken body, had been with him for as long as he
could remember. Beauty was inextricably mixed up with
blood. He fed his fantasies with girlie magazines, where all
the women offered themselves to the men behind the camera's eye. Unconsciously he thought all women were like
this, that the women in the magazines got pleasure from their
actions. That theirs was a chosen degradation, and that all
women would choose it.

His victims were everywhere. All women were a single
Woman. He wanted a love as poignant as intense fear, as the
moment before death. In destroying women he was pene-
trating the mystery of his life.

Still he went around from job to job in the daylight hours;
sometimes the client was a woman and while she was talking

to him he thought about what he could do to her. He saw his female clients guillotined in front of him and he fixed their broken fuses and spliced their wires while he saw their faces contorted and covered with blood. And he said, oh, yes, that's the trouble, you won't have to worry anymore. And their bloody sightless eyes thanked him, and their cold fingers wrote the check, and he left them unaware of their own deaths. And he went home to a blond woman and when the pressure of the music grew too strong he escaped again into the chaos of the night in his van, along the dark empty streets inside his head.

8

The headlines were screaming. SLASHER VICTIM LIVES! It was May nineteenth, and John was drinking coffee in his office; he was the accountant for a medical publishing company in the Helmsley Building, across the street from Grand Central Terminal. The commute from Bayside took an hour and forty-five minutes, sometimes two hours. He took the express bus every morning, and every evening he waited on the corner of Forty-fifth Street and Third Avenue to catch the express bus home. He looked at the people in the crowd as he waited for the bus, he looked at them as he rode the bus home. The man could be any one of those people. That was the only way John ever thought of him: the man. He tried not to think about what the man had done.

John had not known before that you can stop thought. That you can catch and freeze an image and back away from it before it moves—before it hurts you. Sometimes at night in the moments before sleep the image escaped and he saw Cheryl, her head thrown back; he saw the knife.

SLASHER VICTIM LIVES! Could he really do what he had said he was going to do? The woman had been raped, but somehow she had gotten away before the knife. She knew, whoever she was, she knew some of the things that Cheryl had known. Not the last thing, not the blade. What was the last thing Cheryl saw? His face? And this woman had seen his face.

At home in the morning John read the *Times* with his coffee, and every morning as he took the paper out of its blue plastic sheath he held his breath until he scanned the headlines for the Metropolitan section. The *Times* would never deign to put a Slasher murder on the front page. But it was there now, in the lower right-hand corner: WOMAN ESCAPES "SLASHER" ATTACK. And then the *Post* headlines over people's shoulders on the bus. John hated the *Post*. The things it had said about Cheryl—"reported virgin," as though that were shameful. He didn't read the *Post*.

The *Times* article didn't mention the woman's name. It was common practice now in the press not to print the names of sexual-abuse victims. To leave some clothing on the psyche, at least. John had a copy of the *Daily News* in his lap. He had finished reading the articles. He was still staring at the paper in front of him. The *Daily News* hadn't printed her name either. But John had to know.

She had been walking in the West Village at about eleven-thirty at night. She lived in the area. She was blond, "attractive." Twenty-seven years old, a teacher. She'd been walking on Washington Street, one block in from the West Side Highway. Between Eleventh and Bank streets.

John wished he could talk to that woman. The papers had been full for months of comparisons with other cases. They talked mostly about Ted Bundy. There had been one girl,

Cheryl's age, John thought her name was Georgiana. Georgiana was walking down an alley on a summer night, all the windows were open. This was in a college town, John couldn't remember where. There were students leaning out all the windows, Georgiana knew them all. She called out hellos to them as she walked. At the end of the alley was a busy street. Right before the street there was a stretch of alley, about thirty feet long, where nobody could see Georgiana from the windows. She walked into the dark there and never came out the other side. Her body was never found.

John didn't know the West Village very well. He had been walking there several times, years ago. He remembered that there were steps leading down to used or unused basements in front of every row house along every street. There were courtyards in back of some of the houses, with narrow alleyways. They were kept locked—or most of them were usually kept locked. There were odd configurations of buildings butted up one against the other; some of the buildings were triangular. There were small, oddly shaped empty spaces between the buildings. There were empty buildings, for sale. Up near the meat-packing district above Jane Street there were parking lots, underneath the rusted columns that supported a stretch of old, abandoned railroad track that ran for several blocks over near the river. There were schoolyards, shadowy asphalt deserts at night, under surreal yellow lamplight. There was a playground that had been a cemetery in the nineteenth century. In that safe, well-to-do neighborhood there were a thousand places to commit a rape-murder.

The woman, the woman who had seen the man's face, had already been released from St. Vincent's Hospital. The papers had published no description of her attacker. The woman was "cooperating with the police," however, and they expected to circulate a description within twenty-four hours.

When that woman was gang raped and beaten nearly to death in Central Park in 1989, none of New York City's mainstream papers printed her name. The *City Sun,* one of the city's two black newspapers, thought the arrest of five young black men had been a setup, and they did print her name. Protesters stood outside the courtroom every day while the trial was going on and chanted her name next to the television cameras. Cheryl had been very interested in that trial, she had said that if you read the *City Sun* and the *Amsterdam News* you understood why some people were saying it was a frame-up. So Cheryl knew that woman's name but she said she would never have been able to say it out loud.

All morning at work John thought about what to do. Call the hospital? They'd never tell him. At eleven o'clock he called anyway, Admissions, St. Vincent's. "Excuse me, but could you tell me the name of the woman who was treated and released last night in the Slasher attack?"

"Are you a member of the immediate family?"

For one mad moment John thought of saying yes. "No," he said. For the first time in a long time he almost laughed.

"I'm sorry, but we are not at liberty to give out patient information."

"Is there anyone I could—"

"I'm sorry, but we are not at liberty to give out patient information."

Numbers. Columns on a page. How much the new Mac computers were costing versus the figures on typesetting and page makeup for a year ago. What precinct would it be? Washington and Bank. He called information, where they eventually told him it was the Sixth Precinct. As he dialed the number he realized he was frightened. He had to tell himself there was no way the police were going to know who he was or why he was trying to find out the woman's name. But when the phone rang in his ear he still wanted to hang up.

"Sixth Precinct." The voice, a woman's, had no inflection at all.

"Uh—I guess I want the Slasher Task Force."

"Just a moment." The voice was completely uninterested.

"Slasher Task Force. How can I help you today?" This voice was big and hearty; it filled up John's ear. A black voice, Southern.

"Excuse me." John hesitated. "I'm trying to find out the name of the woman who escaped from the Slasher," he said finally; but he had given his hesitation to the policeman on the other end of the phone, like a piece of clothing that can later be used for tracking.

There was a ruminative silence in John's ear; when the voice spoke again it was easy.

"My name is Sgt. Blackman," the voice said, and it laughed. "And I *am,* too." A truly rich voice, multilayered. Now it was friendly and watchful. "And what might your name be?" John said nothing, said, "Uh," very softly. The voice filled the gap. "You know I can't just hand out that information to whoever asks me for it. How about you tell me who you are and why you need to know?"

"Is she all right?" John asked; quite suddenly it didn't matter about finding the Slasher, just for a moment, it was more important that the woman be all right.

"No, she's not." The voice had gone altogether cold. "She had the scare of a lifetime, and she doesn't need any newspapermen knocking on her door this morning."

"Oh, no," John burst out, "I'm not with the papers.

My—" and he stopped in confusion; he had given something away.

"Well, that's good to hear," Sgt. Blackman said, his voice smooth again. John got the impression of a big dog sitting up on a desk at the other end of the line, a big dog with its head cocked to one side and very intelligent eyes. "You know I can't give out her name." There was a pause so sudden and complete that John thought the phone had gone dead.

"It's just that—" he said, and then he stopped and heard nothing and went on, "—but I just wanted to talk to her. I need to talk to her." The air was dead in his ear and then Sgt. Blackman said, very softly, "Why?"

John moved the phone away from his ear because his eyes had filled with tears and he had to clear his throat. He didn't want Sgt. Blackman to hear that but he probably had. John put his hand up to his face and rubbed, hard; he hated to cry. He put the receiver back up to his ear. "I'm sorry," he said briskly, "I guess I'm wasting your time." And he moved to hang up, ashamed of himself and angry, and Sgt. Blackman said, "Wait," a command and a promise.

"I want you to know I'm here, son," Sgt. Blackman said. "You're not trying to hurt the lady, I know that. I think you feel for her. But if you want to know something, why don't you just ask me?"

The voice was every male authority figure, loved and feared, that John had ever known, but he would not succumb. He said, "I'm sorry, Sergeant, but I can't tell you. I have a good reason for wanting to talk to her, and you're right, I'd never hurt her. She's been hurt—" and his voice betrayed him, and he was crying, and he hung up the phone.

*    *    *

He sat at his desk for fifteen minutes and then he went down the hall to Circulation to tell Mary Ellen that he was going home for the day. He'd say he didn't feel well, and if anybody asked, would she tell them?

Mary Ellen was bent over a copy of the *Post*. When she looked up and saw him her eyes were gleaming. "You hear about the latest—oh, I'm sorry." In most people's minds there was a tragic best-seller romance in being the relative of someone who had died so horribly, and John knew he was not tragically romantic. His pain was like Cheryl's latent beauty: if you didn't care you wouldn't see it.

"It's okay," he said. "I'm going home. It made me sick. I wish I could find out her name. I want to talk to her. I think it would do me good to talk to her." John didn't know why he was telling this to Mary Ellen. It could be dangerous later, if he ever did what he had to do.

Mary Ellen's embarrassment was forgotten. "But the paper already printed her name," she said eagerly. "In the Metro edition. Didn't you hear? It was on the radio. They originally printed it but they got a lot of flack from the police and the girl's family, so they printed a Metro Extra edition. They never did that before. So only about eighty thousand copies got out with the name in them."

Suddenly John's heart was pounding. He didn't think he could breathe.

"No, I didn't know," he said. "Do you have that edition?"

"No, I don't get up that early. I think it's terrible they printed her name at all, don't you?" But John had gone.

He went to the newsstand in the lobby of his office building but they only had the Metro Extra edition.

"Excuse me, but do you have any copies left of this morning's Metro edition?" he asked the Middle Eastern man behind the counter.

"We have only what you see. All others are sold."

There was an Eastern Newsstand in Grand Central, where John used to buy the French and Italian editions of Vogue for Cheryl. ("I like to see how much too fat I am for Italy," she'd say; Cheryl was very slim but like every woman she thought she was fat.) What if Mary Ellen were wrong and it wasn't called the Metro edition? He knew about the Late City, that was the last one. There was a Sports edition maybe, or was that the *Daily News*? Did they have any more copies of the first edition? The Metro edition?

"We sold out of that this morning."

There was another Eastern Newsstand at the other side of the building. "We don't have any more of that edition. You like later edition maybe."

There were two newsstands on the first floor. "Only what you see there." "We have no more of that." They sold magazines and newspapers in the Barnes & Noble in the tunnel next to the subway. There was no *Post* at all. "I don't know, if it's not out we don't have it."

"Are you sure?" Every place he went, "Are you sure?" Because maybe they weren't sure, maybe they just didn't want to bother and the name was there, behind the counter, carelessly folded, discarded in a corner, with a ring from a coffee cup obscuring the name of the only person who could help him.

There was a newsstand at the corner of Forty-Second and Vanderbilt. A newsstand at the corner of Forty-Second and Madison. A newsstand next to the Forty-Second Street Library on Fifth Avenue. A newsstand down in the subway, or was there? John paid his fare but couldn't find it. The city had taken out most of the subway newsstands because they were robbed so often. Cheryl had told him that the newsstands were good places to stand beside on the platform, because she felt safe there.

There was a newsstand at Sixth Avenue and Thirty-ninth Street. A newsstand at Sixth and Thirty-seventh. John walked in a daze. It was lunchtime. He didn't quite bump into any-body because New Yorkers have a kind of inborn radar cou-pled with an extreme dislike of being touched. Nobody turned to look at John when he almost bumped into them; there was nothing special in the vacant face, the thoughtless step. There was a newsstand at Thirty-fourth Street, at Thirty-second. John began to think that maybe he would not be able to stop walking, to stop asking. "Do you have—do you have—" "No." "No." He stopped at a street corner, not because he saw the light but because everybody else stopped. A woman standing next to him was carrying a copy of the *Post*.

"Excuse me, is that the Metro edition of the paper?" he asked her.

"I don't know." The paper was folded to the gossip on Page Six.

"May I look at it a moment?"

"I guess so, sure." The light changed but she did not move as the crowd flowed around them. Page three, John's fingers fumbled and he stopped at the article. "—released last night from St. Vincent's Hospital." John looked at the woman waiting for him to give back her paper. About twenty-two. Pretty. Blond.

"You shouldn't be talking to me," he said roughly, shoving the paper into her hand. His fingers were black with ink. "I could be a murderer." He turned his back on her shocked and frightened face.

There had been so little hope, just one woman who had seen the man's eyes, and now there was no hope at all.

*9*

The woman used to sing the boy songs from *The Three-penny Opera*. Her memory was prodigious, she sang from *The Threepenny Opera* and she sang "All the Pretty Little Horses" and Mother Goose rhymes and things he didn't know what to call, *la-la*-ings from the music where they sang, there was one about a butterfly lady and one about a funny word that ended in "mouse." And she read to him from all kinds of books; his favorites were stories from Finland about fat little animals called Moomintrolls. Sometimes in Finland it was night for months at a time.

When he cut himself she would sing nonsense rhymes to him while she cleaned the wound and put a Band-Aid on. *Seesaw, Margery Daw, which is the way to London Town?* He couldn't bear the sight of his own blood.

The man hit the woman. He was afraid of the man. He knew he shouldn't be: he should love him. But he didn't.

When it was just him and her alone together, she sang.

"Und der Haifische, der hat Zahne, un die tragt er im
Gesicht." And they danced. (Her legs were covered with blue
and yellow and purple bruises, and she danced so gracefully
around the linoleum floor in her bare feet.) There was a piece
of music she used to put on the record player when she didn't
feel like singing, he never could remember the name of it, it
was harder than the Haifische even, but his mother told him
it was the music the universe moved to.

She taught him the names of the notes on the staff: *Every
Good Boy Does Fine*. And, to make him laugh, how to tune
a ukelele: *My Dog Has Fleas*. (Sometimes there was a blue or
purple bruise around the delicate skin of her eye.) He could
say the major scale by the time he was four years old: Whole
step, whole step, half step, whole, whole, whole, half. He
thought of the notes going up the steps, they were wide stone
steps like the steps of a staircase in a castle, and when she
played the music the universe moved to, he thought about all
the beautiful frantic notes going up, up, tumbling up stone
steps to the top of the universe.

The man hurt the woman. The boy wanted to grow up so
he could make him stop. "When you grow up," she said,
"you can take care of me.

"When you grow up," she said, "we'll go to London to
visit the Queen."

# 10

He was driving on the Long Island Expressway. It was six thirty-five in the morning; he'd just stopped at a 7-Eleven off Exit 25 and bought the papers. He had a Styrofoam cup of coffee propped up next to the shift bar; he shook it with the top on and pried a triangle out of the plastic top. Lots of sugar, that was good.

It was still night in his head. The ride last night past the old train yards on the Jersey side, the hypnotic yellow lights in the tunnel, the low ceiling. There had been another ceiling, it was the last thing she saw. For some reason he always thought of that in the tunnel. His wife was at home sleeping; he had come in at two-fifteen, just before the baby woke his wife. The baby ate at nine and again at two thirty-five. Every night, two thirty-five. He had lain beside his wife and then he had left before dawn.

After the tunnel the dark streets. Park the van on Perry, two blocks in from the water. He never planned his kills, but he was always ready. The tarp laid out in the back of the van. The hunting knife in its holster on his belt. Mud on the license plates, tape across the logo on the front doors: Wyche Electric.

Should he go to the hookers tonight? The moon was full above him as he parked the van, white through the crazy silhouette the maple branches made. The hookers were always a risk. Some of them weren't even women. That one who blew him a week ago, then it was a boy. Young—sixteen, seventeen. With a black eye and a busted cheekbone after he got through with him.

So lovely she had been, high fine cheekbones like blades; a man could slice his tongue on them. Slanted Latin eyes, rich dark hair. Blond could never put its mouth on him—a sacrilege, an obscenity. But her—heavy makeup, red red lips, slim-hipped. She was small, so small, he could have broken her back with one hand. And then, in the van, her mouth. Expert forgetfulness, mechanical—he liked that. The whores' professionalism pleased him, their lack of sentiment. Their knowledge of their place. The whores down by the Holland Tunnel would do it for five dollars; they were a sorry lot of crackheads, old by eighteen, by twenty dead and gone. The small Latin one had worked him professionally; he caressed her dark hair, held her neck, and found some surcease from pain.

And when it was over she had smiled with blotched lips and offered him horrible things. Had cupped a delicately clawed, red-fingered hand to her own crotch and outlined the bulge hidden there, and had offered things no woman can offer.

A sickening, a tightening in the belly, sharp disgust. Screaming, DO YOU KNOW WHO I AM? not seeing anything, a fist slamming into the soft eye socket, the sharp deceptive bone in the cheek. He had not sliced his fist on that bone; he had heard the bone break.

He had not gone back there for a long time after that, until last night when he had heard the call of the shadowed loading docks. He always wanted the hookers dark. Dark, black hair and dark, dark eyes. Dark for inconsequential pleasure. But last night he had wanted light.

After he parked the van he walked and waited. Not far, if it was meant to be she would walk right up to him. Sometimes he couldn't wait, last night he'd relieved himself right on the street, facing an old brownstone wall.

When he saw her he knew she was meant to be his. The papers said every full moon, but he didn't really think so. There were nights and nights when no blond woman passed by.

This one was walking alone, north, on Washington Street. Eleven-twenty. There was a passage—hardly a passage, an intimation—in Beethoven's Sixth Symphony, the Pastorale, just before the thunderstorm starts, a three-note intimation. He found himself humming it now, *da-da-de,* as the girl walked toward him up the block, now in shadow, now her hair lit yellow under the yellow light from the street lamps. Just before the full fury of the thunderstorm hit: what had Beethoven waited for that made him able to write that phrase?

She was close now, just two houses away. He couldn't see her face. Only the blond hair stirred him. He could remember this much: the knife falling through the air had looked enormous.

Just one house away now. He waited, perfectly coiled, unaware that he was smiling. He wished women had never started wearing sneakers everywhere they went, he missed the romantic echo of high heels on cement. He would have liked to hear that lonely, fragile clack along the sidewalk. But she made no sound. *Da-da-de.*

As she passed him he rose, silent, inexorable, and in two steps he was upon her, one hand over her mouth, the other around her waist, lifting her back and down to the shelter of the basement enclosure.

They almost never tried to scream. His wife had told him a story once, about how when she was eleven she went into the bathroom at the neighborhood library. The bathroom was down a flight of stairs at the end of a long corridor in the basement. As she went down the steps she saw a man standing by the front door—a big man, dirty, with construction boots. She slipped past him down the steps.

When she was in the stall she heard footsteps coming down the hallway. She was not surprised when they came into the ladies' room, not surprised that they headed toward her stall, not surprised to see a pair of construction boots stop underneath the stall door. A large, veiny hand came over the top of the stall, shook it, disappeared. The boots did not move. She scrambled in her little eleven-year-old's pocketbook for a weapon. A nail file. If he tries to go under the stall I can poke his eyes, she thought. If he tries to go over I can poke his hands first, then his eyes. The big hand came back over the top of the stall door. The door shook, held, shook and held. After a long time the hand disappeared, the boots disappeared, and the boots' heavy tread receded away along the corridor.

She had not thought of screaming. She had had the presence of mind to arm herself, to form a plan of defense. But she had not thought of screaming. Even when she opened the stall door and instantly found herself running full-tilt up the stairs to the lobby (having lost forever the time it took her to

leave the ladies' room and run down the hall), she didn't
think of screaming. And she told no one. Every woman had
a story about terror. It was part of them.

He had pulled the woman down the steps and wrapped his
hands around her throat. As always he loved the smoothness
of a woman's neck. A woman's skin was always softer than
his memory of skin.

She had lost consciousness so quickly, and he had been
seduced by her motionlessness. He had forgotten her.

She kicked him. Just before the moment of ecstasy, just
before the knife. She rolled away and flung her leg like a
javelin; she brought her knee up and butted his stomach. In
his shock the knife had hung lifeless in his hand. He had not
thought she would act. She had kicked him then, hard, between the legs, and pain as exquisite as an orgasm had rock-
eted from his groin to his brain.

He could not imagine how she'd gotten away. To have
broken the tableau, to have moved out of step—his head hurt
and he thought of the same thing over and over. His uncle,
who had raised him after his parents died, slapping his face
again and again and saying, "Lazy, stupid, lazy, stupid,"
again and again, and his own head turning with comic jerks,
like the head of a marionette.

Days before the urge to kill came upon him he saw the
highway lights behind his eyes, the tunnel lights, the letters
on the wall of the tunnel, NEW JERSEY/NEW YORK, the way
he'd seen them the day his uncle drove him from the town to
the city after his parents had died.

His uncle had beat him. Not for any offense—for every
offense, for the mud on his shoes or the expression on his
face. For doing or not doing. The garbage wasn't taken out,
the television was on. The whole of his childhood he saw as

through a black screen; in some places the screen obscured everything: he did not remember his parents. In some places the screen was relatively light: baseball, his bicycle, anything outside that stucco house. The ceilings there were high, the long windows let in a lot of light. But still in his memory the rooms were dark.

His aunt was a shadow only, a tentative pat, a rare furtive embrace. He saw her always recoiling from words or blows. Even as a child he suspected that she was relieved to see some of the pain deflected from her body to his. That her love and her shame were the same thing.

He had left that house as soon as he could, and when he left he forgot. He remembered almost nothing now of his child-hood. The smell of summer, the sound a fist makes. He remembered no love. He remembered only the first love. The first kill.

He was a big boy for thirteen, big hands, long legs. The girl was nine years old. He sometimes played with her in the deserted train yards on the other side of Yellowstone Boule-vard in the middle-class neighborhood where he lived with his uncle and aunt. The girl was from some other street, some other neighborhood on the other side of the yards. He didn't have any friends his own age.

He didn't remember her name anymore. They played to-gether through the long summer afternoons; the tracks were live tracks: a train would come. He went with her to every-where. Trains to Paris, trains to Guadeloupe. They never planned to meet; he found her under the weedy trestle, she discovered him hidden in the brush watching boys his own age play baseball.

One afternoon his uncle beat him again. He never knew why, a rage out of the clear blue sky. His aunt watched. He saw again the near-unconscious relief, the barely perceived, ill-hidden survivor's joy: *it isn't me.* Her hair was mouse-brown.

His uncle hit him until he was tired of hitting him. His uncle was not a big man, nor particularly strong; to the boy he seemed strong. The boy did not fight back.

He escaped at last into the summer afternoon, cheekbone bruised and lip bitten in unconscious humiliation. The deserted fields lay hazy under the sun. The girl was under the heavy stone bridge that held the only really live tracks to run through these fields. Sometimes they put nickels and pennies on the tracks and waited for a train to come and transform their offerings into fantastic shapes, currency for a dream world.

The girl had a pocketful of change. She had blond hair; it reminded him of something. He watched her kneeling to place pennies on the gleaming track, and he called her name, the name he had not yet forgotten, called her to come down into the shadow of the waiting bridge.

So far he had only dreamed of sex. A nascent warmth, a suspected pleasure. When she turned her trusting face to his he exploded in a fury wholly unexpected even to himself. While he took her he saw his aunt's face. When he put his hands around her throat he saw his uncle's hands. He did not know whether he was inside or outside. She did not cry out.

At the moment of orgasm he knew that he had pressed too hard: her eyes were pupilless, her lids fluttered and stopped. And the moment was more than the moment, it was a continuation of something long lost, the final piece of a forgotten puzzle.

He looked at the girl's dead face and he felt such love. For a moment there was only the girl's dead face and the unmoving sun and the anonymous buzz of the summer field. Then the enormity of what he had done crashed down around him. He shook her; he could not comprehend his power. She did not move. He had acted, and she did not move.

He left the girl where she lay, in the weeds under the train bridge. As he moved away from the body a train went by overhead, monstrous, a noise without boundaries. It sucked up all thought, like air in the wake behind its echo. He wanted to cry out his power but he only turned away.

A group of teenagers found the body two days later when they went down to the train yards to split a couple of six-packs. Nobody ever found the killer. For days the papers were full of the murder, and for weeks mothers kept their girls close to home. There were no clues. A size-ten sneaker print in the trampled grass. Dark hair on the body. Everyone thought there was a crazed killer on the loose but then he must have moved on.

For years that single act served as the basis for a thousand fantasies. It was so easy to kill. He felt the equal of his uncle at last; he alone knew what he was capable of. A week later when his uncle hit him he saw something in the boy's eyes that made him never hit him again.

He didn't understand how this one could have gotten away. They lay still, they waited to be killed, immobilized by his power.

For the first time his rage was unextinguished. His love had been denied.

When she ran screaming he did not follow her. Better to fade into the shadows up on Little West Twelfth Street, the scream like a single note from a violin string reverberating in his head.

## 11

SLASHER VICTIM LIVES! Zelly sat at the table with the New York papers spread out in front of her. The *Times*, the *Post*, *Newsday*, and the *Daily News*. Whenever she looked up she could see Mary napping like a cat in the puddle of sun that came into her playpen through the late-afternoon windows.

This was Zelly's quiet time. Pat had worked late last night, and he'd taken off again very early in the morning; he hadn't spoken a word. There were always jobs, jobs that took him away all hours of the day and night, but payment was slow, and equipment and supplies ate up every bit of the potential profits. Zelly'd had to ask her mother for a four-thousand-dollar loan just to make ends meet for another three or four months.

Zelly read all four accounts. Raped and strangled but she struggled free: Zelly felt a thrill of empathetic horror. Why had she been walking alone on Washington Street? Zelly didn't even walk on her own safe Washington Street by her-

self after ten at night; when he was home she had Pat go out
for anything they needed.

Of course there was some doubt. The woman had been
strangled, not slashed. The *Post* said there was a knife, the
*Times* didn't mention a knife. The *Daily News* screamed knife.
*Newsday* was noncommittal. A flash of steel, a possible knife.

The paper listed the characteristics of serial killers. Zelly
had read them a hundred places: *The Only Living Witness, The
Green River Killer, The Stranger Beside Me, The Shoemaker,
Killer Clown, The Man with the Candy*. But she read them
again now.

He was a loner, probably divorced, if he'd ever been married at all. A man like that would never be able to sustain a
relationship. But Zelly had read about one in England who
was married, and Ted Bundy had a girlfriend until she called
the police.

Marginally employed, meaning that he couldn't hold a job;
serial killers are generally so involved in their fantasies, and so
busy driving from place to place looking for victims, that
they're unable to hold down a full-time job. But John Wayne
Gacy in Chicago headed a thriving construction business
while he tortured and killed thirty-four young men, and Dean
Corll in Houston had a candy factory.

Has an excessive love of pornography, particularly violent
pornography, which he uses to fuel his murderous fantasies.
But all men liked pornography, Zelly suspected, and all of it
looked violent to her.

There was a strong possibility that the killer was someone
marginally involved with police work: a security guard,
someone who had tried and failed to become a policeman.
But the police always said that, invariably, as though they
couldn't believe that anyone could elude them without the
benefit of their own training.

The killer was a victim of severe childhood abuse, physical and probably sexual in nature. It was a given that sexually abused boys grew up to be abusive, possibly murderous, men. But every woman Zelly had ever asked—every woman—had a story about childhood sexual abuse, from a relative or a stranger, one time or a thousand times. *Every* woman. We should be killing them faster than they can kill us, she thought.

The killer wanted to make a statement to the world with these murders: that was why he left the bodies naked, or half-naked, on the street to be found. But what was the statement? It was one of the tragedies of these cases that no one but the killer ever really understood the killings.

There were footsteps coming up the stairs. The thin sound of whistling, just three notes: *da-da-de*. That would be Pat. He wasn't usually home in the afternoon. Suddenly she felt as if she were doing something wrong, like a child caught reading by flashlight after lights out. She pushed the papers into a nervous pile as the door swung open.

The baby started to cry as Pat came in the door. It was always that way. Zelly kept telling Pat it wasn't him, and it wasn't, he just woke up the baby and the baby woke up crabby.

"I wasn't expecting you," she said as he came in the door. "Is everything okay?"

"I can see the whole family is happy I'm home," he said. He pulled off his black leather driver's gloves, which he wore even in warm weather, and put them down on the table next to the newspapers. Something was wrong. Zelly got up to go to the baby but he blocked her way.

"Let her cry," he said.

"Pat, I have to go to her."

"What about me?"

"Would you like me to get you some coffee? She's just

crabby, you know she cries when she's woken up. I'll get your coffee in a minute."

"I don't want a cup of coffee. Come into the bedroom."

"The baby—"

"Fuck the baby." He grabbed her arm, up and painfully away from her body, and pushed her toward the bed. Zelly could see the baby sagged crying against the playpen netting as Pat threw her on the bed.

She was not afraid. She was extremely shocked—"Fuck the baby"—but she was not afraid. He threw her down and unzipped the pants of his blue workman's uniform and he seemed almost unaware of her. She wanted to say, *the baby,* but she knew he wouldn't hear her. He didn't hear the baby crying. He was smiling.

He didn't ask her to take off her clothes, and he didn't help her take them off. He stood there smiling. Zelly pulled her sweatpants down over her hips; there was a baby screaming inside her head. It was another woman here pulling down her pants, another woman listening to another woman's baby screaming. My husband is raping me, she thought incoherently.

But he reached down and ran his finger along the ridge of her cheekbone. "Zelly," he said: and she thought he was reassuring himself of her name.

"The baby—" she said, and he was upon her. He looked at her eyes; he hypnotized to silence the cry in her throat.

When he put his hands around her throat she felt, as if from outside herself, the voluptuousness of his pleasure. Mary's screaming had become a single blind furious note. Zelly could see her standing in her playpen, holding on to the top bar, her face contorted—but she had not stopped looking into Pat's eyes, could not stop looking. Brown and expressionless, like button eyes on a toy.

With no more conscious thought than a trapped animal she flung her neck to the side and broke his grip. At the same moment he collapsed on top of her.

There was not enough air in the world, there would never be enough air. The weight of Pat's head on her breast was intolerable; she pushed him away and breathed in great gasps that sounded like crying.

The baby was sobbing quietly now. Zelly pushed Pat the rest of the way off her and got up. The room rocked, once, to nearly vertical.

The baby had screamed herself sick. Zelly went and held her and she screamed again, and then suddenly she was quiet, and Zelly's shirt was soaked with milky vomit. Every couple of seconds the baby was convulsed with sobs that sounded as though she were trying to get a breath of air.

"There, there, lamb, it's okay, it's okay, lamb," Zelly said over and over. Pat lay on the bed with his eyes closed. Zelly looked at him until he opened his eyes ("It's okay, lamby, it's okay now"), and then she looked at the floor.

"Is the kid okay?" Pat asked gently; he came and stood next to her, his head bowed to look into the baby's purple face.

"What the hell's the matter with you? You could have waited. You made the baby cry." Somehow that was what mattered, that he had made the baby cry.

"I'm sorry, Mary. I'm sorry, Zel. I just—that was pretty wild, wasn't it?" He was embarrassed.

"I suppose that was something you read about in your—" But she stopped; her throat hurt when she talked. She looked away from him, down to Mary clinging wet to the front of her shirt. If she looked at Mary she could force away the memory of incomprehension, of what she'd thought she'd seen behind his eyes.

"Did I hurt you?" His touch was gentle on her neck.

"No." She moved away. If she screamed at him it would hurt her throat. And it would make the baby cry again. "You scared the hell out of me, though." Petulance was easier than fear or rage; and it was surprisingly easy just to be irritated.

"I'm really sorry about Mary. It's just—I guess you bring out the beast in me."

Zelly wasn't shaking—she *wasn't*—she was just annoyed. "Well, come on, beast, and help me clean up this throw-up." She dared look into her husband's eyes and they were gentle, and his mouth was rueful. "I'm really sorry."

"Next time give me some warning, okay?"

"That would have taken all the fun out of it."

Zelly felt the sticky vomit cold against her skin where it was seeping through her shirt. Her reality was different than his reality. He hadn't been trying to hurt her. He smiled at her, and her throat hurt, but there was now no longer any stranger in her husband's eyes.

## 12

Everything was quiet all along the dead and empty street. Suburban houses, twenty-five feet apart, lawns white with fertilizer, a horsey smell in the air. It was dusk, May twenty-first. Color receded, and arbitrary things stood out with eerie clarity: a clay flowerpot on a shadowy porch, a yellow plastic sunflower on a dark-green plastic stem. Two days since the last attack. Somewhere a woman was breathing who had seen the man's face. The papers had waited hysterically for something more to happen, but the moon was waning and nobody had died.

John had sat at his desk at work like a somnambulist, had sat in front of the television at home like a catatonic. The house his father had left him had gotten bigger since Cheryl died. In the mornings, in the kitchen, the soft May sun fell through the window in motey slants. But whatever room he was in, he knew that all the other rooms were empty. Probably he should sell that house.

He was enveloped in a passionless lethargy from which there was no one to rouse him. He had friends, but after three or four attempts they accepted his transparent excuses of work and ill-health with the mistaken, lazy sympathy that is incapable of recognizing when death has entered into a life and become part of it.

Sometimes John and Cheryl had taken walks together in the evenings. Less frequently in the months before her death, when John was happy to lose her to her new friends, her new experiments with night and beer and smoky selections on the jukebox. But they had walked the night before she died. It was a stupid, sentimental detail John refused to ignore: the night before she died. Like a child's doll in the wreckage left by a hurricane.

Here was a house Cheryl had liked: somebody had built a funny little turret onto the side of a Cape Cod. Here was the cat they could never get to come to them; John did not try now. Here were all the living rooms they had imagined behind plastic-backed 1960s curtains. All the lives they had imagined.

John stood a moment, paralyzed by loss. Well-meaning, inept Mary Ellen had said, standing awkwardly in his office doorway, that surely Cheryl would want him to get on with his life. But who knows what the dead want? Who would want to know?

A cat suddenly appeared at John's feet, a plaintive soft cry and soft fur at his ankles: the cat who would not come. It was crying now, and it had nothing at all to do with Cheryl and John felt tears welling up. The cat twined around his legs and slipped out of reach. As he stretched his hand toward the warm anonymous fur, his eye fell on a pile of newspapers bundled and tied at the edge of the sidewalk. They had been rained on. SLASHER VICTIM LIVES!

The cat cried again; there it was on the front page: the Metro Edition. He knelt and groped at the soggy rope that bound the papers; he hurt his fingers and didn't feel it. An old man on a porch two doors down watched with blank disapproval. Page three, he had cut his fingers on the rope. There was blood on the page now. Seven lines down. One corner of the article tore off and dissolved into ink in his fumbling, bloody fingers. "The victim has been identified as Madeleine Levy, twenty-seven, of the West Village."

John scooped up the unsuspecting cat; it hissed once, with vampire's teeth, and struggled free with ruffled dignity. Madeleine Levy. Her name was Madeleine Levy.

# 13

He drove down the West Side Highway at night, the whores outside the Riverview Hotel waved at him but he didn't slow down. The rearview mirror joggled up suddenly and he found himself looking into the back of the van. Darkness. There was no indication that there had ever been anybody there. He moved the mirror back to its proper place and the darkness disappeared abruptly into the empty street. There. Walking unsteadily along the sidewalk, blond hair an untidy Marilyn cloud. But when he saw her face she smiled a groggy invitation. Not a whore, never a whore. The easy, the obvious. The virtuosic touch was in knowing: that all women desired death, that Woman subjugated herself to the superior force, the obvious necessity of death. The whores got into death's car a dozen times a night, they could be killed like cockroaches and who would care?

It angered him that the papers said it was the moon—that all the loonies come out when the moon is full. It wasn't the moon. He wasn't a pickpocket or a prostitute killer or a fare evader down in the subway. As though the eternal, ineffable tableau he created were the product of the same forces that made crabs sidle up the beach or dogs bark in their backyards.

Hadn't that one that spoke to him—the one whose voice he'd loved, her honey voice—come to him on a night the moon was not quite half full, an irregular blob in the pitch of the sky? Because the dark one had been unsatisfying. The dead dark eye, the mouse-brown softness against his fingers against her neck. That was the only one he was sorry about. He had wasted his seed and his power on that one. And the next one had come soon, sooner than expected, and it was not a sacrifice to any moon but to the honey light that glittered in her hair.

He had played this neighborhood out. Here on the highway the hookers would not stop soliciting if a cloud of locusts descended on them. And that was good; there were times he needed them, them and the ones up on Little West Twelfth Street, when the soft familiar flesh of his wife was bland, like bread or cereal, when he needed dark flesh and dark hair.

Why had he put his hands around his wife's throat? That memory had the same quality as the others; as if his wife had been, for a moment, one of the others.

Why had he forced himself on her? She never refused him. She was not meant to be a challenge.

He had frightened her—he felt a kick in his gut, deep inside—that was dangerous, she was his wife. She was meant for ordinary pleasure, not for passion. And she was the mother of his child. She must never be touched by the things he did.

He drove. Red-capped Guardian Angels patrolled the blocks. Women walked in twos or with boyfriends or not at

all. They had begun to wear hats, caps, and patterned scarves
to cover their honey or ash or yellow hair. Stores on West
Fourth Street, stores along Bleeker and Hudson, all carried
the same sign in their windows: YOU ARE SAFE HERE. IF
YOU ARE THE VICTIM OF A CRIME OR FEEL THAT YOU ARE BEING
THREATENED, COME INTO THIS STORE. The signs con-
tained safety tips: DO NOT TRAVEL ALONE AT NIGHT. REPORT
ANY ABNORMAL BEHAVIOR OF ANYONE DIRECTLY TO THE PO-
LICE. DO NOT TALK TO STRANGERS. The signs gave the num-
ber of the Slasher Task Force.

The task force had been set up to deal with the hundreds of
leads being offered from all parts of the city. People were
calling and saying it was their neighbor, their teacher, the
Con Ed repairman. The killer was murdering one woman for
each year of his failed marriage. The killer was somebody's
son-in-law who drank too much, stayed out late, and had a
penchant for blondes. Somebody's brother who beat his
blond wife. Somebody was killing a woman for each astrological sign.

The air on the Village streets vibrated with fear. No longer
were there strolling couples and groups of friends laughing
down the busy streets. The West Village had always carried
a holiday aspect, to his mind. Now the crowds were quieter,
and people looked behind them more often. Couples had
stopped sitting hidden behind old ivy on the worn stone steps
of the century-and-a-half-old brownstones. The steady hum
of people on the streets, in the cappuccino joints, the stores,
had stuttered and skipped a beat; a new note had entered, a
faint, insistent, shrill note like the echo of a scream. There are
thousands of ways to die, and all the vibrant young blondes
were going to die someday—but they didn't want to die with
a madman's hands around their necks, a madman's sperm
between their legs.

To have such power was like a drug. The labels in the paper didn't trouble him: psychopath, sociopath. The psychological profiles: marginal man, underachiever, victim of women. There was no one who knew him. He pushed the memory of his wife's frightened face away: no one.

That one, there. Slight and dark, leaning up against a lamppost, probably because she was too stoned to stand up straight. Since there would be no love tonight, that one would do just fine.

# 14

There were seven M. Levys in the Manhattan phone book. John took an uncomprehending bite of his ham-and-cheese sandwich and pushed a page of calculations away from a Diet Pepsi can. Two on the Upper East Side, one on the Upper West Side. One in the Thirties, in Murray Hill. A full four within the boundaries of the Village. Horatio Street, Thompson, Greenwich Avenue, Bank Street. No Madeleines, just M.'s.

John always assumed that an initial meant a woman's name. How many M. Levys would hang up on him when he said, "I'm calling about the Slasher attack . . ."?

Greenwich, Bank, and Horatio were all in the right neighborhood. The Horatio Street address was pretty far east, he thought; he wasn't sure how the addresses ran in the West Village. For the rest of Manhattan it was up from zero in either direction from Fifth Avenue. Two hundred West Thirty-ninth Street would be about Seventh Avenue. Four hundred East Fifty-sixth Street would be about First Avenue. But John wasn't sure about the Village, where all the streets ran cockeyed, many had names instead of numbers, West Fourth Street crossed West Twelfth, and Waverly crossed itself.

He would try the Horatio number after the Greenwich and the Bank numbers. Thompson was in the middle of the Village, where tourists and people from the boroughs went. Where Cheryl had gone the night she disappeared.

John pushed the ham-and-cheese angrily overboard into the wastebasket. He hadn't bought a knife yet but he knew it had to be a knife. A gun would be safer but he had absolutely no idea of how to obtain one that couldn't be traced. And he didn't even know how to use a knife, didn't know how to kill; a knife was entirely outside the realm of reasonableness and practicality—but it had begun with a knife, and so it had to end with a knife.

John dialed the first M. Levy quickly, before he could think about it. One ring, two. He knew what he would say. If it was the right one she would not hang up.

Four rings, five. Suddenly John realized that it was the middle of a workday. Even if she hadn't gone back to work yet she might not be there. He would probably have to talk to a machine.

"Hello, we can't come to the phone right now. Please leave your name, number, and the time that you called after the beep." John hung up without saying anything and was immediately sorry for leaving silence on a woman's phone. "Whenever I hear a click and a silence," Cheryl had told him once, "I know it's probably a wrong number, but it could also be somebody calling to find out who lives here and whether I'm home."

John suddenly felt impossibly foolish. He would have to

call back, to talk to dead air and never receive a reply. Why should they call him? Every M. Levy would be made afraid.

He dialed the next M. Levy. Action was better than no action. Bank Street. A man's voice, belligerent; a bulldog of a voice: "Hello?"

"Hello," John said pleasantly, as though he were some sort of salesman. "My name is John Nassent. I'd like to speak to Ms. Madeleine Levy, if she's at home."

"If you're the press you can go to hell." John's breath escaped in silent, jubilant thanks.

"I'm not the press, I promise you. Please tell Ms. Levy that John Nassent wants to speak with her." There was a pulsing silence on the line. Madeleine Levy would recognize the name of one of the women who had died. "Please," John said again.

"The number was supposed to be changed yesterday," the man said. "Fucking telephone com—excuse me. What do you want to speak to my daughter about?"

"When she hears my name I think she'll speak to me." The man considered, was gone. John listened to the reassuring static of the open line. He waited a long time. By the time he heard the woman's voice he was a long, sad way away.

"My father said your name was John Nassent." No hello.

"Yes," said John; he was chagrined by her anger.

"One of the girls who was killed was named Cheryl Nassent."

"She was my sister." A beat of quiet for that, a tribute.

"How do I know you're not from some scummy rag, trying to trick me?"

"You tell me if that happens and I'll kill the son of a bitch."

"How do I know you're not the Slasher, then? Calling up with a pretty good story."

"Ms. Levy? You have no reason to trust me. But the same

man that hurt you murdered my sister. And I need to talk to you about that."

"The papers all said that I had 'escaped unhurt.' That I didn't have any 'serious injuries.' "

"I need to talk to you, Ms. Levy. Maybe I can help you."

"Help me? Oh, right. Like the press helped me. Like the police—"

"I'm not the press, Ms. Levy, and I'm not the police. Listen, you can call information and get my number and call me back. I live in Bayside. I just want to talk to you."

"Oh." Madeleine Levy had run out of steam. "I guess that sounds reasonable—I don't know. My father wants to talk to you."

Her father thought it was a good idea, too. He would call that night at nine o'clock. He sounded neither suspicious nor afraid. He sounded like he would kill John if John hurt his little girl. John liked him.

After John hung up the phone he stared for a long time out the window; there was no view. Madeleine Levy was very, very angry. John liked that, too. If she hadn't gotten angry she might be dead. If Cheryl had gotten angry earlier, years and years earlier—if she hadn't been such a quiet girl, so careful never to worry or to hurt—if she hadn't been such a "good" girl—she might still be alive.

# 15

She had been walking west on Bleecker Street, walking backward and calling something across the street to a group of people. She was wearing blue jeans and a black blazer. Cigarettes? Going to get a pack of cigarettes. Meet you—and an anonymous voice saying something—"Cheryl?"—but the words were tossed away by the wind and the traffic.

Her hair hung heavy gold almost to her waist. She walked and he followed her. The van was parked two blocks away down on St. Luke's Place and his wife was home putting the baby to bed. The streets were busy, with a festive air. The benign moon hung above a gabled roof. The girl walked with a gangly, unself-conscious stride, she almost bumped into somebody and giggled and apologized; she was tipsy. At the corner of St. Luke's Place she stopped. Her foot stopped first and then the rest of her body, and she did an awkward, pretty little shuffle to keep from falling, and she giggled again.

There was a black cat a few doors down St. Luke's Place.

It stretched, and rolled, voluptuously, on its back. The girl walked a few steps toward the cat, speaking softly; he couldn't hear, across the street, what she was saying. He wanted to be ahead of her, waiting, but he couldn't get past her without her seeing him. And there were too many people out to risk jumping her this close to Bleecker Street, anyway.

The girl crouched down to touch the cat, and her hair swung down and touched the ground. When the cat ran away she remained crouching, unconcerned, and he watched her as he walked toward her. Somebody in a gray car honked at him, but she didn't notice that. He stopped about ten feet behind her. When she stood she didn't turn back toward Bleecker, she just stood uncertainly and he was sure she was smiling. When he came up alongside her she turned her smile toward him. It lit up her plain face.

"Excuse me?" she said; she hadn't heard him.

"The Midtown Tunnel," he said. "I'm afraid I've gotten myself lost again."

"Oh. I do that, too. You go—you've got to get up to Fourteenth Street and then east—it's easier if you go up Bleecker, I mean east, until you get to—wait, I can't remember if the park goes down that far." She was pointing the wrong way; a minute ago she had been pointing the right way. Her voice was astonishing, young and honey-pure. It was the first time he had ever heard one of them talk—and he knew she would be one of them. And he wanted her to talk some more.

"Like the scarecrow," he said, crossing his arms and pointing in both directions. The girl laughed. "Like the scarecrow," she agreed. They had begun walking west down St. Luke's Place, although she seemed unaware of it; "I don't know this part of the Village," he said.

"I don't either. I'm the worst person to ask for directions."

Like honey, like spun sugar. He could listen to her forever.

"But you know once you get to Fourteenth Street," he said.

"Oh, everybody knows that. Oh, sorry. I guess not, huh?" Her laughter was beautiful too. The cat for some reason followed them for three or four houses, a small black shadow out of the corner of his eye.

"I can't remember how far down the park goes," she was saying. She didn't seem to mind walking down the street with him, after all the street lamps were bright and there was a young couple across the street, arm in arm (and not seeing them at all), and a group of guys up ahead in muscle T-shirts, earnestly talking (and not seeing them), an old woman talking encouragement to her squatting dog (and he could see that she didn't see them either). In the middle of the city, in the middle of a crowded street, there would be, he knew, no witnesses. And she felt safe.

The cat dropped back, abruptly sitting to wash its hindquarters. The image was burned into his mind now, one leg stretched up and away like a can-can dancer's, dark against a dark pocket of space that the streetlight didn't reach: he thought about the cat as he walked along and chatted with the girl. It was a spring night, ten o'clock, and across the street the couple walked with melded hips, and the moon hung like a stage prop.

When they got to Seventh Avenue he expected her to be put off by the sudden rush of traffic, the barren corner; crossing Seventh Avenue meant changing neighborhoods, from the Village proper to the West Village, away from the tourist haven of Bleecker and MacDougal. He expected her to look south where there was nobody, just red taillights running in rows like a vast, undisciplined school of fish. North the lights were white. They emphasized the bareness of the corner, the shelter of the dark residential street behind them and the darker leafy street far away across the intersection. The girl was telling him about the time her aunt's sister-in-law drove her car the wrong way toward the entrance of the Midtown Tunnel during a road test; she stepped into the street and he moved his arm to stop her and he almost touched her. She stepped back up onto the curb and laughed and looked around. White lights, red lights.

"Oh," she said, "what is this, Sixth Avenue? I don't think I've been this far west—" She took a step backward. He could feel her wholly conventional apprehension: she didn't want to be impolite.

"If I could offer you a lift—" and she took another, more resolute step away from him, and he knew he had misjudged her drunkenness. "God, that was a stupid thing to say, wasn't it?" he asked, shaking his head ruefully. "I'm sorry. Sometimes you forget, you know, how dangerous it is for women. How careful you have to be. I'm really sorry." It was easy to forget that it was really just like talking to any girl.

"Oh," she said, "that's all right. I was looking for a place to get cigarettes, actually—" as though she owed him an apology for her suspicion—"and I seem to have gotten lost myself."

"I think there's a candy store about a block down St. Luke's," he said, moving into the street as the light turned green in front of them. There was no candy store. "I'd offer you one but I quit about six months ago." He held his empty hands out and his wedding ring caught the light from above— the streetlight, the moon.

The girl shrugged and followed him. "My car is this way," he said. "I was having a few beers with some friends and I'm on my way back to the car. But I forgot to ask how to get back to the Midtown Tunnel."

"I'm with friends, too. They're waiting for me back at—I forget the name of the bar. Kenny's something?"

"Kenny's Castaways."

"If you know so much, how come you don't know how to get to the Midtown Tunnel?" He suddenly became aware of the saliva in his throat, his clenched teeth: don't leave me now, don't turn away—just a little bit more, half a block—don't leave me. She wasn't talking any longer and he was afraid he had spoken aloud. "I've always—"

"Look at those curtains," she said, pointing. "I've always wanted lace curtains. But John says they make him think of old Italian women." John. The lover? The husband? She was very young, and she wore no ring. The boyfriend, John. It always amazed him when he read the things they said in the paper, later. It amazed him that they knew anything at all about what he was doing. This girl was his, given to him out of the sky, the moon; she could have no antecedents. "My car's up here," he said casually. "The store is on the corner, up ahead. I just want to get a map out of the glove compartment, just a minute. Then you can show me what everybody else already knows."

"Just from Fourteenth Street."

"I remember I came down what, Second Avenue?" He reached casually for his keys. The couple had turned the corner at Seventh, and there were no dog walkers along the length of the street, there were no figures at the windows of the old brownstones, there were no lovers sitting in the shadows of the ivy-covered stoops. She was standing two feet away from him under the arc of the streetlight, digging through her purse. She was completely unconcerned, unaware of any danger. He wanted to hear her speak again.

"I've got a map in here somewhere," he said; the van door let a flood of light out onto the sidewalk. Her lips were pursed with the particular female concentration of trying to find something in a pocketbook. When the light hit the sidewalk she looked up and smiled. "This darn bag," she said, and he was touched by that "darn"; that would become part of the memory. That, and her voice, and the way the light hit her hair.

She walked over to the van, right up to the door, and turned her back and held up her pocketbook at an angle to catch the light from inside the door. What was she looking for? She had come with him. She had trusted him. Now she was waiting for him. There was an old handle of a hammer in the glove compartment, something he had never used before but had always wanted to use. It felt light in his hand, as though it were only an extension of his hand and not a separate thing.

Just as he reached for her she started to turn. "I think I remember," she said. "You go—" Her surprise was so great—her honey head bent, a little spot of skin at the nape exposed, the silver dangle of a feather-shaped earring at her ear, her honey voice music at the altar of his sacrifice—that for a moment he didn't do anything. They stood, his arms around her in a parody of love, and then he struck her with the handle, just like that, silent, and her breath was a tiny *ooh* of exhalation and she slumped and he caught her. There was no sound.

The simplicity of her falling, of his striking and her falling, enraptured him. He held her dead weight a moment and everything else was silence, and then he felt a familiar throbbing in his groin where her back slumped against him. He held her with his right arm while with his left he opened the sliding back door of the van. It made a terrible noise, rusted and full of accusation, and he scented up and down the street for movement, commotion, but there was none. The door squeaked and there was no one else at all on the street and the young woman in his arms did not move.

As he shoved her limp body into the van her pocketbook dropped. Nothing spilled out. He could see lipstick and tissues and a silver key chain, an address book, a nail file, bank-machine receipts—all the commonplaces of an anonymous life.

When he drove away he stopped partway down the block to look in the rearview mirror at the quiet street behind him: was there a telltale gleam in the gutter under the streetlight? A lighter, a compact, a lipstick case that had fallen from the girl's purse and rolled under the van? There was nothing. She had never been there.

She had lain in the van while he drove west. He hadn't hit her very hard but he had hit the tender skin above the first vertebra. He had driven all the way over to the West Side Highway before she stirred. A low, guttural animal moan. He wouldn't have recognized it as that honey voice.

He stopped the van; of course he was where he wanted to be, over by the Riverview Hotel, where the whores flagged down the cars on the highway and the clientele changed every fifteen minutes. He had turned the van off onto a side street, Bank or Eleventh or Horatio, where it was quiet, where there were sure to be no dog walkers, no loving couples. The action was on the highway; there was nobody in sight here on the quiet street.

The girl stirred, and moaned again, and he was above her, with one hand on her neck and the other unzipping his fly. For a moment she did not struggle. Her right pupil was enormously dilated. Her face took on an exaggerated look of surprise, like a character's in a comic book. It was funny. What did his smile look like to her?

With his hand on her neck she was silent now. Her eyes closed much too quickly and he almost spoke to her, but he would have had to loosen his grip to keep her conscious. He didn't know that the next morning he would be reading her name in the papers; there was only this moment, and this was something that was happening only to him, this heat between his legs, this fluttering pulsebeat under the thumb of his right hand. Her open mouth emitted a low, hollow counterpoint to the cacophony in his head, the images colliding as they always did: he could not tell whether he was in his van or on cold asphalt, could not hear the cars passing on the highway a block away. The voices were inside him or outside, screaming or singing. The hollow moaning went on and on and on, like improvisation on a cello. The pulse fluttered and his groin expanded and she opened her eyes abruptly, like a doll, toward the ceiling, and mouthed something—"Please"—he was coming, hacking at her and coming, there were tears in her eyes, the knife in his hand like part of his hand, echoing something—lazy, stupid, lazy, stupid—a violin was screaming and the blood was as dear as his own blood, she was looking up and there was a propulsion like coming, a red spurt and her eyes were open and there was nothing to see there at all, just the dirty ceiling of the dirty gray van.

# 16

There were footsteps coming down the long hallway: the skittering clack of a woman's high heels. He was crouched somewhere, behind a wall or under a stair, where the space was too small for his man's body.

High heels against cement. The footsteps were getting closer, and faster as they got closer, and with the fall of each stiletto heel against the cold cement came the sound of shattering glass.

There was only one way to stop the footsteps (which had gotten heavier, louder, a man's heavy workboot now). He had done it before. There was something cold in his hand. The footsteps were running and they were almost to the room where he crouched hidden; there was somebody pounding at the door.

The knife was cold in his hand. "I can't let you in, even if you have her blond hair. I killed them all. I will kill them all.

All the pretty blond ones." He raised the knife and the heels left a skid on the dirty linoleum floor and she was looking at him and he raised the knife and she said, "You killed me too. You killed me too, you killed me too," and he drove the knife into her eye.

# 17

He lay in the bed next to her and his breathing was innocent. There was something wrong, very wrong. Here in the dark, Zelly was forced to recognize that.

The strangling had badly shaken her. She didn't know what to think about what had happened. When he put his hands around her neck she was not surprised. The shock of her unsurprise was deep and numbing, she could not analyze it. Like all women she had been brought up to believe that most men are sometimes violent, and that all men are sometimes cruel. She was more hurt than angry at the virulence of Pat's possession of her body; what she minded most was that he had let the baby cry.

Two days ago Pat had gone with her when she took Mary up to Elysian Park, at Tenth Street. It was a Saturday. Pat had forgotten how badly he'd frightened her, if he ever knew it. He put Mary up at the top of the slide and caught her as she came down, on her back with her feet crazy in the air. Mary laughed and laughed. Zelly wanted to say, *Why did you do that to me?* but she knew he wouldn't know what she was talking about.

"I love spring," he said, looking around the park, which wasn't even really a park but a cement playground set amid bare dirt for a dog run and a few yew bushes, with a high iron fence over by the water. Mary stood teetering, holding onto two of the bars. (Zelly had once counted every bar of the fence, walking along looking out at the river, to make sure none was missing.)

"Maybe we'll see the Circle Line," Pat said, but a white boat like a ferry went by, and then an enormous ocean liner, and he picked Mary up and stood with her in one arm with the other around Zelly's waist; he and Zelly pretended to be greatly excited by the ocean liner but the baby had something in her hand—a single palm frond—which she was trying to eat. Zelly felt Pat's arm around her waist and she held on to the cold bar in front of her and looked out at the water.

Zelly couldn't sleep. Who was her husband: the man who had strangled her or the man who held her baby up to look at the *Nordic Queen* as it passed by on its way to the open sea? The man who said, "Women are easy to kill," or the man who whistled Schubert's *Lieder* to his little daughter to make her laugh?

There had been something in Pat's eyes. Something that disturbed her—but this was her husband. This was the baby's daddy. He had never been abusive. What if he were to become abusive now? Pat moved next to her in the bed. For a little while on Saturday it had seemed as if nothing were different. Lying here she could almost think that nothing *was* different. You are rationalizing, her mind told her; but since she didn't know what it was she could be rationalizing it was easy—almost—just to let it go, just let it go and go to sleep, to sleep, the *Nordic Queen* had been big as a city block, white and gleaming in the sunshine, one bird flying in the sunshine—"I'm sorry," Pat said next to her. Zelly jolted awake.

"I will," he said unclearly.

"You killed me too," he said distinctly. Zelly felt a ripple of cold over her body. His voice was getting louder. "You killed me too," he screamed suddenly. "You killed me too," and he reared up and slammed his fist into the wall next to Zelly's head.

## 18

Easy Blackman loved everybody—which was why he was so often hard. He had grown up in the Deep South, in Hazleton, Alabama, an entirely black town where all the houses and trees and the one main street were gray; sometimes people in cars—white people—came off the interstate looking for a rest room or some gasoline and Ezra suffered the indignity of watching their eyes. His mother grew geraniums in a box in the window of her house at the end of the one gray street. Every morning when Sgt. Blackman walked past the geraniums in the planters on either side of the door to the Sixth Precinct precinct house he thought of Hazleton, Alabama. He had learned to love in a desert of hate and neglect; that was, quite simply, why he loved. And why he was hard.

"Hey, Scottie," Blackman called from across the squad room, "you got Quantico's description of the van plugged into the computer yet?"

"Sure do, boss."

Blackman walked into Scottie's glassed-in cubicle with two cups of coffee.

"The people who helped Madeleine Levy saw white tape or paint across the right-front-door panel. It could be a co-incidence, but it jibes with what the Feds are saying."

"That report hasn't been released to the public yet."

"It's not going to be. Listen. I got something a couple of days ago that's been eating me." He told Scottie about John's call, reading off the notes he'd made in his small, neat, indecipherable handwriting. When he was finished talking he was pretty sure he had remembered all of the conversation. Scottie was certain he had.

"What do you think?"

"You think this guy might have been the Slasher?" Scottie sat down on the edge of Blackman's scarred desk.

"No. But I have an intuition." Blackman's intuition was legend in the Sixth Precinct. He had an extra eye; he saw connections where there were no connections; more than once other officers had come to Easy with unsolvable conundrums to which Easy had supplied motive, suspect, reasonable cause, all the pieces of the puzzle settled neatly, incontrovertibly in place. It was not only that he was more intelligent than the men around him—although he was—nor was it only the leap of imagination or faith that lets some know what may come ahead, or what has already happened, without firsthand knowledge. It was not only these things: Easy Blackman had made a lifelong study of the human heart.

Scottie knew how much this investigation was costing Easy, was costing them all. Scottie felt as if he ate and drank this case; he dreamed about it at night; he hadn't really thought about anything else for four months, and he knew Easy hadn't either.

All the officers on the Slasher Task Force were paying

dearly; even though they liked to think they were hardened to misery they couldn't stop thinking about the women who'd been killed. Some of them turned it into a macho contest; Scottie pretended not to care at all. Easy pretended to care on an intellectual level only. He and Scottie, partners for four years and partners now on the Slasher Task Force, talked the way they'd always talked, about their chances of catching the perp, about their onerous work hours; on a case like this one they wouldn't talk too much about their own families, because thinking about anything other than the case could be painful. They drank a lot of coffee. And they never admitted to fear or adrenaline, although they complained often of boredom. They were New York cops.

"He wasn't a crank." Easy watched a man being led by outside his glass wall. The fluorescent light made everybody green and old. In every cop movie Blackman had ever seen, in every television show about cops, the open space outside the glassed-in offices was always full of prostitutes, who were almost always shown as beautiful young women wearing short, tight dresses. There were no beautiful young women out there now. The prostitutes of Paris are said to be beautiful. Blackman had never been to Paris so he didn't know.

"And he's definitely not crazy. Did you catch that 'my—'?" Scottie knew that if he walked away Blackman would keep talking. Sometimes one of the men would come into the room and hear his soft, deep voice talking, and he was never embarrassed or ashamed. "Not a crank," he said to Scottie or his coffee cup. "That boy was crying. Only two of our girls had husbands, is that right?"

"Linda Swados and Belinda Boston."

Blackman held his fist up against his mouth, he tapped it unconsciously against his upper lip. "I want you to pull everything we have on those husbands. This boy's voice was

pretty young—mid-twenties, I'd say. How about boyfriends?"

"Let's see. Nassent—no. Moscineska, yes. Moscineska had
a boyfriend out in Brooklyn."

"Pull him. This boy wants to get to Madeleine Levy. Why?
He damn sure wasn't the press—they all know her name
already, and anyway they know better than to try a stunt like
that with me. I already told her daddy to get the phone number changed. There's no professional angle going on here.
Get me everything you can on that boyfriend." Blackman's
fist tap-tapped absently against his lip.

"You'd better get me files on all the male relatives of the
victims," he added. "I think we have a civilian here who
wants to do our job for us."

# 19

Madeleine's father proposed a meeting between himself, his daughter, and John two nights later, May twenty-fourth, at a restaurant in the West Village that John did not know. John parked the car too far away and walked through the streets and they were haunted. The middle of the Village, Bleecker Street, Sullivan, was a pretty place. Until quite late the streets were full of shoppers and strolling couples and groups of friends and the stores were open late and it was safe there. It was not where Cheryl had died.

John walked away from the safe, tourists' Village and got lost on unfamiliar streets. It was beautiful there on a spring night, Grove Street, Morton, gingko trees seemingly lit from within by yellow-green light, century-old ivy twined around stone balustrades and the ancient, faceless lions that guarded the front stoops of the brownstones. The moon was invisible; it had waned to nothing. Seventh Avenue, big and impersonal, Hudson Street. The West Village proper. Cheryl had been found on the side of the West Side Highway, down by the water. No one knew what streets she had walked to get there, or with whom. No one had seen her, a blond girl of medium height and slight build wearing blue jeans and a black blazer.

The police had come to his house and asked him Cheryl's bra size, her pantie size. Certain articles of clothing had not been recovered with the body. John had understood and wanted to help, but he had hated those policemen. He had gone into his sister's room and read the labels on her panties, on her bras. Thirty-four C. It had felt like incest. After the police left, John sat for a long time in Cheryl's defiled room and then he realized that no matter how long he sat there she would not send a sign of forgiveness.

The restaurant was near the water, a sleek place with glass and hanging plants. John had walked blocks and blocks out of the way. It was so easy to get lost.

He recognized Madeleine and her father immediately, even though neither of them was what he'd been expecting. Mr. Levy was small, much smaller than his voice on the phone, but he sat eyeing the door with bantam belligerence. The woman next to him was small too; John had expected a big girl. Her hair was almost mouse, darker than Cheryl's. She was pretty, heartbreakingly pretty when you knew what had happened to her. John knew it was wrong to think that. Beauty and suffering. As though the plain do not suffer, do not die.

He walked toward their table and felt himself very far away. There was nothing in the world but this woman's eyes, this woman who had been violated and punished for no reason at all. By the same hands that had violated his sister. "Thank you," he said instead of hello.

It was a tense meal; Madeleine had the free-range chicken,

her father had the penne, John had sweetbreads, and nobody ate anything. Now that Madeleine was in front of him John didn't know what he wanted to say. Tell me what he looks like so I can find him and kill him? But Madeleine's father already knew that.

"Just what is it you expect to accomplish by seeing my daughter, young man?"

John looked at the brains on his plate. An odd choice. "I want to know as much as possible about the man who murdered my sister."

"I didn't really see him," Madeleine said. Her face was as fine as a pen-line drawing; her eyes were neither green nor blue. Often she reached up one long-fingered hand to push a strand of hair out of her face. She did not smile.

"The police also want to know as much as possible about the man who murdered your sister," Mr. Levy said. "I feel for you—how could I not? But I don't see what you're going to accomplish this way. You're just hurting yourself."

"I have to know. Madeleine—Ms. Levy—"

"Madeleine."

"Madeleine. You must know how sorry I am to be asking you these questions—"

"That's exactly what four police officers said." John stopped in confusion. "I know you are," she went on, "and I'll tell you what I told them." Her father put his hand on her arm but she shook it off. "I've told it so many times it almost seems as if it didn't happen to me. Almost." She took a sip of wine and smiled an inexplicably kind smile at John, like a parent about to teach a child a particularly painful lesson.

"I was walking home from a friend's house. It was about eleven-thirty. Of course I'd heard about the Slasher, but you've got to live, don't you? Some of the girls I know have dyed their hair. Everybody wears hats. But this isn't even really blond, you know? I used to streak it so people wouldn't keep calling it brown. Anyway, I was walking home, there were people out and everything. West Fourth Street always has people on it, so I walked up West Fourth. There were people on the benches in front of Lattisimore's cappuccino joint, that dog was there I always see around, a Doberman, his master wears a dog collar around his neck. They've got the same nose. The dog's coat is shiny and the master always wears these shiny black pants, I always think the master's name is Spit and he calls his dog Precious." She started to cry.

Mr. Levy touched her arm without awkwardness; this father and daughter were close. "You don't have to tell me," John said. "It's none of my business."

"Oh, but it is. I understand exactly why you want to know. Need to know. It's okay, Daddy, I'm okay."

"You sure? The young man says you don't have to continue. I personally don't want you to continue. This is our private grief, it's not for strangers."

"Oh, but Daddy, wouldn't you need to know? If it were me, Daddy."

Mr. Levy looked down at his plate for a long moment. He nodded without raising his eyes.

"I turned down Charles Street." Her voice sounded stronger. "I like Charles Street. Do you know this neighborhood, Mr. Nassent?"

"John."

"John. It's very pretty. I live really far over, on Bank, near the river. There are some hairy scenes at night. The transvestite hookers come down from the meat-packing district, and there are regular hookers too. Daddy hates it that I live so close to that, but where I am it's really safe. *Was* really safe. And it's pretty, did you see any of the old brownstones on the way over?" John nodded.

"He was waiting for me in a stairwell on Washington Street. I didn't see him. Even when he was—he grabbed me from behind. He was tall, I told the police that. They wanted to know if he smelled like anything. I don't think so. He just—he grabbed my neck. He pulled me down into the stairwell and I hurt the back of my head when he threw me down. I kept my eyes closed. He never took his hands off my neck, I don't know how he did that. Always one hand. He had enormous hands. It was like that was all I could feel, his hand on my throat. Not any of the other.

"He didn't say anything. Even his breathing hardly made a sound. I heard this terrible noise, this wrenching sound like the last breath of something, and I realized it was me. I heard it from a long way away. And then suddenly I heard a jet engine. This is so strange. This is what it sounds like to die. Like a jet engine going over in your brain—I can't explain it. A very, very loud noise, and when I moved it was just reflex. The whole time I hadn't believed it was happening and then I knew it was.

"I kicked him. I wanted to kill him. Not just stop him, *kill* him. I knew a little bit of what he must be feeling: it would have made me very happy to kill him. That's not something anybody should ever have to feel. Anyway, I kicked him and I guess I startled him because suddenly I was running screaming down the street. I don't really remember how I got away. I was just running."

John was ashamed to be listening to her. "This couple walking their dog helped me. They took me up to their apartment and gave me clothes and called the police. All the lights were on up and down the street but these were the only people who helped me. I wish I could tell you more, I really do. But I knew if I opened my eyes he would kill me."

"How do you know it was really the Slasher?"

"The police said it fit his M.O. I didn't know about the strangling part. And he had a knife."

"How do you know?"

Madeleine put her hand on her thigh. "He cut me," she said. "Nobody knows about that. I think the cops didn't want people to know it was the Slasher. But somebody talked. He cut my leg when I kicked him. I don't know how. I didn't even feel it. I don't know where the knife was while he was choking me. I guess next to him. I guess he reached for it when I kicked him."

"He's fast, then."

"He's a monster. He's not real. But that's not the worst thing, is it? The worst thing is that he's not a monster. He's a man, just like you." She looked down at her plate and a strand of hair fell into her face and she pushed it away with her hand.

"Mr. Nassent," said Mr. Levy, "I agreed to let my daughter meet with you because I know what you must be going through—my Madeleine is very dear to me. But we can't help you get over the loss of your sister. I don't think you just want to know what happened for sentimental reasons—even though I would want to know too. I think you're looking to turn this into a personal vendetta, Mr. Nassent, and though in my heart I can find a place where I want just what I think you want, I can't be a party to helping you find and harm this man. That's what you want, isn't it?"

"I don't have a chance in hell of finding the man, Mr. Levy," John said truthfully.

"But you want to try."

"I don't know what I want. I guess I just wanted to see the woman who'd escaped what my sister couldn't escape."

"Well, we're happy to help you there. But I won't allow my Madeleine to get involved in a vendetta. If you'll excuse me, Mr. Nassent. Maddy, if you see a waiter, order me a cup of coffee, would you?" Mr. Levy got up and headed toward the men's room.

John sat uncomfortably. He didn't know what to say; there was nothing of Cheryl in this woman.

Suddenly she leaned forward and touched his hand. "I want to kill him, too," she said. Her voice was low and her touch was cold. "I can help you. I did see his face. Daddy didn't want me to tell you, he knew what you wanted. But I want it too. Listen, the police will be releasing a sketch in a couple of days. The police artists have been wonderful, but it won't be him. I tried and tried, but I can't get out what's in here," tapping her temple with her cold fingers. "A general description, yes, but not the eyes. Not the mouth. I saw his face and it's trapped inside me and I have to get it out or it will drive me mad. I couldn't make the police artists see him—*really* see him. But I see him all the time, John. I'll help you. I'll help you find him. But you have to promise me something." Over Madeleine's shoulder John could see Mr. Levy on his way back from the men's room. "Anything." he said.

"That you'll kill him. I don't want to sit in the witness box in front of the whole world and say my name out loud. I want you to kill him for me."

# 20

The van was parked on Hudson Street, down by the park next to the water. He could see the Midtown skyline splayed out and sparkling across the river. From the other side, Hoboken was nothing but a swatch of darkness at night. Across the river everybody was afraid, and nobody knew where he was. It was his city now.

He got out of the van and walked around to the side doors. Tonight there was no tape over the logo. Across the street an old woman was walking an old poodle. She looked into the van and saw nothing. There was no trace of the body that had lain there.

The tarp lay rolled up now at the back of the van. The old lady and her dog had gone away ignorant. He turned on the overhead and looked at the equipment spread out in front of him on the floor: a pile of newspapers, a white bottle of Elmer's glue, scissors, several sheets of heavy construction paper from a multicolored pack, a pair of skin-thin rubber gloves. These things reminded him of school supplies, and how he had always loved school supplies.

He took out his pocket diary. The diary was the week-at-a-glance type; his heavy script ignored the ruled boxes as it crawled down the page. He needed a challenge. He checked the date in his pocket diary: May twenty-sixth. The summer symphony season was about to begin.

He slid the gloves onto his hands; this was awkward, and it would take a long time, but when he slipped the final creation into an envelope (Number 10) and mailed it (Series A stamp) from Staten Island or Bay Ridge in Brooklyn or Riverdale in the Bronx, he would have played the first note of what was surely going to be his greatest part. He reached for the scissors, pulled the stack of newspapers close, and began.

## 21

Stacy Iocca stopped walking. She stood at the corner of Fourth and Hudson streets. She often walked this way in the evenings; the lights of Manhattan looked pretty across the river. Stacy was exhilarated by the spring air, by the big white clouds moving over the river. They made her happy to be alive.

Lately she hadn't been so happy. Her friend Rosalie had been dead for almost three months; their babies had often played together in this park. Rosalie and Stacy had gone out for Japanese food several times, leaving their husbands home to watch the babies. (Her Joey was home now with his father, who thought Stacy was overly moody of late and needed to get out more.) They always sat in the same booth and ate sushi and drank three or four little porcelain cups of warm saki. They had told each other their childhoods. Since Rosalie had been murdered that horrible way—the knife coming out of nowhere, the baby alone on the bright green lawn—Stacy had learned what death was.

She had never thought much about death before. She was twenty-six, healthy. Her husband and the baby were healthy. But now she knew that only the thinnest membrane separates us from death at any moment. The membrane is as thin as a breath. She could look at the clouds and be happy and the next moment she could be dead. Even a heartbeat is not faster than death.

Stacy stopped walking. There was a dark van parked midway down the block. Its doors were not open and she couldn't see any light, but the stereo was blasting music into the night sky: classical.

For some reason, for no reason, the dark van on the dark street blaring classical music suddenly seemed horribly sinister. The van reminded her of a hearse: black for death. Only her breathing separated her from the dead. Abruptly Stacy turned and walked up Fourth Street toward the lights and bustle of Washington Street.

# 22

Zelly sat on the floor in front of the closet looking at the pair of panties in her hands. They weren't hers.

She had been meaning to clean out the small, overstuffed closet for months now. It was June first. Mary lay happily entangled in a heap of pants Zelly had decided really never would fit again. And should she just throw out the blouses she used to wear to work? Would she ever be able to wear anything again without getting applesauce on it?

Then she found a bag way at the back of the closet. A plastic bag from the QuickChek down the block. The bag had a pair of panties in it. It was on top of a pile of particularly repugnant pornography.

Zelly held up the panties. They definitely weren't hers. Even before the baby her hips had never been that small. She gingerly held the panties up. Lilac satin, white lace. She turned to the inside tag, feeling like a voyeur, feeling horrible: size five. Not Zelly's size. Zelly wore a seven. And not new.

Pat hadn't made love with her in two weeks. He wasn't normally an adventurous lover; even when they made love more often, before the baby, he had seemed content with ordinary touch and gesture, fashioned over the years into their own comfortable ritual. Before he tried to strangle her she would never have expected him to initiate anything kinky, in spite of his pornography. If he wanted spice he had never shown it. If Zelly wanted spice she had never dared tell him. With Pat some silences were inviolable, and his silence surrounding the sexual act was sacrosanct. Zelly never knew whether Pat's silence came from Pat or from Zelly's own sympathetic imaginings—that some woman had hurt him terribly, that he had been duped by tragedy and that sex was for him not a joyous act but a field of intimated betrayal. He seemed almost afraid, even after eight years, to let himself go, to experiment. Some perfunctory cunnilingus, a few missionary thrusts, and Zelly with the wet spot on her side of the bed. The only time she had attempted to perform fellatio on him he had shoved her away brusquely. But there was pornography in the closet, pornography stuffed between the mattress and the box spring. He didn't want her but he wanted those paper women. He didn't buy lingerie for her, but he had lingerie hidden in a bag on top of his filth.

Zelly began to cry as she stuffed the panties back in the bag. She'd heard about things like this. The baby looked at her, startled, and started to cry herself.

"Oh, Mary," Zelly said, scooping her up and hugging her against her breast. "Daddy's sent away for this stuff in the mail, I'll bet. I've heard about this, honey. Mommy's okay. Sometimes men send away for things like this at the back of girlie magazines." She pushed angrily at the pile of slick-shiny books. Mary started to really wail. "You don't know what a girlie magazine is, do you, honey? Come to Mama.

Mama needs a hug. We won't say anything to Daddy, will we?" Zelly rocked the baby and cried. Mary grew quiet.

"Unless—" She looked inside the bag again. There might have been a reptile in there. She reached in; she didn't know that she closed her eyes when she did it. Lavender silk, a white-lace bow. They could have come from one of those places at the back of the magazines. But they could have come from someplace else, too.

The late nights. Size five—she must be a slim woman. Lavender—a romantic color. The whole scene came to her, like a memory: a slim-hipped woman, half turned away, pulling the lavender panties down her hips, her thighs. Under the garish impersonal light in a motel room.

The emergency calls Pat just had to answer. The slim woman reclining (was she blond? brunet?) on anonymous hotel sheets. Zelly's imagination lent the scene an orange neon sign blinking outside the window. A brunette? Younger than Zelly, slimmer.

He talked in his sleep. What had he said? "I will." The panties lay in her hand and she couldn't stop looking at them. Lavender silk, white lace. So he had another woman. What else had he said, that night at dinner? Something about the greatest love. He was gone all the time and he had another woman and he had tried to strangle her the day after one of the Slasher victims had escaped, he talked in his sleep he hit the wall, but he had another woman that was why he was never home.

A loner, probably divorced. But Ted Bundy had a girlfriend until she called the police.

Marginally employed. But there was John Wayne Gacy in Chicago.

So busy driving from place to place. But he had another woman.

Has an excessive love of pornography. A slim-hipped brunette.

The late nights. The distance. The odd, disjointed things he sometimes said. I *will*.

An adulterer. A murderer. Zelley stared at the panties in her hand. *My God.*

## 23

Madeleine expected him to have a plan. "You know that the only way you're going to catch him is if something preposterous happens," she said over dinner at the same restaurant a few days later. June first, and it was pouring rain outside. "So you're going to have to put yourself into preposterous situations. You don't have any kind of training, do you? As a private investigator or anything?"

"I'm an accountant."

"I forgot."

"That's how you know somebody's an accountant. If you forget." She smiled; Madeleine Levy didn't seem so angry tonight. She was able to smile—but when the waiter's arm crossed in front of her face as he reached to pour the wine, Madeleine started and began to cry. John liked it that she didn't apologize. He wanted to touch her arm, as her father had done, but of course he didn't.

Now she expected him to have a plan. "You are aware,"

she said, "of the ridiculousness of our position?" The papers had printed Madeleine's description of her attacker, and a police artist's sketch. Caucasian male, twenty-six to thirty-two years of age, six foot two to six foot four, approximately two hundred pounds, dark hair, brown eyes, no distinguishing marks or scars on face. The sketch showed a surprisingly handsome face with a thin nose, large black or brown eyes, a mobile mouth.

"That isn't him," she said now. "There was something about the eyes, I can't describe it. See how they're almond-shaped here? So that they look almost Asian? Well, that's not right. His eyes did look almost Asian, but it wasn't the shape. He's definitely not Asian, or even part Asian. It always seems to be you white boys who do these serial rapes and killings, if you don't mind my pointing that out. But there was something . . . and the mouth. The artist got the shape right—the lips were that full—but we couldn't decide on the expression. The artist tried cruel and he tried angry and he tried petulant even, but he didn't get it. We couldn't find implacable, and that's what it was. It didn't come to me until after. And that set of the mouth is characteristic, unconscious, I know it is. It determines the entire cast of the face. This is not the man. I wish it were, but I couldn't bear to tell the police artist how unlike him it really is. He was really wonderful, he tried so hard."

"Those sketches don't usually look like the real guy, anyway," said John. Her face looked so pretty across the table. She had been so used. "When they catch the real guy I never think the sketch looks like him. When they caught Berkowitz they had, what? Two, three sketches that all looked completely different." She had not asked him anything about Cheryl, and he didn't ask her anything more about the attack.

Every man who walked by their table looked at Madeleine.
John saw her flinch under their looking, and he felt such guilt
for his sex. But he was careful also not to *not* look at her; he
stood on the thin line between her shame and her rage.

He was overwhelmed with the knowledge that this woman
had been raped. He had read a statistic that said that one out
of every four American women will be sexually molested
during her lifetime. He knew now that hundreds of women
he passed on the street—thousands that he had passed in his
lifetime—had been raped. Horror need not be tattooed on the
arm, need not turn the hair white or the eyes old.

But John and Madeleine were comfortable together, really;
they were like children conspiring under the dining room
table. She didn't seem to be interested in what he might be
thinking.

"You don't know a thing about the West Village, do you?"
And he gladly ceded his ignorance. "Well, you're going to
get to know it." She was like a ten-year-old: this was her
house and her toys. "You're going to get to know it as well
as he does. I've been reading about serial killers." John nodded; so had he. *The Stranger Beside Me, The Boston Strangler,
The Nightstalker.* Some of it was sensationalistic pulp and
some of it was riveting, terrifying. "These people," she went
on, "tend to drive around the same area again and again and
again, looking for targets. And they all seem to be into pornography and hookers. A lot of these guys kill hookers, and
when that's the case the police go to the hookers themselves
and ask them which of their johns—" here she smiled—"their
*clients,* are particularly kinky. Sadistic, like they beat up the
girls or they need something special, violent. Of course in
this case the guy doesn't go after prostitutes, but he may go
to them anyway, for whatever kind of sex he wants when he

isn't killing. We know he probably can't—perform—very well in a normal domestic setting. And the books say he's unlikely to have a lot of steady girlfriends."

"Ted Bundy had a girlfriend."

"And she turned him in to the police. This guy's not going to have a wife or girlfriend. Who could live with that kind of weirdo and not know it?"

"The books say that this kind of sociopath appears to be completely normal. That it's almost impossible to tell by his everyday behavior."

"Do you believe that? While he buries twenty-nine bodies underneath the kitchen floor. I think a woman would have to be awfully stupid not to figure something out. Anyway, the books say he probably doesn't have anybody. And I'll wager he doesn't get a lot of dates. So where does he go? The meat-packing district."

"The what?"

"Where were you born?"

"Queens."

"That must be a lot farther away than Idaho. That's where I was born. Funny place for a nice Jewish girl to come from, isn't it?" Madeleine had grown up on a farm, where there was no such thing as rape. Her father had grown up in New York City and didn't want that life for his family, his children. Two boys, two girls. All blond, like their Swedish mother. Her father used to say that he had sired a bunch of Nazis. It always surprised Madeleine that he could joke about that. He had fought in the Korean War. She adored him, and by extension she had always liked and trusted men. She was by no means a fool or an innocent, but she had always found women quick to judge and quick to talk, and she was comforted by the predictability and trustworthiness of men's silences. She was a woman who claimed not to understand women, whereas men had never been a mystery. Now they were a mystery and a terror.

"Anyway"—John kept loosing the thread of what she was saying in the music of how she was saying it—"the meat-packing district is just above the West Village. It's where most of the beef that comes into the city is processed." Maybe her voice was ordinary, but it didn't seem ordinary to John. "I'll take you there," she said, "it's kind of neat. But the thing is, at night it's what's known as a 'haven of prostitution.' There are hookers all over the place. It's right next to this guy's turf. There's a twenty-four-hour deli up the street from me that nobody goes to after about ten at night because all the hookers and transvestite hookers and their buddies and their pimps and their johns are there. I'm really sorry about that word."

"It is an unfortunate name."

"No, it's not," she said, and she smiled again, and John knew that for that moment she forgot that she had been raped. Then she looked down at her wine and he knew she had remembered. "The hookers," he prompted.

"The hookers. There are hookers all along the West Side Highway, too. That's all right around this guy's stomping ground. You're going to have to take some time off from work."

"I have time coming."

"I'm on vacation already. I'm a teacher. Third grade. The kids think I'm in Yellowstone National Park." She was quiet a moment. "You're going to have to go places I can't go, so I'm going to have to show you those places during the day. I won't walk alone in the meat district anytime, but during the day I can go with you and show you where the hookers go. And we can drive through at night—you have a car. You're going to have to get to know this whole part of town as well as he does. You're going to have to talk to anyone he might talk to. You're going to have to ask the hookers if they've got a kinky john who fits the description. With a peculiar set to the mouth. He might beat them—and he probably goes for blondes. You think you can do it?"

"I think you're wonderful, Madeleine."

"Do you think you can do it?"

"I'm sorry."

"You're a nice guy, John. Maybe if I didn't find men revolting right now—all men—I'd like to get to know you better. I had a boyfriend. Three years. He wanted to know if I felt anything. I knew what he meant. So right now I think you're all kind of disgusting, okay? It's nothing personal."

"Sometimes I think you're right."

"I wish I had known your sister," she said suddenly, and at that he could not speak. "Now *I'm* sorry. Do you pray?"

"Yes. I don't like to talk about it, but I do."

"Well, I never did before. But you've got to know we don't have a chance in hell of actually finding this guy. So I think I'm going to start praying, John." She held up her glass: an apology, an acceptance of an apology.

"To prayer," he said, and they smiled at each other over the garnet in their glasses.

# 24

Blackman and Scottie sat in their patrol car at Little West Twelfth Street and Greenwich. Manhattan's notorious meat-packing district. The windshield wipers hit the bottom of the window with a magnified, repeated thud. The cement island across the street blurred and came clear, blurred and came clear. The neon sign of a restaurant shone eerie orange beyond the island, up the block. Across from the island a line of hookers waited on a loading dock under an old wooden awning. The force of the rain sent a line of little stars exploding up off the pavement in front of them.

"I hate coming down here," Scottie said.

"You know the drill. This is Slasher turf. Our man operates out of the West Village, the meat-packing district borders on the West Village. If he uses prostitutes, he's likely to use them here. And he may like to rough up the girls, if they've met him they'll remember him."

A gray car appeared out of the sheeting rain and slowed at

the island; a tall woman in bondage heels skipped across the cascading street, her shoes making little fountains of flashing silver on the shiny asphalt. She leaned over the passenger-side window and then disappeared inside the car, carefully shaking each foot before closing the door.

"We've already been here twice. I've got a bed at home, you know," Scottie said, looking dubiously at the hookers across the street.

"This is police work at its finest," Blackman said dryly. "Dogged determination, strict dedication to every particular—"

"Bullshit. A real bed, with pillows."

"Pussy." Blackman got out of the car.

There were eight hookers. Most of them were smoking. Two big transvestites stood apart, their heads close. Five white women leaned across one another in animated conversation. They wore tight, short skirts, and the tops of their stockings showed. One of them had very high hair. Another's eyes were all but closed by false lashes and liner. One was younger than the rest, with straight blond hair parted in the middle, the way girls wore it in the seventies. Her face was without makeup; her eyes were dim with drugs. She saw the policemen and smiled, completely without subterfuge or feeling.

The big whore who'd gotten into the car had been talking to a little blond-wigged black woman, who stood now as if unplugged, a cigarette in midair. A little way away from the others stood a slim woman, leaning against the wall; her back was directly under the edge of the awning, and rain hit her buttocks but she didn't seem to notice.

"Evening, ladies," said Scottie as he and Blackman walked up. "And gentlemen," nodding to the big transvestites.

"—mother," one of the transvestites muttered without

malice, turning away. She took a cigarette out of her bag and made an elaborate ritual of lighting it.

"Don't worry," Blackman said briskly, "we're not out to roust anybody tonight. We just want to ask a few questions." The whores looked down, looked away. The young blond one was still smiling vacantly at Scottie.

"We'd like to know," Blackman went on, "whether any of you've noticed any of your johns acting strange lately."

"You know, Officer," said the blond black woman, coming a step closer out of the dark, "it's the oddest thing you should ask." She was shaking her head, all concern. "Every man who comes by here seems to want to get his dick sucked."

Blackman sighed. "Don't bust my chops, Dixie."

"You're looking for the Slasher again," said one of the transvestites in a bored voice.

"This is just a routine investigation," Scottie said. Dixie squealed with pleasure. "Oh, I *love* it when you say that! Hey, Angel, honey, it's just a routine investigation. Come on out, honey."

The girl over at the edge of the awning turned an indolent swan's neck and looked at Dixie. For a moment there was no recognition in her eyes. "Dixie?" she said, but the voice was male. As she moved toward the light her delicate face seemed to shift and split: one cheekbone was higher than the other, and swollen, and the white of one eye was red. "Huh?" she said; again the male voice. But the wounded face was wholly feminine.

"We got a Spanish guy likes to beat up on the girls," one of the white whores was saying. "We don't nobody go with him anymore."

A car door slammed and the big whore stepped away from the gray car. "Hey, Twinkie," Dixie called, "we got company. These guys want to know if we've seen any rough stuff lately."

"Hell," said the big whore affably, "we got people here specialize in the rough stuff." She laughed, and nodded hello to the cops. "It's all done with mirrors," she said to Scottie, who was staring at her feet.

"Where do you guys go for shoes, anyway?" Scottie asked disgustedly; Twinkie laughed again. "There's a place to buy anything, honey. *Anything*." Then, to Dixie, "They want to know about the rough trade? What for, they going to arrest them for assaulting innocent women?"

"You look like you'd be a match for anything that came along, mister," Scottie said brusquely. "We're here to talk to the ladies, all right? You and the other gentlemen needn't concern yourselves."

"You there," Blackman said softly, "Angel." The slim form stiffened, the head went up like a dog's head scenting a sudden wind. But she didn't say anything. Dixie took a step toward her. "Angel," Blackman said gently, "where'd you get that broken cheekbone?"

"Come on, Easy, he's not even a woman. And he's Puerto Rican—he sure as hell isn't blond." Dixie stepped to put an arm around Angel's shoulders. "Honey?" she said softly.

"He's so out of it he doesn't even know we're here," Scottie said disgustedly.

"Leave her alone," said Dixie, "she don't need no attention from you. Last time you said he'd go for blondes. So it's still blondes, right?"

"We're acting on that assumption, yes," said Blackman. He was still looking at Angel's cheek.

"We are looking for the Slasher," he said suddenly, turning from Angel to the women. "And we need to know if any of you have noticed any peculiar behavior from any of your clients. I mean behavior out of the ordinary. We're particularly interested in any episodes of asphyxiation—if any johns have tried to strangle the girls."

"I'd like to fixiate—" one of the whores began; another cut her off. "You mean a guy who chokes the girls to get his rocks off?"

"Yes, that is what we mean," said Scottie with exaggerated patience.

"We got the one guy, he's Spanish. That what you looking for?"

"No. No," said Blackman.

"We're not going to get anything here," said Scottie.

"Wait. Have any of you seen a van? A dark van, recent make. It might have tape across the front door panel."

"We get vans," said Dixie. "We get vans, Range Rovers, Coupe de Villes. And we get guys want it rough—guys want a golden shower, guys want to haggle the price. We get everything there is to get here. And all for the price of a meal at that fancy steakhouse up the block there. You know I never been to that fancy steakhouse. Four years. I'll be twenty next week. You want to take me to that fancy steakhouse for my twentieth birthday, Blackman?"

"We've got girls dying," Blackman said matter-of-factly. "We've got five dead already—"

"The papers say four."

"Five. And the body count is going to rise."

"What's dead don't want our help," said Angel suddenly from the shadow. "You think you know so much, Mister Man. Well, you don't know nothing. Do we see a dark van? This is our *life,* here.

"You don't want to catch that man. You want to come up here in your uniforms and make yourselves feel like you're doing something. Well, *we're* doing something.

"You're not going to find him. Maybe he'll find you some-day. Ain't none of us going to live a long and happy life here." She stopped as suddenly as she'd spoken, and walked away out of the shelter of the awning into the pouring rain.

Blackman watched her go. He sighed. "We'd appreciate it if you would call me or my partner at this number," offering a card, "if any of you think of anything, or remember any-thing."

"That your private number, handsome? Any special time you want me to call?" Twinkie was looking at the card over the shoulder of the young blonde; he was smiling hugely.

"I don't want *you* to call—" Scottie snapped.

Blackman put his hand on Scottie's arm; as they turned to leave he watched the slight form of the Puerto Rican trans-vestite, Angel, as she leaned in the front window of a blue station wagon. She listened, said something, listened again, then shrugged and got in the front seat. Blackman watched the car as it cruised slowly up the block through the pouring rain and disappeared around the corner.

# 25

Diapers and wipes and talcum powder and zinc ointment. Zelly was crying. Extra sheets for the crib and socks and six of the little Onesies Mary wore for underwear—she would have taken more but the rest were at the laundry. The stuffed pink poodle. Where had the panties come from? She had been crying all afternoon. On the phone with her mother when she could only say, "I need to leave him, Mama." He was gone almost every night. Blankets and her eye-makeup remover and underwear. Only jeans and T-shirts; she would get the rest later. Later didn't exist. She cried while she was changing Mary's diaper; that wasn't a good idea, because Mary cried too. Zelly kept seeing the images of women hidden underneath the mattress, vulnerable, excited, afraid. A few times she stopped crying but she would pass by the closet or she would see the picture of herself in her wedding gown that hung over the sofa and she would start crying again.

Twice she heard footsteps in the hall. When the wind blew

through the back windows the front door rattled a little bit; she thought she was used to it but now it frightened her. It kept rattling while she packed her bag on the living room sofa. All morning long she heard his fist hitting the wall next to her head. Pat never came home in the afternoon—but he had come home the afternoon after that girl got away.

She was weak from the adrenaline running through her hands. Once when she picked up the baby she almost dropped her. She had washed her face over and over again and redone her mascara, her foundation. At some point she stopped trying to stop crying. Her eyes were racoon-ringed and they hurt.

The baby was finally asleep: she had picked up her mother's anxiety and become fussy and difficult. It had taken her a long time to fall asleep. He wore the same pair of black leather driving gloves no matter how hot it was. Now Zelly looked at the two bags on the sofa. Only the baby's crib toys were left to go into the blue bag. And when she put the book she was reading—*Wasted: The Preppie Murder*—on top of the clothes in the gray bag she was done packing. She tried to remember when he'd started staying away at night. January; Belinda Boston was murdered in January. She stood for a long time over the open bag. The baby woke up and started to cry again. "There is a certain elegance to using a knife. A certain *appropriateness*." Outside there were sirens, police going by. When Zelly closed the bag it shut with a sound like a gunshot.

# 26

Madeleine was drinking steamed milk; it made her think of her childhood even though they'd never had anything like that on the farm. She put whipped cream from a can in her milk and thought about cream from cows. Winter mornings and cream on the milk: her father would milk a bucketful by hand and give her the cream that rose to the top. The Slasher had written a letter to the *Post,* and he had mentioned her name. It was a long letter, surprisingly poetic. THE PATTERN HAS BEEN BROKEN BUT THE MASTERWORK WILL NOT BE LEFT UNFINISHED, it read in part. ONE DISCORDANT NOTE DOES NOT DESTROY A SYMPHONY. WHAT IS BEING OFFERED IS NOT A SACRIFICE TO THE MOON BUT A TRUE AND BEAUTIFUL MUSIC PLAYED UPON THE THROATS OF THE GUILTY INNO-CENTS. I SPARED HER, BUT I AM NOT A LACKA-DAISICAL KILLER. THE BITE OF MY TOOTH IS

THE VIOLIN OF BEETHOVEN. THE STORM OF MY
POWER HAS YET TO BE UNLEASHED. THE RIVER
THAT SEPARATES ME WILL RUN MELODIOUS
WITH BLOOD. They were calling him the Symphony
Slasher now.

The letter had been pieced together from newspaper print,
words in Times Roman, words from the *Post,* words from
*Newsday.* The newspaper said, "The killer made reference to
the latest victim, the twenty-seven-year-old woman who escaped an attack in the West Village in May, by name, apparently cutting her name from an article run in this paper the
day after the attack." That part of the letter, the paper reported, was heavily stained with brown liquid, most probably coffee.

He was an intelligent man, a poetic man. He was a handsome man. He drank coffee. He had sat somewhere and put
together this letter, painstakingly, out of newspaper print,
while drinking a cup of coffee. He knew her name.

The fact of his existence was overwhelming. She was
breathing and he was breathing. John's sister was not breathing; if Madeleine had died, what state of decomposition
would her body be in now? He knew her name. There were
thousands of people and how could he find her again? But he
had found her once. And now he haunted her like an absent
lover. Even John—the night they'd met for dinner he'd
walked toward her down a crowded street and he'd been the
man, the motion of his innocent swinging arm the prelude to
the tightening iron grasp. All that in a moment and then it
was just John, and her heart had lifted toward him and she
had discovered something about herself.

Madeleine didn't want to fall in love. She knew that she
could separate the grotesque thing that had happened to her

from the simple act of loving or being loved—a kiss is not, she knew emphatically now, just a kiss. But she was in no way ready to take on the absurd responsibilities of love: the awkward striptease of the clumsy heart, the opening of the self to hurt—or even to happiness. In a very short time Madeleine had learned how to live without happiness. She didn't know if she could so quickly give up a certain, safe numbness for any real feeling at all; she thought that virtually any emotion might hurt her now.

It was her boyfriend who had inflicted the blow that left her numb. His own unanticipated pain had been so great that two days after the rape, when Madeleine still could not close her eyes to sleep without the man being there, her boyfriend had asked her, "Did you feel anything?" And three years together came down to four words.

She had been unable to answer him. Not for her soul would she have answered him. What she could not forgive was that he had made her ask herself the same question. Not that she was afraid of the answer, but her mind grabbed the question like an idiot dog with a bone, and it could not let it go. What had it felt like? The space between her legs, the secret, once-inviolable space: what had it felt like?

It hadn't felt like anything; not anything she could put a name to. Certainly not sex. A soundless bludgeoning of incredulous flesh, nerve endings refusing even to answer the indignity. A well of pain that she became aware of having felt only later. It was the thought of him that seared her, then and now. The thought of his unasked presence inside her—where even a lover has only the momentary rights we choose to bestow. She had felt nothing, and she would feel him inside her until the day she died.

When Madeleine first came to New York she needed at

least the reassuring illusion of love to gird her against the indifference of the crowded streets, the sheer weight of restless, inanimate energy given off by the buses, the cars, the subway trains, and the endless circling jets. When her boyfriend asked the question she had told him to leave. He had packed and gone in the space of an afternoon, and he had not fought to stay. Madeleine had felt curiously little watching him ready his things; it had not seemed to matter. He did not love her; she was not surprised to find that she had never loved him at all.

She spooned whipped cream off the top of the milk. The letter was "untraceable." The man made a promise: THE SYMPHONY SEASON IS ABOUT TO BEGIN. MUSIC UNDER THE MUTILATED MOON, WITNESSED BY THE EYES AND THE SILENCE OF THE TREES. WITNESS TO THE PERFECTION OF MY VIRTUOSITY. WHAT WOMAN IN THE CROWD IS WAITING TO DIE? WHAT WOMAN WILL FOLLOW THE MUSIC TO ITS LOGICAL CONCLUSION? THE CODA WILL COME BEFORE THE FINAL NOTE. THERE WILL BE NO MISTAKES. THIS TIME THE KNIFE WILL NOT FALTER. THE MUSIC WILL BE SWEET. IF YOU TRY TO STAY MY HAND YOU WILL MAKE SCHUBERT ALL THE SWEETER. The Slasher Task Force released a statement that interpreted the killer's words as a direct threat to murder someone at the next New York Philharmonic concert in the Concerts in the Parks series, in Queens' Cunningham Park on Friday, June nineteenth. Every year the Philharmonic gave a tour of free concerts in New York City's parks. Schubert's Quartetsatz was scheduled to be played, along with Beethoven's Sixth Symphony and two pieces by Delius and Sibelius, composers Madeleine had never heard of. SYMPHONY SLASHER PROMISES HARM AT PHILHARM, read the

*News*. KILLER AT THE CONCERT? asked the *Post*. SERIAL KILLER
THREATENS TO COMMIT MURDER AT OUTDOOR CONCERT, said
the *Times*.

Madeleine liked Schubert. She found Beethoven too heavy.
She was thinking things idly, stirring her canned whipped
cream: Beethoven, Schubert. The particular shade of brown
of John's eyes. It was going to happen again: it had to. She
had watched the cut on her thigh heal; of course she'd known
it would happen again. The cut was clean and small and it
healed quickly. When it was gone it left a red mark, like a
brand. Once the murders began they didn't stop until the
murderer was captured or dead. She and John were simple-
tons. This man was not a man he was a force, like a hurricane
or plague; you cannot kill a hurricane.

Her steamed milk was getting cold. Her father had gone
back to Idaho three days ago. "I'm okay, Daddy," she'd said,
and it had been so hard to lie. She had never lied to her father
before. The Slasher was not a force of nature. If you cut him
he would bleed. The symphony season is about to begin, is it,
buddy? she thought grimly. As she finished her milk she saw
John's face again, dear, and accepted it. I don't care how crazy
John and I are ("The killer made reference to the latest victim"), it's open season on bastards like you, that's what it is.
And she smiled, and felt something giving way, deep down,
like seismic activity beneath a quiet surface: a shifting of
plates. And she pushed her hair away from her face and got
up to call John.

# 27

Zelly sat with red eyes in her mother's sun room, cradling a cup of tea. The tea was cold, but the heavy mug felt good in her hands. She looked at her mother; there was a sewing pattern-half lying on the sofa next to her, it made soft crinkly sounds every time she moved. There was a pile of threads on the pattern, different shades of purple. Her sewing scissors caught the light and sent it back in a bright beam that hurt Zelly's eyes. Mrs. Thuringen had been talking about other things, Zelly's sister Linda's upcoming wedding in St. Louis, her brother-in-law Jack's new podiatry practice in New Mexico. As she talked she hemmed a dress she was making for Zelly's sister Emmy. Two shades of purple. Now she sat quietly, waiting for Zelly to start.

"I guess Mary's finally down," Zelly said. She was biting her lip. She wanted a cup of hot chocolate.

"I would cry too if my mother hauled me out of my house and took me to Grandma's and stuck me in some playpen and expected me to go to sleep," said her mother. She put down the purple dress. "What happened, honey?"

Zelly breathed deeply. "I think—of course I don't know, but I think—that Pat may be involved in something pretty terrible."

"What something, honey?" Her mother's voice was gentle and all-accepting: there had never been any fear or any sin or any monster that she could not understand. In spite of having so many brothers and sisters Zelly had never felt neglected or unloved; her mother's love was a high-powered beam that shown with equal intensity on whatever child it happened to fall. And Zelly was still the baby. "You haven't been at all like yourself lately," her mother said, running her finger unconsciously over the smooth steel of her sewing scissors, and Zelly felt a child's tears welling up. She looked up from her cup. "Mama, I want a cup of hot chocolate," she said suddenly. She didn't want to talk about it in the sun room, where there were a thousand fragments of happy memory.

Here in the womblike comfort of the house where she'd grown up, Pat's recent actions seemed less sinister, and more humiliating. The house stood next to the Stevens College campus; most of the other old Victorians had been converted into dorms long ago. Mrs. Thuringen's ten children had grown up in a warren of nineteen rooms; there was a servants' staircase that they'd all thought was secret, there was an old pool table in the attic, there were endless halls and doors and closets to hide in. Every room had three doors, or four, and every room led into every other room or into long, off-white halls. When it rained all the children played hide-and-seek for hours at a time.

Zelly knew every corner. Her favorite place to hide was behind the heavy curtains that hung over the bay windows in the sun room, a bright circular room that faced the backyard on the first floor. Behind the curtains were child-size window seats, where Zelly and her sisters had curled up with books: *Jane Eyre, Half Magic,* the Narnia series. It was a different land behind the curtains, it was every land they read about and it was very far away from the dining room next door or the sewing room or the pantry down the hall. Zelly had overlapping memories, from all the times she'd hidden there, layers of sun and snow and rain together, and the smell of old brocade, looking at motes floating in sun or not able to see at all for the gloom, cold or too hot and sweating, a hundred times, five hundred times, like a chrysalis safe in a cocoon.

She'd shown all her hiding places to Pat one Thanksgiving afternoon, she and two brothers and a sister, flushed and full of turkey and pulling Pat from one insignificant site to another—over here, remember? Under the great old wooden table, behind the northeast-corner door. Until Pat begged off for the football game.

What could she say to her mother? I think Pat is having an affair, or—what? At the table where she'd had five thousand breakfasts. He's got another woman's panties in the closet? To her mother. He tried to strangle me to get his rocks off? The father of her child. The red-brown curtains hung at the windows as they had hung for thirty years. "I'm just tired," she said.

"That's nonsense," Mrs. Thuringen said genially, "but you'll either tell me or you won't," and Zelly felt again the unbearable comfort of this house, the unbridgeable distance she was from it now. She was not a child; she had lost the child's right to unexamined safety.

They went into the kitchen, Mrs. Thuringen carrying her sewing. They were silent as she made the chocolate, one cup for Zelly and one for herself. Zelly stared at the black-and-white linoleum floor until the perfect squares swam out of their boundaries and leaped up toward her eyes. She promised herself she wouldn't cry and took a sip of her chocolate and started to cry.

Mrs. Thuringen busied herself about the stove. If her back were turned maybe that would make it easier for her daughter to speak. "Well," said Zelly, "at dinner a few weeks ago he said some really disgusting things." That wasn't where she wanted to start.

"What did he say?"

"He said women are easy to kill."

"I don't know what to—"

"Well—I did say that if I killed a man I'd use a gun."

"For heaven's sake, Zelly, sometimes I don't understand you at all." Mrs. Thuringen sat down and fiddled with her cup. "Actually," she said ruminatively, "I'd use arsenic."

"Mama! How Victorian!" Zelly laughed.

"Exactly. Nowadays nobody would be looking for it." Mrs. Thuringen poured more hot chocolate into her daughter's cup. "Now," she said, "tell me all about it."

"There isn't really that much to tell. I think he's just tired out from working so much. You know he's been away a lot of the time—I know he's just starting his own business, but for God's sake, it's been eight months and he hardly brings home a penny."

"He's got overhead, doesn't he—tools, gas, I don't know. But you can't expect him to be making any money in the first year. I've been waiting for you to ask for another loan for some time now."

"I was planning on it."

"And you shall have it. Now, how often does he get home late? Didn't you tell me once he's sometimes gone all night?"

"Not all night. He just gets in late. Maybe once a week. Two, three o'clock."

"I thought you were saying a couple of weeks ago that it was later."

"No, not really. He does late calls, and then I think he just drives around or goes to get a beer or something, to calm down. He's awfully worried about taking care of me and the baby."

"Does he smell different when he gets home?"

"Oh, no, he doesn't really smell like liquor."

"That's not what I mean. Does he smell like another woman."

"Oh. No. No, he doesn't. It isn't that, we're fine." Slim-hipped, younger. Why not just say it?

"I know this is hard to talk about, and it's hard to ask about, too, believe me. But is he treating you badly at all?"

His hands around her neck, the breath stopped. "No. Oh, no. He's just—distant, I guess. He's been kind of inside himself lately."

"Then maybe he really is just worried about his business." Zelly was looking at the floor. "But you don't really think so, do you?" her mother asked, reaching over and touching her daughter's hand. "Let me tell you something about your father. This was a long time ago. While he was waiting for the results of his bar exam he used to go play pool three nights a week. It drove me crazy. One night at about midnight I went storming in there expecting to see Arthur with a redhead on each elbow and what was he doing? Setting up a bank shot."

Zelly and her mother laughed; Zelly's laugh had a glass edge. Mrs. Thuringen stopped laughing and looked into her daughter's face.

"Zelly," she said gently, "do you think he's having an affair?"

A blonde, a brunette. His eyes above her like the button eyes on a toy. "No."

"You said that too fast. Are you sure?"

Zelly became aware that she was tearing at the skin of her lip with her teeth. "Mama, who knows? You watch TV or the movies you get the idea every man—*every* man—has an affair. Or is ready to."

"We're not talking about TV."

"I am sure. I don't think he is. He's just—"

"Marriages go through phases, honey. I don't know what girls expect today."

"I found a pair of panties in the closet," Zelly said abruptly.

"Were they yours?"

"Mama!"

Mrs. Thuringen got up from her seat at the table and went over to the stove again. Zelly thought she didn't want her to see her face.

"Do you remember Alice McDowell? Well, she moved away when you were little. But Alice and I were close friends. Her husband was a lawyer too. He was away from home a lot. She had two little ones at the time—a boy and a girl. The boy was two; the little one was just eight months. Alice started noticing things about her husband—he smelled different some nights. As though he were wearing perfume, or a new aftershave. And he started dressing a little bit different. He kept coming home with new ties. And he stopped wanting her to have dinner waiting. Little things. Well. Her husband had an extensive stamp collection—"

"Like Daddy."

"Yes. Like Daddy. And one day Alice was looking through his stamp album—I don't remember what she was doing, cleaning the drawer it was in or something—and she found love letters. It was unmistakable—they had a lilac scent, I remember that. And Alice had to decide what to do. She had two small children and a third one on the way." Mrs. Thuringen was looking at the window but she wasn't seeing the window. "She could have confronted him. She could have left him, I guess. But she didn't do either. She knew in her heart that he loved her. She knew he would come back to her. So she waited."

"I don't know if I could do that."

"We were brought up differently in my generation. We thought of men differently. Sometimes I think our way is better—we hurt less because we didn't expect as much of them. So. Alice waited. And after a while her husband started coming home early more often, and he put away the new ties and then one day a year later she screwed up her courage and looked in his stamp album and the letters were gone."

"But what if he hadn't stopped? What if it just went on?"

"Then she would have had to make a decision." Zelly thought of her father's stamp album up in the master bedroom, still in the top drawer of his dresser where he'd always kept it. Her father had died when Zelly was seventeen. Her mother gave away his suits and his shoes and his razor but she kept the thick, untidy stamp book just as he had left it.

Her mother was smiling at her. "Have you talked to Pat about any of this?" she asked gently.

"Mama, you know Pat. We don't talk. Our marriage isn't based on what we say, it's based on what we don't say. You know?"

"I know. Your father and I were the same way. I don't understand the mania these days for telling all. A marriage needs its secret places."

Zelly thought she was going to cry again but she laughed instead. "But sometimes those places get too secret, you know what I mean?"

"Well, of course, if it's gotten to the point that Pat may be having an affair—"

Zelly took a breath and looked away, into her cup. This was hard. "The other day—this was actually almost two weeks ago—Pat came home early, in the middle of the afternoon, and he never does that. And he—wanted to make love and the baby was crying and he—" But the truth would not come: *my husband tried to strangle me.* "There are people who think—who think that if you do certain things it heightens sexual pleasure. And Pat—Pat wanted to—he asked me—he wanted to put his hands around my neck." There was a long silence and Zelly didn't look up from her cup and when she did, to find her mother looking at her, her mother's face made her want to cry again: *what if I had told her the truth?*

"Zelly, honey, I'm sorry—I just never heard of such—that is truly disgusting. It really is beyond the beyond. You must have been scared out of your mind."

"Oh, no. He didn't do anything. He just talked about it." She realized she was biting her lip again and stopped.

"But even to talk! It's just so appalling—"

"It's something some people do, I've heard about it. They think it heightens sexual pleasure."

"Whose?" Zelly couldn't help smiling. "I swear I do not understand anything anymore," her mother said.

"But Mama, the thing is—" This was the hardest part (slim-hipped, and there would be an orange neon sign blinking outside the window). She wasn't sure what she was going to say until she said it. "I think that was the day after that woman got away from the Slasher."

Mrs. Thuringen looked at her daughter. There was something—for an instant of an instant, compassion, comprehension, an inner calculation—and she nodded her head very slightly. Then she laughed sadly. "Oh, Zelly. Oh, darling. Tell me."

"You'll think I'm crazy."

"I have never thought any one of my children was crazy. Even when Denise joined the Army I didn't—"

"Oh, Mama!" she burst out, "you don't know what I've been thinking! It was much worse than an affair. You're going to think I'm crazy.

"Mama, I was beginning to think Pat was—was— mixed up in something terrible."

"Darling, I've been meaning to talk to you about how much time you've been spending by yourself. Linda says you haven't called her first since the baby was born."

"Mama, you know how much work a first baby is."

"Indeed I do. But you haven't been talking to any of your brothers or sisters, and I never hear you mention any other friends."

"I do, sometimes. Sometimes—"

"Honey, it doesn't matter. Just tell me everything—and slowly. You never did know how to tell a story."

"I told you Pat's been gone an awful lot lately. But it's really been since—" she took a deep breath—"since just before the Slasher killings started, in January." Her mother said nothing, watching, nonjudgmental, over her cup of chocolate. Suddenly Zelly didn't know what else to say; she couldn't find anything in her mind: no single coherent thought, no rock of fact. There was a woman waiting in a motel room, that was all. "And, well, serial killers drive around an awful lot. They cruise their territory. And they drive around aimlessly, living their fantasies and reliving their crimes." No word or look betrayed any feeling on her mother's face. Zelly swallowed hard and continued. She was aware that she was talking too fast. "Serial killers are never able to support a family because their fantasy lives take up most of their energy. And that night at dinner I was talking about, Pat knew something he couldn't have—shouldn't have known. He knew that the killer strangled his victims before he knifed them. Or he said something like that. I figured it out later. He said he would kill a woman by strangling and then knifing her." Mrs. Thuringen's eyes were wide. Zelly began to talk faster. "This was before that one woman got away and it was in all the papers. And he said some terrible things about women."

Mrs. Thuringen picked up her scissors and began snipping at stray threads along the purple hem. "If every man who said terrible things about women were a serial killer," she said gently, "there wouldn't be a single one of us left." She scrutinized the hem, her head tilted to one side; she looked like a bird and Zelly started to cry again.

"And darling," her mother went on, "you know you could probably come up with ten different ways to kill somebody without even thinking about it, what with all of your reading. Pat's just been listening to you too long."

"That's what a friend said at the time. But there's more. You know that I think that murder up on Stevens' campus was done by the Slasher. That's something. The killer's got to be from Hoboken or familiar with Hoboken—"

"I don't really see—"

"But I haven't told you everything. Pat has a terrible pornography collection."

Her mother was quiet for a moment. "Zelly," she said at last, sadly, "a lot of men have pornography in the house."

"I know. But it's all rape and knives." It didn't sound like anything. Pat has a terrible pornography collection. When so many men have *Playboy, Penthouse*. There must be a woman who wore lavender silk, size five. There must. Zelly was miserable with shame. "And then there were the panties."

Her mother said nothing, lips pursed, snipping. "But my explanation is a little more believable than that Pat is a serial killer."

"First I thought maybe he must have sent away to one of those places where you get used underwear through the mail."

"One of those—don't tell me. I don't want to know. That sounds much more farfetched than what I said."

"There are places like that."

"I said don't tell me." Zelly and her mother laughed again.

"This already sounds stupid," Zelly said, "but he talked in his sleep the other night."

"What did he say exactly?"

"He said he was sorry. I couldn't sleep—I was just lying there. And all of a sudden he said, 'I'm sorry.' And then something I couldn't understand, 'I will,' or something—I thought later it could have been 'I kill.' And then he said, 'You killed me too.' He said that twice. And he hit the wall."

"You were frightened."

"I was scared out of my wits. He didn't even wake up. It sounded like he was talking about killing people."

"You know what people say in their sleep doesn't mean anything, Zelly." Her mother was looking carefully at every stitch along the hem. "If he hit the wall I'd say he's got a lot of unresolved anger, but the part about killing—"

"I know. It's just that it was all beginning to look like something, when I put it together."

"Darling," said her mother, "you do have something strange going on here. If your father ever thought I might like being throttled—well. You have enough to warrant going to a marriage counselor, that's for sure, especially if what you thought about the lingerie is true—that he sent away for it. That is the most ridiculous thing I have ever heard, you know. Do you need saving stamps for something like that?"

Zelly smiled again into her mug.

"But, you know, I think it's all something much more easily explained," her mother was saying. She had put her sewing down. "I can imagine how you might actually convince yourself of such terrible things about Pat—because the very ordinary truth is, in a way, so much more terrible. Pat's not a monster, Zelly, he's a man. He's not a serial killer—but he may very well be an adulterer. And that's a hard, hard fact to swallow.

"Now, I want you and the baby to stay here with me tonight, and in the morning you can think about what you want to do. What you *really* want. You have to sit down and do some serious thinking about what's going on in your marriage. If things are bad enough so that you start having these fantasies—you're alone with the baby and you don't see enough people and your mind starts running away with your brain, if you know what I mean." Again she reached to pat Zelly's hand. "I think Pat is having an affair, darling. That's what all the signs point to. The question is, are you sure? And even if you are sure, are you certain you want to leave your husband?"

"I don't know what I want. I was sure of something this afternoon. It all seemed to make such sense. Now I—I don't know. You must think I'm a real idiot."

"No, I never think you're an idiot. I know how hard this is for you, believe me. You're going to have to make some very hard decisions. Why don't we see how you feel about it tomorrow?"

"I guess I was being a little melodramatic."

"With the serial killer thing, yes. It's those books you read, I've been meaning to talk to you about—" The phone rang. Zelly took the last sip of her hot chocolate. The phone rang again and they both knew it was Pat. They looked at each other for a moment and then they both started to laugh. "It's the Slasher, Mama. You want me to get it?"

"I thought it was the Hillside Strangler," her mother said, getting up.

"Maybe it's the Green River Killer."

"Or the Boston Strangler."

"Or the Nightstalker."

"Or Ted Bundy."

"He's dead," Zelly said, and they dissolved in laughter and her mother went to answer the phone.

## 28

The message on the answering machine said, "We're at my mother's house. I don't know when we're coming home. I think we have to stay here for a couple of days. Please don't worry. I'll call you as soon as I can." There were tears in his wife's voice.

He listened to the dead air and the click of the machine and his wife's voice echoed in his head. He would kill her before he would let her go. A wave of anger rose up over his consciousness, a sunrise of adrenaline and rage. He stood immobile in front of the telephone. His fingers stiffened and clenched. He reached for the receiver. He heard the noises of traffic outside the window like the roar of a seashell; when a voice answered he was surprised. He heard himself ask the old woman to speak to his wife and then he heard nothing but the seashell roaring and the rage welling up from somewhere unfathomable.

"Pat?" Zelly's voice was entirely unfamiliar. I can let her

go and be free. I can forget her. She repeated his name. "Pat?"

"Zelly, what's going on?"

"Pat. I didn't expect you to get in in time to call tonight."

"Zelly, I want to know what's going on."

"I—I just thought I should get away for a couple of days. Things have been—Pat, I think we have to talk."

"What do we have to talk about?"

"I've got some things I've got to get sorted out in my mind."

"What things?" There was a long pause, and he filled it with remembered screams. What did she want? Was she leaving him? His face was hot, it burned. "Are you leaving me?"

"Oh, Pat. No. I just—I've got to have some time to think. I didn't expect you to call until tomorrow morning. I guess I just don't know what to say. Things haven't been—we haven't been communicating, Pat." You have no idea how well I communicate, with what music I play my sweet message, on what instruments.

"I don't know what you're talking about, Zel. I know I've been preoccupied with business—you know, being the sole provider for two lives is not an easy thing." His voice sounded stilted in his own ears.

"I know, I know." You do not know what they know, now.

"It's just that—you've been gone an awful lot, and we're still where we were six months ago. I have to borrow more money from my mother, but that's not it, that's not the problem, you're just gone so much—" The lights against the eyes, bright and dark, bright and dark. Driving, the thousand uncounted hours outside of even thought.

"Zelly, you know I have to take late calls. Like a doctor. And I don't understand, if I drive around some nights to clear my head—you don't know what a responsibility it is, taking care of you and the baby."

"Well—" The silence was relenting in his ear. There was rage in his head and there was a need, overpowering even rage, to keep at least his home inviolable, unchanged by the passions that ruled him. But there was still rage.

"I miss you and the baby." You are mine: you promised yourself to me.

"I just need a little time to think." I could snap your neck like a chicken bone.

"You and the baby belong with me." I will say when you leave.

"I just think I want to stay at my mother's for a few days."

"I know I haven't been there for you and the baby. It's just that business hasn't been going well and I know I haven't been—"

"I found women's underwear in the closet."

The phone would break if it were bone. The trophy—a prize of the kill. Tainted now, its sweet memories tainted by innocence. "Honey, I don't know what you're talking about."

"I'm talking about underwear! Panties. I found a bag in the closet."

"Way in the back?" You interfering bitch I will break your neck. "That might be stuff Karen left, at the old apartment. Zelly, is all this about underwear? I'm sure my old girlfriend must have left it—the one I lived with before we got together. Karen. I thought I threw all her shit out. Honey, you can't really have gone to your mother's because you found underwear in the closet. There's got to be a real reason." On the other end of the phone Zelly was crying. "You're not giving me a chance here. The least you could do is come home and talk about it. I deserve that, at least."

"You haven't talked to me in such a long time."

"Give me a chance before you run away. I deserve a chance."

"Pat, I don't know."

"I want my girls home with me tonight."

How long does a baby cry before it dies?

"Oh, Pat. I guess I didn't think about how hard this would be on you."

But no, the baby's breath was soft like flowers, like fur.

"Zelly, I just want you and the baby to come home."

Zelly sighed. Her breath was soft, too. "We'll come home in the morning."

"No, now." My wife, my baby.

"But Pat, the baby's sleeping."

"Zelly, I want you now. It's been a long time since I made love with my wife. I'm sorry about the other day—you know—that was just an experiment. I know you thought it was too kinky—that's one of the reasons you're doing this, isn't it?"

"Yes." The voice so ashamed—as though she were the one who had done something wrong. It would be a pity to kill her.

"I need my girls home."

"Okay, Pat." The silence was breathing again. "You can come get us."

## 29

"Thank you for meeting me here today." John sounded stiff; he felt stiff, when all he'd wanted was to see her again. To see her somewhere outside the unfamiliar streets that were her home, where everywhere he looked he saw melodramatic death. He saw her everywhere now, on the express bus on his way to work, her half-profile lit golden by the morning sun in the window; he saw her out the window, walking a dog, turning a corner, turning away, moving away always; the nape of the neck, the line of the hip, the flag of hair blown out straight by the wind.

For ten days Madeleine had escorted John around the West Village and SoHo. The mid-June weather favored long night-time walks. They had seen the corners where the hookers stood at night, the gay bars, the all-night delis, the thousand separate places where a killer could hide and wait. They visited the spots where the bodies had been found—even Cheryl's. Madeleine had stood silently while John cried, helplessly staring out over the river toward the undistinguished Jersey coast—a long green building, a train station or a factory; a low arched building half demolished; the Maxwell House sign, a never-ending drip into a giant tilted cup: GOOD TO THE LAST DROP.

She had agreed to meet him at the Twenty-sixth Street Sunday flea market. There were card tables set out in the sun, laden with every imaginable thing; there were overstuffed Empire chairs and ornate mirrors, cartons of books on tables and under them, boxes of ends of lace, of sweaters and old metal pots and rusted keys delicately engraved, rows and rows of blue glass, green glass, murky yellow glass, rows of flowered, chipped plates, of salt shakers and little metal pillboxes and porcelain pillboxes and sorry old stuffed Mickeys and mechanical banks and painted cannisters and stereoscopic slides. John saw Madeleine disappearing into the subway kiosk at Fifty-seventh Street, he saw her waiting for the light on Queens Boulevard. When he thought about Cheryl he sometimes saw Madeleine's face instead. He hated his shallow and unfaithful memory: at times Cheryl came back to him with a paralyzing, fantastic instantaneousness—the whole of Cheryl, palpable and engulfing—and he was left with a miserable emptiness and dejected guilt.

Madeleine had begun to seep into the fissures of his grief. When his wife, Molly, had left him, the grief he felt was not this subterranean pain, molten-lava pain, seeping relentlessly over his heart, searing his heart. He had missed Molly and then he had not missed her, like a habit. Cheryl had worn a rosy scent; he could not say what Molly had worn. Madeleine wore iris, and iris permeated the emptiness of his grief, the depth of it, and the color of her hair, the line of her naked forearm, permeated the emptiness. The void—palpable—became for instants again only memory, when it was filled, obliterated, with memories of Madeleine.

"I love flea markets," she was saying. "My father and I used to drive all over Muscatine County when I was a kid, looking for lawn sales." He did not tell her how much Cheryl had liked flea markets, that he had been here before.

They walked among the tables not speaking; Cheryl would run ahead and then back to him, holding aloft some little treasure: the top-hatted china robin the size of her thumb, the round brass medallion commemorating the twelfth annual running of the hundred-yard dash at Emerson High School, Illinois, in 1910. "Look, darling, I've gotten another venerable," she'd cry, mimicking an ancient great-aunt who used to visit them at Christmastime when they were children; if John remembered correctly, Christmas dinner had always been judged "detectable." Cheryl had been the repository not only of his childhood but of the whole of his family history, John realized sadly; without her there was no great-aunt, no Christmas, no past not entirely his own.

Madeleine picked up a battered coffeepot and held it up in her hands as though it were a living thing. She fingered fragments of lace, ran her hand over a peach-colored teacup with a rose painted on the inside bottom. "The sides are sometimes so delicate you can see through them," Cheryl would say, holding up a cup to look through the china membrane at the sun. Madeleine did not lift the cup, but her fingers traced the rose.

Now she stood next to a glass case of odds and shining ends; something silver caught the light. John looked at her and saw for a horrible moment not Cheryl, not even a promise for his own future, but only what the man had seen. What he had seen when he tried to murder her.

She was not innocent now; she had been robbed of even the illusion of innocence, of being unknown. He thought that she must know what he was thinking, what all men were thinking all the time, now that she had been raped. A woman scratched her thigh or straightened her skirt and that was an invitation. The leg, the cowboy boot or the stiletto heel; the black tights like skin over the buttocks; the shirt that could be unbuttoned or pulled over the unresisting neck. The eye caught—an invitation. The eye aloof—a challenge. The woman walking ahead of you up the subway stairs is yours, her ass is yours, in your mouth, spread out like a sacrifice under your pumping thighs. And then you get to the top of the stairs and she disappears like mist. The woman walking toward you, her breasts bouncing gently underneath a silk blouse, is yours, the nipples between your teeth like ripe fruit and you plunge it into her and she screams and passes by and you never even saw her face.

The late-afternoon sun cut a shadow across Madeleine's throat, throwing her face into darkness and her body into sharp relief. She looked trustingly at him: a man who has just lost his sister to the monster would not be like the others, "revolting." He lowered his eyes.

Reflected sunlight winked at him. He leaned closer: rows of silver rings on a bed of blue velvet. An untidy pile of amber glass beads, green beads, shiny silver metal beads. And next to them a winking eye: a knife. A short green scabbard, intricately designed, a heavy silver handle, the blade obscured. Madeleine followed his eyes.

"Perfect," she said softly; she might have been in church.

"It can't be traced," said John, and she lifted her finger quickly and brought it up to his mouth. The gut kicked, tensed and twisted and breathed, and John hated, for a moment, his sex.

The man behind the counter showed them the knife; they handled it reverently, feigning indifference. And in the sun in front of two or three hundred people they bought the knife, their talisman.

## 30

"There's a guy in Queens who's looking good," said Scottie. "Three different people have called in I.D.'ing him as the Slasher. Seems he's a musician, plays the trumpet. Not jazz, classical. And he has a history of altercations with his neighbors—particularly his blond neighbors. He tried to strangle the nineteen-year-old who lives downstairs. This was after he sent her several letters—the girl's bringing those in today."

"I want to see them."

"I don't know who's been assigned the questioning—"

"I'll be able to get the questioning, don't worry about that. What else do you have on him?"

"He's suspected of poisoning a neighbor's cat. He complained several times to the owner that the cat was getting into his apartment and leaving blond hair all over his furniture."

"What else?"

"An old girlfriend. She said he tried to strangle her during an argument once—almost made her pass out. And he used to write letters to the papers, one was something about the moon."

"Have you been able to get a hold of any copies of the letters?"

"Nobody ever followed up on the original call. I was meaning—"

"Why didn't you tell me?"

"—to tell you."

"Damn, man, I want in on this one! When did these calls come in? When—"

"We're getting hundreds of goddamn calls a day. You're answering the phones yourself. We're all answering the phones. Do you have time to interview every person who calls in?"

"I want in on the questioning of that neighbor. And pull me the name and number of the ex-girlfriend. I want to talk to her as soon as possible. And don't forget, the relatives and friends of the victims. You've held me up on that—"

"I know, I know, but I've had to input all this other crap—"

"Just hurry up and get me the name of that girlfriend."

## 31

"Pat?" Zelly said hesitantly; she was afraid.

"What?" The restaurant, a new Italian place a few blocks from their apartment, was busy. There was a wall of brunch conversation around them; their high-backed booth was as private as a monastery cell. Pat was drinking coffee; he drank a lot of coffee, with lots of sugar. Zelly had a cup of tea in front of her but she wasn't drinking it. Mary dozed improbably in her booster seat, every moment about to topple into the bowl of mashed potatoes in front of her.

"I wanted to talk to you," Zelly said.

"Sure, hon. What about?" The sports pages were in front of him.

"I want to talk to you about our marriage," she blurted. The paper came down and to her surprise he was smiling.

"Our marriage? You know, I've never thought of it that way, as if it were some thing, like a pet. Our marriage Fluffy."

"Pat."

"It just struck me as funny. Our marriage. What did you want to say to me about our marriage?"

"Our Fluffy."

"Yes."

"Well. This is so hard." Looking at her eggs, which were slicking over now. "I wanted to know—I need to know—am I a good wife to you?"

Pat put the paper all the way down, and as he talked he smoothed the edges with his palm, back and forth. "Of course you are, Zel. What do you mean?"

"I mean—do I make you happy?"

"This is about when you went to your mother's a week and a half ago," he said.

"Yes." All slicked over shiny, the way they get after you're done. Zelly couldn't stand the sight of food after she was done eating. They had not talked about their marriage that night. Pat had held Zelly while she cried, and then they had made love, very gently. They had not talked the next morning. Pat had been neither angry nor unapproachable, but he had not been chagrined either; he had not behaved like someone whose actions had driven his wife and baby from their home. He had played with Mary on the living room floor, and when he looked up at Zelly standing in the kitchen doorway his eyes were innocent, and Zelly could think of nothing to say. As afternoon stretched into evening and into night and the next day and she said nothing, it became impossible to say anything. It had taken twelve days to screw up her courage.

"About the panties," she said now.

"I told you about those."

"I know. I know, it's just—"

"You think I'm having an affair." There was something in his voice almost like pleasure. Mary let out a little snore and they both laughed. When she met Pat's eyes they were both still smiling.

"I'm not having an affair," he said.

"I guess—I guess I knew that. But you've been away so much—nobody has their house rewired at eleven o'clock at night."

"Actually people do, sometimes. But you're right. Not about the affair—but a lot of times it's true that I just don't come home. I can't explain it—I need to be alone, to be outside, to drive. It's a male thing. I don't drink, and believe me, I don't fool around with other women. But I need my freedom, and I need my privacy."

"I know that. But the money hasn't been coming in—"

"The money! Is that what this is about, the money?" His fingers came up off the paper like a mime creating a glass wall.

"No. It's not about the money. Pat, you haven't had a real conversation with me in months. It's about that. And—just you're being gone, and not talking. And then I found the panties and I thought—"

"Zelly, those were Karen's panties. I told you."

"And you've been carrying them around for eight years like old love letters?"

"Let's say more like library books I forgot to return. Come on, honey." His anger passed just like that. He was all conciliatory now. "Why would I carry around some woman's underwear?"

The paper was smooth under his fingers. They were talking about the one thing he could never forgive her. She had touched the lavender silk.

"—in the back of one of those magazines," she was saying. She looked sincere. He could not imagine how she thought his magazines were any of her business. He would have gotten angry again but he could see that would be inappropriate.

"Zelly honey," he said softly—she was, after all, his wife, and "wife" was a word with meaning and reverence—"those magazines have nothing to do with you. With us." (How utterly truthful he was being!) "Nothing at all."

"But you don't know how they make me feel," she said. He had never thought about how they would make her feel. He could not even imagine her looking at them. Her reality was limited to the time he spent with her. When he was gone she didn't exist. Her thoughts, her suppositions, were of limited interest to him; he needed her to be there when he got home.

He never thought that her fascination with serial killers was any danger to him. Even after she found the panties he was not afraid. Angry, but not afraid. She thought he had mailed away for them from someplace at the back of one of his magazines! She thought he was having an affair! He was quite safe. Now he listened from inside himself while he made quieting noises. That part of his life and this, the baby's head tipping farther over perceptibly now with each sleeping breath, and the memories of resisting muscle and unresisting flesh, were not connected in any way.

"—member when we met?" Zelly asked wistfully.

"Yes, I do."

"You asked for clear nail polish."

"I'd been there three times in one week and I couldn't think of anything else to ask for."

"I thought you wanted it for your grandfather. I thought you had an old Italian grandfather who played boccie ball and painted his pinkie nails with clear polish."

"I was desperate. I kept coming back and you just weren't getting the hint. I thought if I asked for something stupid you'd realize I didn't want anything except to see you."

"I did. But you could have just asked me out."

Pat smiled into his coffee cup. "Not my style," he said, and Zelly felt a rush of love for him; it hurt. Imagine if he knew what she'd been thinking!

Pat was the only man Zelly had ever slept with. Sometimes she was embarrassed about that and sometimes she was proud.

"You're everything I know about love," she said suddenly. His palms stopped smoothing the paper. "I just want to be a good wife," she said. "That's all I've ever wanted. You know that, I never wanted a career for myself, really—just to be a good wife and have lots of babies."

"Having babies is a career."

"I think so. But, lately I've been feeling like I've failed you."

"Because of the underwear?"

"Because—because we haven't been close."

"That time I put my hands around your neck—that was just something I was trying out. I thought you might like it."

"I didn't like it."

"I know. And I'm sorry."

"That's not even it. It's the communication. I guess I think you should have known I wouldn't like it—or you should have asked me. We haven't really talked for a long time. Not since before—" the first Slasher killing, she almost said, and stopped herself.

"Since I started my business, I know."

"What do you want out of our marriage?" she asked him. He looked down at the table for a long time. Then he looked at her and the depth of sadness on his face frightened her.

"Peace," he said.

# 32

"Pat wants to go to the Philharmonic concert in Cunningham Park on Friday, I forgot to tell you," Zelly said to her mother on the phone. Her mother called her often; sometimes for days on end the only person Zelly spoke to other than Pat was her mother. In the two weeks since Zelly had taken the baby to her house Mrs. Thuringen had called even more often. Each time she asked gently after Zelly's health and each time Zelly said, "I'm fine, Mama." Once her mother had asked her if she "had sorted out that problem with Pat" and Zelly said she thought they'd worked it out. Her mother didn't probe; she knew her daughter would come to her when she needed her.

"You're not going to drag the baby to that?" Mrs. Thuringen asked now. "It's been in all the papers that the Symphony Slasher practically said he was going to murder some poor woman at that concert. It's going to be a madhouse, with policemen every two feet and the press all over the place and every weirdo in New York out there under the stars with the music. Why does he want to go to that?"

Why indeed? THE SYMPHONY SEASON IS ABOUT TO BEGIN. Every year the Philharmonic gave a tour of free concerts in New York City's parks. MUSIC UNDER THE MUTILATED MOON. June nineteenth, the day after the full moon. IF YOU TRY TO STAY MY HAND YOU WILL MAKE SCHUBERT ALL THE SWEETER.

"Pat was hoping you would watch Mary that night," Zelly said carefully. She didn't want to go but she did, too: to be that close. She didn't know she was biting her lip. It was frightening and exciting at once. Like being in the laboratory when a difficult experiment is being performed. She felt guilty about being excited but she couldn't help it. It wasn't as if she wanted somebody to get hurt.

"You know I'm going down to Oak Ridge to stay with Emily," her mother said. Emily, Zelly's second-eldest sister, was nine months pregnant and counting, and she wanted her mother to be there to help when the time came. Mrs. Thuringen was always there, at weddings and births and divorces and at deaths, too; when Zelly's father died it was the mother that comforted the children, not the children that comforted the wife. "Zelly, you can't let Pat drag you both there. It's too far for Mary, and honey, you've got such pretty blond hair."

"But I'll be with Pat, Mama. And now I guess the baby will, too." *And I'll be there to*—she thought, and stopped herself. Nerves and loneliness. *There is nothing wrong with Pat.* "Anyway, he really wants to go. It's the Beethoven, and the Schubert. They're his favorites." Schubert's Quartetsatz was one of the few classical Pat had once told her that the Quartetsatz was the music the universe moved to.

"I know. I know, honey, but it's just not someplace I think

you should be. And wait a minute, I think there's a bad moon that night." Zelly heard rustling; that would be one of her mother's astrology magazines. Mrs. Thuringen considered herself something of an expert in astrological matters. She called her children to warn them that Mercury was going retrograde or there was a particularly nasty aspect between Uranus and Mars. When she came back on the line she sounded worried. "That's the night after the full moon. It's in Scorpio this month." Zelly said nothing. "Scorpio," her mother repeated. "It's a very violent moon. And there's a square between Mars and Venus. That's action—and sex. Violence. Full moon in Scorpio, Mars square Venus. The last time I remember seeing something like this was when that poor jogger got raped and beaten almost to death in Central Park."

"Mom, it's not the full moon, you just said it's the day after the full moon. And anyway—"

"You know the full moon is in effect for one day before and one day after. All the primitive types will be affected for at least three days altogether. And the square is right on that day, seven forty-nine in the evening. Oh, Zelly, that's right when the concert is."

"Eight o'clock. I'd stay home—I really would, I believe you—but you know how Pat is about astrology. Whenever I tell him you told me something he says maybe Venus is in the International House of Pancakes. And he's going to be with me and the baby. It'll be good for her, she can crawl in the grass. And what could possibly happen to me with Pat there?"

And I want to see, she thought to herself guiltily, I want to see for myself if something happens.

## 33

He would go to the whores tonight. The familiar loading docks, shadows at night where shadows moved and sucked, the familiar smells of animal blood and human sweat, were refuge, sanctuary. Only the memory of the boy tainted their sweetness. He would go, and if he saw the whore-impostor he would kill it.

But as he drove the clouds broke unseen overhead and the full moon winked silver light along the roof of the van. Suddenly he stopped the van; if you asked him his name he wouldn't have known it. There was no one on the street—nothing—except the sudden moon.

The whores could wait. He got out of the van and walked without thinking: there were no words for the things he was looking at in his mind. He saw the knife fall and there were no words for it; the blood spurted out in a perfect arc, there was blood on his hands. He clenched and unclenched his gloved hands as he walked down the street.

He had followed the one he got in the vestibule. And afterward, under the anonymous fluorescent light, he had taken off her clothes, and nobody walked by. He had had her one more time after he got her clothes off, why not? Anyone could have come by and nobody did. She lay there all night and nobody did.

Now he watched the woman walking ahead of him. She had her shoulders hunched against the cool night wind. Blond hair. His hand around her throat, in their own bed, why had he done that? Even her blond hair on the pillow unresisting had never before prompted such a response.

He moved behind her like a cat. He could see the upward slope of her cheekbone and then her hair covered it, blown gently by the balmy June air. Her high heels made a glittery, satisfying sound. Much better to have been ahead of her, to have been waiting. But she did not quicken or slow her pace as he approached. She did not look behind. So many women make that mistake: they don't look behind to see what might be catching up with them.

He kept about half a block behind her; when her steps did begin to quicken he saw a flash of silver: she had taken her keys out of her bag. Where was she coming from, alone? He could see her dead already. Feel her.

To be free of the knife must become the knife, to re-create what had been destroyed. The moment of perfect love.

# 34

Leanore Haller. Twenty-two years old. Last seen, by her friend Elizabeth Steen, outside Vivaldi's, a cappuccino café on Jones Street, at ten-thirty the night of June eighteenth. Leanore wanted to get home in time to tape *Ninotchka,* with Greta Garbo, which was due to air at eleven o'clock. Leanore had never mastered the timer on her VCR; she couldn't even get the clock part to work. She loved Greta Garbo, though. Loved old movies, especially silent movies, loved the atmosphere of old movies, the clothes, the mannered dialogue and different ways women's faces have been made up to emphasize different, desirable aspects of the female ideal: in the silent era it was eyes, large and black-fringed, and the mouth was played down, made smaller, poutier, like a child's mouth. To emphasize innocence, when innocence was a premium of sexual enticement. In the forties the women had great square shoulders and erect stances; in the twenties they stood stooped, with their abdomens thrust forward in a parody of a little girl's posture. In the movies today the women have very big, open lips, so that men necessarily think of what those lips would be like opened more, and lowered, and filled. Innocence no longer excites, and the current ethos demands at least the promise of a prostitute's expertise.

Leanore Haller painted her mouth very big, in bold red slashed across the skin above and below her rather thin lips. Midnight Rose. She affected long fringed shawls and very high black heels. The grainy shot that appeared in the newspapers the morning of June nineteenth was one that had been taken the summer before, when Leanore and her then-boyfriend, George DuBasky, went on a canoeing trip down a river upstate which the papers were never to get right. Leanore sat against a gray outcropping of rock, staring off somewhere into the middle distance. The Ramapo? The Delaware? She had a tiny half-smile on her unpainted mouth. They got her height wrong, and her middle name. The picture didn't even really look like her. Not Rose, Rosie. Because her mother loved the sound of it, and wanted Rosie for her proper name, but her husband said no one would ever take the girl seriously if her name were Rosie. And five foot eight, not five seven and a half.

Leanore Rosie Haller was found lying on her back at the bottom of a stairwell on Greenwich Street. Her blue jeans had been wrenched off one leg; the zipper was broken. Her left high heel was some two feet away, lying with the heel straight up in the air. The contents of her purse lay scattered across the sidewalk: tissues, a spiral notebook, Midnight Rose. Her blouse was undisturbed, her royal-blue fringed shawl was matted and torn under her. It was determined later that her keys were missing; they could not be found anywhere on the sidewalk or the street. That part of Greenwich is sometimes rather deserted, but Leanore had told her parents in Ohio that she was not afraid. The papers would quote her mother: "She said that she understood the dangers of the big city but she was willing to make sacrifices for her art." The lead in the high school play, the drama club in college. A pretty fair portfolio put together by a gay male photographer friend who lived down in SoHo. Nights spent waitressing or, as on June eighteenth, a Friday and Leanore's night off, spent in the company of friends.

Her throat was mottled gray and purple from the force of the hands that had encircled it. The white of her left eye was red. She had apparently died before the knife wounds were inflicted—a fact to which her mother in Ohio would cling for many years—and so the eleven cuts did not bleed much. Four in the area of the left breast, two on the right breast, four in the abdominal area, one lower down, on the upper left thigh next to the pudenda. In the newspaper picture her face was not clearly visible, just the attitude of the mouth and the self-conscious stare. At the time Leanore was thinking about how Alla Nazimova had looked in the 1921 silent-movie version of *Camille*.

Leanore's hair was ash blond, and she wore it shoulder length. Belinda Boston had yellow hair; she had had an abortion when she was nineteen. Linda Swados, whose light brown hair was lit with gold streaks in the summer, had also had an abortion, and she had been molested by her grandfather throughout most of her childhood. Elizabeth Moscineska, eighteen years old, strawberry blond, had wanted to be an opera singer when she was a child. She was attending Parsons School of Design at the time of her death. Rosalie Howard had plans, with her friend Stacy Iocca, to start a mothers' group in Hoboken. Six or seven babies, neighborhood moms, a chance to get out of the house and talk to people. Dark blond hair, dyed. Cheryl Nassent looked, in her

newspaper photograph, like a very sweet person; it was
something about the eyes. Her hair was very long, honey
blond, and a silver feather earring showed at her left ear.
Leanore had been stabbed eleven times, Cheryl five, Linda
eighteen. Rosalie had been cut only once, Elizabeth six times.
Belinda had been stabbed eight times. Leanore went to auditions for television commercials, Linda was an assistant pro-
ducer for the local public television station. Rosalie liked to
gossip, although of course she didn't call it that, and Cheryl
loved cats. Elizabeth hadn't yet gotten over how big New
York City was; her eyes were used to a distant horizon, and
she could not accustom herself to the glass canyons of Sixth
Avenue. Leanore was going to be this generation's Gloria
Swanson, a gaudy ambition that was absolutely meaningless
to the men who asked her her background at the commercial
auditions. Belinda loved to cook.

Would the Symphony Slasher keep his promise? The newspapers betrayed a subdued indignation: he had said the nineteenth. The city had been planning to put into service every
available police officer the night of the concert. The cordon
was provisioned to run approximately two and a quarter
miles around the wooded and open perimeter of Cunningham Park. The police were "cognizant of the gravity of the
situation and fully prepared to go forward" with their original plans.

The papers ran the picture of Leanore Haller, but fully half
the day's space was taken up with speculation. In 1977 David
Berkowitz, who called himself Son of Sam, promised to kill
on the anniversary of his first killing. He wrote a letter to
Jimmy Breslin, saying so. As the day approached, the media
became more and more shrill, peremptory: Why do you only
kill women with dark hair? Blond hair is the American dream.
Why do you only kill women with long hair? Short hair is

sexy too. Why do you only kill women in Queens and the Bronx? What's the matter with Brooklyn? Brooklyn is synonymous with New York. And the anniversary came and no one was killed.

The media screamed betrayal. All their deadlines had been met, space allotted in the next day's edition for the victim's picture and her history. And the next day—or the day after, not any later than that—Son of Sam murdered a Brooklyn woman with short blond hair. And the papers were grateful.

Would the Symphony Slasher keep his promise? Would he come out again to kill, the blood of his latest victim barely dry, his seed in her barely dry, her body lying on a mortuary slab awaiting autopsy—would the Symphony Slasher keep his promise to New York?

Leanore Rosie Haller had just gotten a bit part in a beer commercial, but they hadn't had a chance to notify her yet.

## 35

The last light gathered at the apex of the sky like drops in the center of an inverted bowl. An airplane high up, on its way to Europe or Iceland, was lit white by the rays of the unseen sun, which had set ten minutes ago, leaving the crowd below in shadow and the trees in sharp relief against the darkening sky. Zelly sat cradling the baby on the spread of a blue woolen blanket that stood out unearthly against the deepening dusk. Certain shirts in the summer crowd stood out, red or yellow or green, a white beach chair like a beacon, a red plastic beer cooler seeming to float above the dark sea of the grass. Girls wearing pastel dresses, men in shorts or blue jeans, materialized out of the formless crowd like chalk-faced ghosts, walked by, and disappeared. Bits of conversation floated by, inane and compelling: "—the eighty-seventh one tonight—" "—two-bit madonna—" "—the beat was wrong, it should have been sliced—" The trees were papered with a saturnine face, a sharp nose and an uncertain mouth, hun-

dreds of times duplicated in the deepening gloom. HAVE YOU
SEEN THIS MAN?

The baby was lying on her back looking at the sky, getting
sleepy. Pat stood, a shadow against azure. Zelly watched him
scanning the crowd, his sharp nose appearing and disappearing as he turned his head, a fox scenting the wind. He was a
tall figure in his work overalls, all dark blue with a white
stripe where his name should have been. He'd torn off all the
name labels when he started his own business, he said having
your name on the pocket was for flunkies. He looked almost
military, precise, a dark blue silhouette. It was nice to see him
interested in people, in being with people. Zelly didn't even
care when his eyes followed a pretty woman. All the women
were pretty under the kindly rising moon.

It was the Schubert that had him so excited. He kept disappearing into the crowd and reappearing. But Zelly knew
that when the music began he would sit and calm down; she
had seen the music's snake power, the way it hypnotized his
restlessness.

He had been out late last night, at eleven-thirty when Leanore Haller died. He had been gone last night, but this morning he had been cheerful and ordinary. He had played with
Mary while Zelly tidied the apartment, and he spoke several
times of the concert that evening. He was anxious to get a
good spot on the grass, up close to the orchestra. One nig-
gling point of suspicion remained, like the last germ of a
virus: it could disappear or it could fester and grow. Here
under the moon, among the soft undulation of the crowd,
suspicion almost disappeared.

Cunningham Park is a big green bowl of grass surrounded by
a wedge of brown woods, which in turn is bounded by suburban houses and a stretch of much-used highway. At one

end of the woods is a police storage facility where horses and motorcycles and blue-and-white police cars are kept. The woods run down from there, well traversed with narrow dirt paths and dotted with picnic tables, until they meet the gravel road and the green, where there is room for four baseball fields and a stretch for football tackle practice. In the sixties and early seventies up to two hundred teenagers wafted onto the field each night to drink wine and smoke dope, and they hardly filled the edge that borders the front of the park.

Cunningham is considered a safe park. Years ago there was one incident of a man stalking young women in the woods with a bow and arrow, creeping up toward them where they sat talking together at a picnic table or at the foot of a tree, but even he never actually shot anybody. There is the occasional rape in the neighborhood, but mostly there are car thefts; that part of Queens is famous for the number of car thefts that occur there.

Couples in white play tennis under big white bubble ceilings in the winter; in spring the bubbles deflate with a rush and the tennis players come after work to the well-lit courts to hit balls about under the moony sky. Baseball games go on well into murky twilight, and laughter carries all the way across the field into the windows of the cars passing by on Union Turnpike. An upper-middle-class neighborhood, privileged and secure.

Tonight three police vans were parked along the turnpike. TV vans lined the rim of the parking lot. TV journalists with microphones were interviewing female concertgoers who had blond hair. The women stood nervous and proud: potential targets, the chosen, blond American dream.

The previous night's murder had not relaxed police vigilance. Uniformed officers were stationed conspicuously throughout the crowd, and a blue line of police formed a

loose cordon where the woods met the grassy green; one
uniform every forty yards. The cordon had to stretch not
only across the woods and around the field but also back
along the perimeter of the woods, at the street, half a mile on
either side of the park. There were not enough policemen.
The mayor and the police commissioner had had a series of
very public arguments about the proper allotment of men,
and the commissioner had lost. But the police here in the
dusk had a reassuring solidity about them, strung out like
Christmas lights all along the perimeter of the dark woods.

Madeleine held tightly to John's arm, because somewhere in
this sea of faces there was one whose eyes only she knew.
Nobody seemed to be talking about anything else. Children
were running about among adult legs; hide-and-seek, tag.
She and John had parked the car three blocks away and followed the crowd. They were part of a steady stream of people flowing from the street into the wide round bowl of green
field under the sky. Young people laid out cheese and wine
and old people set up soft plastic lounge chairs and put their
faces up to the night sky.

Madeleine had almost chickened out. From Union Turnpike the crowd looked like a carnival. Madeleine thought of
what her grandmother used to say: When people are walking
there's something afoot. He could be anywhere; he *was* there,
undoubtedly, undetected. Madeleine couldn't stop looking at
people's faces: somebody might kill, somebody might die.
Ahead of them a teenage girl laughingly shook her long blond
hair. "Come and get it, you son of a bitch!" she called to the
line drawing on a passing tree.

"John, I'm scared," Madeleine said; it was stupid, John was
right next to her, she was in a crowd of ten thousand people.

"We can leave," he said; not the first time. She could hear

his regret. He looked out over the crowd, scanning every male face for the full enigmatic lips, the foxy nose, the Asian eyes. The face that stared, imperfect, out from every tree.

The crowd was in a high hysterical holiday mood. To Madeleine it looked like a scene in a funhouse mirror. The tight, exaggerated smiles, feral teeth and cruel, "Hey, Judy, you'd better look out, you're just his type!" "Bet the Slasher'd dig getting his knife into that one over there, huh?" The women laughed too, all of them cruel, they walked on bodies raped and bloodied, they had blood on their hands, on their feet. The orchestra tuned discordant, the notes were tiny cut-off screams. Madeleine looked at John's face and saw an eager echo of the madness even there.

There was another couple ahead of them, older, walking silently with their green-and-white plastic chairs, their faces radiant expectations of pleasure only. And for a moment there was no murderer in the crowd, no waiting eyes. The sun had only just set; the people seemed to be floating on the dark grass. The older couple stood out with reassuring solidity. "It's okay," Madeleine told John, and it was, and then she saw the man's face. Slanting eyes, his mouth open in an obscene, skull-like grin. "John, it's—" and a man she had never seen before bent to give a lollipop to his little boy. "I'm sorry," said Madeleine. "I'm being really stupid."

"No you're not." John's hand on hers, his gentle arm. The man didn't really look anything like that. "I'm seeing things," she said.

They made their way through the crowd toward the stage. John loved Schubert. Madeleine did to; they had both been coming to these concerts for years, in the same crowds, unseen. It was a pleasant surprise to her that John liked classical music, and an unpleasant surprise that the Slasher seemed to.

There was no room on the grass; every available inch

seemed to be covered in blue, in white, in old heavy olive drab, with sheets and tarps and blankets with holes. Above them Venus showed herself like a beacon in the west, but Jupiter, the navigator's anchor, was not straight above, the fixed point, where Madeleine had been accustomed to see it in the rich night skies of her childhood. The police were everywhere, searching the many-faceted face of the crowd as Madeleine searched it; there was a constant vibrating hum of conversation, with valleys and sudden, excited peaks—a woman screamed. Madeleine turned and saw his face. A teenager being tickled by two boys. No killers here.

The notes from a violin rose clean and pure from the gentle cacophony of the stage as the musicians tuned their instruments; five notes, four high and one low, rich on the warm air. Madeleine and John found a place for their blanket and the basket he had brought. Madeleine felt a childlike anticipation. John set it down with a self-conscious flourish. Red wine, wheat crackers, Stilton cheese, little green Cornichons. A tall man with high cheekbones; suddenly she grabbed John's arm.

"Madeleine, what?" He followed her frightened eyes; she relaxed her grip. "Nothing. I just—for a moment I thought I saw him. I know he's here. What if he sees me? Oh, John, this is horrible."

"We can leave. I'm sorry. I thought it would be a good idea. I don't want to upset you." She could see something here that was invisible to him. A face. "We'll go."

The man had been looking right at her. Every detail about him shone out for one instant. He was wearing some kind of uniform, dark blue. There was a white stripe over one pocket; she couldn't read anything on it in this light. The lights from the tennis courts made a nimbus around his hair, and his eyes were like drills, staring with insolent interest at her face.

There was a kind of pride about the mouth; he had smiled and then he was gone, and she was looking at a blond woman on a picnic blanket, glimpsed through legs—there was a baby crying, that was what had caught her attention. "No. I'm being ridiculous."

"Maybe we really should leave."

"No. No. It's like when your boyfriend has a blue Impala, when you're a teenager? So you see blue Impalas everywhere. It's what he was wearing." The man had been wearing a mechanic's uniform when he attacked her. "It wasn't him. If it were really him, believe me, I'd know. We knew we wouldn't really see him here. This place is a zoo, there are police every two feet."

"Then let's just listen to the music, okay?" The musicians had stilled their instruments, the stage was hushed, quickly the crowd hushed, in a smooth wave that moved out from the stage. As Madeleine took a cracker spread with Stilton from John's hand she could feel the imperceptible shiver of his desire. A silhouette menaced the corner of her eye: a woman. A dark-haired woman bending over a little girl. Madeleine met John's eyes, their fingers touching, and she smiled.

Zelly looked at Pat's serene profile. The baby drowsed in his lap. She had crawled around, making friends with the people around her and trying to eat grass, while Pat had walked back and forth into the crowd. Even from where she sat on the blanket Zelly could feel the tension running up and down his vertebrae. Then when the orchestra went suddenly silent and the crowd became silent he was back, his agitation evaporated, his smile for her easy, his hands gentle against Mary's neck as he sat next to Zelly on the blanket. She had brought lemonade and Cheese Doodles, as well as a big bag of things

for Mary: diapers and wipes and bottles and a change of
clothing and the stuffed pink poodle, an extra sweater, a rag
to wipe up with, a dropper bottle of Ambesol for her teeth,
teething biscuits, a jar of banana baby food and a spoon, an
extra blanket, and Mary's favorite pink teething ring, which
the baby held clutched in her hand as she slept on her daddy's
lap.

The conductor walked onstage to a burst of applause. Zelly
couldn't remember which one he was: somebody famous.
Funny to think about how many undercover policemen there
must be in this crowd. Zelly had been trying to guess which
ones they were. That man over there, looking at all the girls.
He didn't have a blanket or friends. That man with the blond
woman; they didn't look like a couple. Was she undercover
too?

Everybody was Slasher-watching. There he goes, that one
there, look at that guy. The man on the poster had a nose like
Pat's. It had jolted her when she first saw it: Pat's nose. A
coincidence. A hundred guys had sharp noses, feral mouths.
When Zelly and Pat first sat down she'd even heard it behind
her: "That guy there, with the baby. Jesus, it's him."

"He's holding a baby, dorkbrain. You think he's going to
commit a murder while he's holding a baby? 'Excuse me a
minute, sweetheart, I'd like to slice you but I've got to diaper
the kid.' "

"He's with a blonde." Zelly suddenly couldn't breathe. So
easy to jump to conclusions. She remembered his face across
the restaurant table, the touch of his hand against her own.

"Nice. But that ain't the guy. They woulda found baby-
food stains at the scene of the crime."

"Maybe they left that part out of the papers."

"Yeah. So they can ask the guy when they question him,

'Was that applesauce you left next to the body, or was it rice cereal?' " But she had seen the posters: it was not him.

"That rice cereal, it looks kind of like come."

"You're disgusting. Look at that guy, the one standing over by the redhead with the tits. Now, that looks like the real McCoy."

Zelly knew no one would see him. He had already killed. Even if he chose to kill again he would kill somewhere far away, or he would kill on one of the side streets in this peaceful neighborhood, mocking the police who jumped at his command. It was a false lead—it had to be. So that he could flagellate the city with his power. Just this morning he had taunted them with a body.

Was he standing on the street outside the park, listening to the Beethoven? Sitting in a car in the parking lot, watching the line at the Mr. Softee ice cream truck? Two blocks away, the Beethoven a whisper at the whim of the night wind? From the street the stage would be small, a pocket of light, brighter than the moon, the crowd a soft undulation of demicolors. Pat sat next to her on the blanket, his eyes closed, his face rapt, Zelly reached out a hand and put it on Mary's bootied foot. Pat turned his face toward her for a moment but she couldn't really see it; she thought he smiled. The music seemed to be going up, the stars were listening.

All through the Beethoven Madeleine had kept thinking she saw him. His face was blurring as she saw pieces of it in this face or that one, the nose the nose of a sixty-year-old man, the eyes for a moment above a blue mechanic's uniform, the cruel line of the cheekbone on a teenager's downy cheek.

The mouth that butchered sleep, the animal eyes that drove her gasping from sleep, had receded into only a dream—a blessing and a betrayal. How could she forget that face? The tactile memory was fading too, the skin against her skin that she had thought she would never stop feeling, like a burn, like a brand—that was fading too. She had taken a shower before meeting John and had realized, as the soft, warm stream of water washed soap from her body, that her skin felt clean, reclaimed. It was once again her skin. She listened to the music, and if she closed her eyes she forgot, for runs many notes long, that she was no longer Madeleine Levy but Madeleine-Levy-who-had-been-raped. Who had looked at her own death and said no. Now she closed her eyes against the garish light of memory and listened to the opening notes of the Sibelius.

"Zelly," Pat said. "You fall asleep?"

"Oh, no. I was thinking—do you really think there'll be a murder here tonight? It makes it hard to concentrate on the concert."

"I'm enjoying the music very much. Don't you think there'll be one? He said there'd be one, and he doesn't seem to lie."

"He. He killed somebody already, yesterday. They don't usually do it twice in two days. There are exceptions—I just can't believe it's a real person, somebody who was somebody's baby once." Mary stirred and began to wake.

"Here, you take her. I'm going to get us some ice cream."

"The line will take forever. I don't even dare use the ladies' room, the line is always twenty minutes at these things."

"Intermission is usually about half an hour. I'll be back by the time the music starts again. Wouldn't you like some ice cream? I think Mary would," he said, clucking her tiny chin; she smiled with her whole face.

"So she can have something else to throw up in the car? I'd

love some. One of those Calippo things, the ices you push up from the bottom."

"Cherry?"

"Cherry. And an ice cream sandwich for Mary."

"You'll like that, won't you, lamb? Keep the blanket warm. I'll be right back." Zelly watched him disappear into the crowd.

"Dante, we can't go into the woods. There's cops all over the place." The girl spoke with friendly exasperation—Dante and his ideas. Even though they were hidden behind some bushes across the road and thirty feet from the nearest policeman, she whispered. With Dante under the romantic moon it was an adventure. Under the romantic moon, she thought: this will be a memory someday. Me and Dante under the romantic moon. "Sure we can," said Dante. "It'll be like crossing the enemy lines at Nuremburg or wherever it was."

The girl laughed. Her name was Ariadne. Ariadne and Dante under the romantic moon. The wine they'd been drinking made everything float. Dante had been her boy-friend for seven months and he liked to do it outside, in strange places, almost in public for God's sake. Now he wanted to sneak past the cordon of policemen and do it in the woods.

"See that one there? He keeps looking over at the band-stand. He's not doing his job. We can sneak past him easy."

"What about that other one?" The wine had not dulled Dante's quiet step. From close enough to touch him Ariadne thought she was talking to a shadow. She giggled.

"Hush up. We've got to be real, real quiet. This is going to be a blast. This is going to be good." He ran his hand up the inside of her thigh. The shadow of the policeman turned the indistinct white blob of his face toward the warm yellow light of the bandstand. "That other one is looking at the girls," said Ariadne.

"You'd give him an eyeful, baby."

"I thought we didn't want to give anybody an eyeful. I thought we want to get into the woods."

"We're going to get into the woods. Look—when I say. We'll run—quiet. Crouch down when you run. See that bunch of bushes right in the middle there? Right toward that. I'll hold your hand." They knelt, shadows in their dark shirts, Ariadne's legs incandescent lines of light, her hair a pale cloud of blond light. The incidental sounds of the crowd above the music—the unmoored phrase, the laugh, the baby's cry—intensified and then faded, the Sibelius lifted up pained and fluid notes toward the distant, romantic moon, a policeman leaned against a tree and looked up at the moon, and two shadows swept across the narrow tar road and into the silent woods.

This must be the madness a vampire feels when it smells blood. Each frail carcass a receptacle only, a delicate stamen that holds the nectar that will make him whole. It is not their sex he wants but their blood, to be inside the blood, to control the blood, the breath, the beat of the heart. Here the music is silent, the stage empty, the crowd thin. He paused and looked at the bandstand, the perfect yellow arc of light and the empty space. What had she said she wanted? Calippo pops. Somebody is going to die tonight.

The knife hung embarrassing and unusable on its short scabbard underneath his untucked shirt. It mocked him, in its decorative green sheath. Like a stupid adolescent fantasy. What would he have done if Madeleine really had seen the man here? (Sibelius had been gentle as a prayer, resigned to some ancient, heavy sorrow, but light, light, on its way to a distant unhearing heaven.) What would he have done? Plunged the foreign unfamiliar blade clumsily into the man's monstrous face, destroyed the sight that had seen so much, stilled the hands that had stilled Cheryl's short, hopeful life? It was not that his nerve failed him but that his sense of the ridiculous cast up images before him: He and Madeleine jumping over picnic baskets and recumbent couples, knocking down old men in lawn chairs, knife held high, with war cries of rage and righteous anger. Or just him, crouched behind a station wagon in the parking lot where he had tracked the man, crouched down waiting as a thousand people thronged past him to get to their cars. Or he and Madeleine in his car, the killer six cars ahead in line as they inched toward the exit of the parking lot.

Madeleine seemed to be dozing beside him; he dared not move, he didn't want to touch her—not yet. To frighten her. His feelings were like a flower growing in a wound. He respected her pain, he would gladly wait forever.

He turned and dared to look at her. She could have been sleeping. She could have been dead. He had only recently seen death; before that he had only lived with the rumor. His mother's coffin had been closed against her smashed face, Cheryl's against his grief. But he had seen Cheryl defenseless on a slab in the morgue, he had been there to validate her existence in death. To say, that is the body that matches that name, those statistics on the driver's license; these are the lips, the face, the eyes behind the compact case and the Pink Lily lipstick, there, and the pathetic cracked funnel of mascara, broken he would never know where or how.

On the grass Madeleine stirred and opened her eyes. She smiled and said, "I'd like some ice cream. Want to be a gentleman, or should we both go?"

*       *       *

She couldn't see; the bright light of the bandstand at the corner of her eye as they ran across the road blinded her now, in the dark with Dante's hand sweaty in her own, leading, clenched. There'd been a sickening adrenaline rush as they swept past the two policemen, waiting an eternity of a split second to hear angry, authoritative voices; then the scuttle of gravel under their feet, loud, so loud, at the far side of the road; then sudden cool air on her face.

They stopped then, just inside the safety of the trees, branches like arms surrounding them. They did not move, and they did not breathe. Ariadne heard a hysterical little intake of breath next to her ear, and Dante's sweaty fingers squeezed her own.

Her breath was ragged and loud in her ears, a thunder in her head. But the vague shapes at the bases of the farthest trees had not moved. Dante squeezed her hand again and they disappeared into the forest, a shadow and a shadow's shadow.

Far behind, the violins took up a plaintive strain and played it to the sky. Ariadne's footsteps were louder than the music. Dante ran his hand up inside her blouse as they walked, his fingers were hot and her skin was cool. They were laughing; they could dare now to make noise.

The web of darkness in front of Ariadne's eyes was dissolving into moonlight and branches. Dante's hands were all over her as they walked. There was a dirt trail and, past picnic tables looming like crouching animals, a little path up a steep incline. At the top Dante stopped to bury his head in Ariadne's hair; she arched her neck and looked up: the full moon smiled back at her. It was light enough, when they moved again, to see a small toad hop up and away, to catch moonlight reflected from the leaves at the corner of her eye. Anticipation of pleasure built between her legs, along the soft down of her arm. Ivy brushed her naked ankles, year-old leaves crunched under her feet, something white shone on the path ahead.

"Dant—" But his whiplashed arm struck her back; a sapling branch struck her cheek. Dante moved ahead, but before his shadow obscured it Ariadne saw: a white calf, a forlorn foot, dark shorts, an obscene expanse of back, blond hair. One arm stretched out above the head, one supplicant hand. The fingers were stained dark. The moonlit dirt under the head and neck was dark. The clotted moonlight could not reflect on that dark puddle. One staring eye, one reaching hand, one forlorn naked foot. When Ariadne started screaming the policemen at the edge of the forest at first mistook the sound for violins.

He had wanted to shout his exultation to the moon, to throw back his head and release the animal roar within. He had stood above her bloody body, blood feeding the earth beneath her neck, the little ants already gathering, surely, to wet their feet in the good sticky nourishing flow. He had stood above her, spent, and as always he was grateful. He could hear the orchestra tuning up an eternity away. His breath was too fast and his hands were sticky. He focused his attention on the discordant, exploratory sounds, catgut and the slow sweep of an arm, air forced upward in a sweet exhalation. Until this moment he had been listening to his own music.

He would have to leave her. She had been given to him, and he had loved her, and now he would leave her to the ants and the forensic experts. Her stillness moved him, caught his groin, but he could not risk having her again. He had to be back before the Schubert began.

He walked softly through the woods, within sight of the lights of the road and the silent dark presence of the police, until he came to the tennis courts. There was a couple playing a desultory game, with twice-bounced balls and laughter. The policeman stationed there was watching the game: when he materialized on a rise above the courts he was not noticed; he was invisible. Walking across the empty parking lot to the van he was invisible; he took off his bloody uniform and changed into an identical one and stepped out onto warm asphalt, invisible. He washed some of the blood off in the van, with washcloths in a bucket half full of water, and he washed his hands again and slicked back his hair with water at a fountain near the tennis courts. The couple was still playing. A policeman regarded him suspiciously. He smiled and nodded reassuringly and the blind man was reassured.

Zelly opened her eyes. The Schubert was beginning. The baby had fallen asleep again where she lay on the blanket, with Zelly's hand on her back. Zelly had fallen asleep herself, the crowd's seashell murmur around her, the air like a blanket, the stars above her as she lay with one hand on her daughter's back.

The bottle of wine on the blanket next to hers was almost empty now; two teenagers lay back looking at the sky, two others were engaged in heated discussion. The old couple on the other side were holding hands. The boys in back of her were quiet: they were not looking for killers anymore. Mary's tiny hands twitched in her sleep.

Zelly looked over toward the ice cream truck; the Schubert had started. A liquid, longing fragment of a melody, a prayer to the sky. There was some movement behind the stage, some change of shift of the police guarding the woods, perhaps: a growing knot of blue. She watched as a rivulet of people drained off the crowd, like a rain stream caught in a seam in the sidewalk; it flowed down and around the corner of the stage, toward the woods. Zelly began to sit up to see better when out of the corner of her eye she saw her husband coming toward her smiling through the crowd, in his upheld hands an ice cream sandwich and a Calippo bar.

# 36

There was something—in her dream it had been an insistent image, like a drumbeat. Imperative to remember it. Imperative. Something about that word: *imperative*. The high, keening cry cut through the image like a blade through cobwebs; the word and the image and the silent undercurrent like a drumbeat, or a heartbeat, were dissolved like cobwebs. The baby was crying. It had been on the shoe and the baby was crying. Zelly got out of bed and went to her with nothing in her mind at all. Two thirty-five. The cries weren't loud; Pat slept. Zelly's breasts were full and sore; she thought she had been dreaming something unpleasant on account of her sore breasts. There was milk on the mattress again, soaked through the sheet. Zelly brought the baby into bed and lay her on a towel on the damp sheet. There had been something sticky in her dream, something on her shoe.

There is no tiredness like the tiredness a mother feels at two o'clock in the morning. It obliterates linear thinking; all her actions are the actions of an automaton: the crooning words, the gentle touch without thought, a ritual undertaken without even resignation. Whatever the mother has been dreaming will continue to possess her consciousness while she suckles her baby; rain will fall in her mind or she will walk down empty streets.

Zelly lay on her side and looked out the window at the dead light of the street lamp while the baby drank with small, excited snuffling noises. Sometimes there were people up at this hour, spillover from the two bars, one catty-corner across the street and one down the street about a half block.

Mary quieted a little, her tiny breath slowed: milk. Try not to fall asleep, have to put the baby back in the crib. The little mouth was only a faint pull, the little heart beat next to her own. His shoes had had blood on them. Zelly snapped awake; the street lamp shone like the last street lamp on a deserted Earth. The baby breathed easily in sleep. Ought to put her back in her crib. In her dream his shoes had had blood on them. The shoes in the closet or the shoes he had been wearing Friday night? He had several pairs, black and identical, which stood lined up in the hall closet. Blood on the toes, blood down along the side of the right foot where she could see it on the brake pedal.

Zelly hadn't looked at his shoes at all at the concert Friday night. Mary had started crying as the rumor spread, and Zelly couldn't pretend to be calm either. The agitated murmur of the crowd overcame the Schubert, which although it did not stop seemed to halt and die away. Blue poured in from everywhere, and cordon ropes appeared, and the eager crowd began to swarm toward the woods behind and to the right of the stage. Pat sat, his face rapt toward the musicians, his eyes closed and his ears oblivious to rumor. Zelly craned her neck and almost followed the crowd, but Mary on her lap held her back. Legs and feet flowed around them, to the right and behind the stage. The whispers became louder and more shrill. Zelly was anxious for the baby but she felt a nauseating visceral thrill: there had been a killing. Ted Bundy, the superstar of serial killers, had once taken two young women out of a crowded park in Washington State in one day, one after the other, in broad daylight, in a ruse involving a papier-mâché cast and a trailer and a mythical boat, but there had been no police, however shorthanded, to protect that weekend crowd. What evil hand of coincidence had prevailed this night? It could not have happened, but it did. Even Pat was moved to suggest they at least shift their blanket out of the way.

Zelly would have gone with the curious if she'd been alone. Not to see—someday in a book about the killer there would be a black-and-white picture of the naked back, the matted blond hair. There would be a caption: "Forensic experts examine the remains of—" She wouldn't have a name until the morning papers. But she rippled through the crowd like a dirty joke, titillating and embarrassing. Some of the women in the crowd were crying, it was true—the same women who had earlier laughed and tossed their hair and taken it as a compliment to be offered up as appropriate for sacrifice.

The face on the fliers looked out, implacable. Zelly had looked at Pat's profile against the night sky and known why the boys behind them thought he looked like the killer. Suddenly she had to get out of there: knifed—naked—found by a girl and her boyfriend after they'd sneaked through the police line for a little fun in the woods. The girl was reportedly hysterical; the ambulance that came screaming over the grass at the edge of the woods was for her. The second came quietly and slow, because the dead don't mind waiting.

Pat had been gone all during intermission, even until the

Schubert had begun playing. But he had brought back ice cream. He couldn't have had time: men do not rape and murder and buy ice cream sandwiches to bring back to their babies.

In her mind Zelly had kept seeing the hands lifting the body, the sudden insect scurry and the mulch dropping off in little clumps. They would not have moved the body yet, and she wanted to leave before they did. And in the car—the baby's cries a counterpoint to the real and imagined ceaseless murmur of conversation around them in the other cars in the parking lot—or in the closet, the foot pressing down on the brake too sharply, making the van lurch: in her dream Zelly had looked down at his foot on the pedal and there was something on his shoe. There was something like a drumbeat, a heartbeat, but it was becoming fainter and there was something about a boat, an old woman who lived in a boat, she was trying to wash something off the side of the boat, it was creeping in a dark stain up the side of the boat and Zelly was asleep.

## 37

He was proud; he was so proud. WHEN I LEFT HER SHE WAS RADIANT WITH MOONLIGHT. DID YOU TASTE HER BLOOD? There were newspapers spread out around him on the floor of the van; there was a bucket of bloody water. It was Sunday morning, June twenty-first. He needed a *T*. "Frightened." WERE THE CHILDREN FRIGHTENED AFTER THEY FOUND HER? The papers would leave out this detail. The bite mark would measure one and three quarter inches. There would be found at the scene various dark brown hairs, both from the head and from the pubic area; there would be footprints, size ten and a half. Probably a tall man. Footprints in big strides led west away from the body, but only a few feet away they mingled with footprints left by Dante and Ariadne, by the police who came when Ariadne screamed, prints from the homicide detectives from the 107th Precinct, from the ambulance attendants. A crumpled pack of Lucky Strikes would be found—impossible to know if that had belonged to the killer—and gray fibers that would be analyzed and categorized as the type used in the kind of rug commonly found in automobiles. There would be blue fibers of the type commonly found in workmen's uniforms—it was all detritus.

KELLY WAS HAPPY TO GO WITH ME, TO BE MINE FOR INTERMISSION.

Her name had been Kelly Dearlove; she had arrived at the concert with her husband and sister-in-law. By a fortunate coincidence she had been one of the young blond women interviewed on-camera for network television news. All three channels played a seemingly endless loop of Kelly's smiling face: "Of course I'm not afraid, I have my husband with me."

Kelly had gone to buy ice cream, and she didn't come back. No one had seen her near the ice cream truck; after she got ten feet from her husband and sister-in-law (who would have gone with her had she not felt sleepy and chosen instead to doze on the blanket) no one saw her at all. She had been eaten by the crowd and spit up half-naked on her face in the dirt.

So little was known, two days after the concert. Brown hair, crepe-soled shoes, workman's uniform. An ordinary hunting knife, which could have been purchased at one of any number of sporting goods stores. The man was said to be six foot two to six foot four. There was the poster. There was the FBI personality file, printed in the Sunday papers: a loner, probably unable to hold a job; unlikely to have any close familial ties; physically, and probably sexually, abused as a child; may have had abnormally close ties with his mother as a child; may have lost one or both parents in childhood; above-average intelligence; may be a collector of some sort, possibly of stamps or baseball cards; drives a dark van, probably of recent make; unable to form or sustain a relationship with a woman; probably a blue-collar worker, good with his hands—a carpenter, a construction worker; high school education; does not have a true or deep-seated love of classical music; has contempt for authority, probably stemming from childhood; may believe he has musical talent, may in fact at one time have been a member of a rock and roll band.

The police and the media and the FBI were building a mighty edifice, one which would stand shining and unshaken for many years to come. The edifice built around the actions of Jack the Ripper, for example, has stood for a hundred years, and sneaking Jack, with his poor draggled backstreet London prostitutes, has been forever buried under a more glamorous Jack, product of movies and articles and books and Hollywood, a society Jack, a Jack who can even claim royal pretensions.

Kelly Dearlove was lucky to be numbered among the one-time loves of the Symphony Slasher. (How he liked that name!) Lucky to be suspended forever in youthful extremis, never to grow old, never, in a sense, to die. Her lovely face (which had in mundane reality been somewhat heavy of jaw and brow) would eternally stare out of books and old newspaper clippings, and actresses would comb her life for clues as to how to portray her going toward the ice cream truck— eager, like a child? Or aimless, watching the crowd, unaware that her life was about to end in pain and terror? He killed them once, for his own untranslatable purposes, and then society would continue to kill them, over and over, for pleasure and instruction.

He was tired. Two in two days. The first one had already faded, even in his own memory—he felt sorry for her. That had been an impulse, a prank, sort of like a bachelor party the day before the wedding. Her picture would always appear next to Kelly's but it was an unglamorous death. Ten thousand people, after all, had seen Kelly die. Only he had seen Leanore die. But their blood was mingled in the dented pail.

He needed an *L*. "Love."

What if a witness were found? But there would be none. A dark figure, tall, carrying something bulky—who would not have alerted the police at the time they saw it? For he took his own risks, too, and was aware of his own death competing with him, as it were, for the prize of a death, each time—and each time he gave it theirs instead. His own tribulations were of course of no interest to the press. He was tired. His arms hurt. The first one—Leanore—had fought hard. Baseball cards! He snipped out the *B*. She'd practically put his eye out but the next day it wasn't even red. Unusually close to his mother, he didn't remember anything like that. It's remarkable how easy it is to get a person to talk to you, if that person is in what she believes to be a safe place. When there is no safe place.

TRUE RAGE SEEPS THROUGH DOORS AND WINDOWS AND BLUE POLICE LIKE WATER OR FIRE.

That would be good. How easy it is to get a person to take a few steps out of her way, if you are gentle—and have you seen a little boy? About so high. Brown hair. With just the barest level of urgency in your voice. (A rock band!) Over that way, toward the road? I just turned my head for a moment—oh, would you? Thank you. An *O*. So easy. And she will go in the general direction you are going, wanting to help find the child but needing also to keep you in sight in case she does find the child. Asking his name but you are so intent, in your completely understandable distress, that you do not answer, and she follows; you are calling something, softly, she assumes it is your child's name, and then you pause, at a particularly dark spot—you and she have gone rather far from the ice cream truck, which is all the way over to the left, now, and are standing across the narrow road from the shadow of the woods. And she comes up to you— this nice, normal father (the boy is just four, tall for his age, with dark brown hair)—and she stands next to you, panting a little because you have been moving fast, with fatherly concern scanning the crowd and moving toward the periphery of the dark woods. Does she notice all of a sudden that there are no people right here? That out of all the crowded park there are no people standing or sitting just here, where the woods loom dark across the road? And the police are just dark blobs to the right and to the left. And you move toward her as she steps back—but she is not going to be impolite, you have after all just lost your son. So she does not move fast enough, and a man with very strong arms who has done this before can cut the breath from the windpipe in a second, can cut off a scream in the throat in a second.

A *D.* "Blood." While he was running across the road with her limp body he got hard, instantly, because that was the only moment when he was really naked—not back when he first saw her, not when he spoke, not when she followed him all unsuspecting, because nobody saw any of that—but when he was in the road he was naked, even if the police were woefully understaffed (which of course he knew from reading the newspapers), even if the police were spaced only one every forty yards one of them might have seen him, she was so light, though, and he had a hard-on by the time he got across the road.

WHEN I LEFT HER SHE WAS RADIANT WITH MOONLIGHT. DID YOU TASTE HER BLOOD? WERE THE CHILDREN FRIGHTENED AFTER THEY

FOUND HER? KELLY WAS HAPPY TO GO WITH ME,
TO BE MINE FOR INTERMISSION. MY SON IS NOT
MISSING BUT THE POLICE WERE. I LEFT MY RIGHT
INCISOR CHISELED INTO HER NECK. I LOVED
THEM ALL. I LOVE THEM ALL. THE PEOPLE WILL
KNOW ME, FOREVER, LIKE JACK. I DO NOT COL-
LECT CARDS BUT HEARTS, I STOP THEIR FOOLISH
BLOODY BEATING. YOU CANNOT STOP ME,
THEY DO NOT WANT YOU TO TRY THEY ARE
MINE. WE WILL MEET AGAIN BUT NOT WHEN THE
MOON IS FULL. I AM NOT SO SHALLOW WHY A
VAN? WE WILL MEET AGAIN.

## 38

"What more have you got on that guy in Queens?" Blackman asked Scottie.

"Right age, right race, right height, right coloring. Wrong car."

"But he could be driving something other than a van. The van that couple saw the night Madeleine Levy was attacked—"

"Could have been anybody's," Scottie finished. "I know. He looks good. Hasn't held a job longer than four months in the last two years. As far as the girlfriend knows, unemployed now. Has a history of altercations with women, threatened to kill his girlfriend that night outside a restaurant, according to the woman and six witnesses. Called her a 'blonde ball-cutter' several times."

"You think he's the one?"

"I can't hope. He looks good, that's certain. But we still haven't talked to him. That's been set up for Thursday."

"Three days from now."

"Listen, I got something for you on our mystery caller."

"God, yes."

"I talked to Elizabeth Moscineska's boyfriend," Scottie said. "He's got a Brooklyn accent you could spread on rye bread with pastrami. He didn't sound like your guy. And he didn't fit the type. He kept pounding his fist. And he kept saying, 'What was she doing out so late by herself, anyway?' Like she was two-timing him. He's not our boy."

"Scottie, the reactions of the nearest and dearest always amaze me."

"After I went through all the files I had," Scottie went on, "I talked to one of the husbands—Ken Swados. Basso profundo. And the other guy—Belinda Boston's husband—you're going to love this, he already knew Levy's name. Seems he gets the *Post* delivered. You ever hear of anybody getting the *Post* delivered?" Blackman shrugged and took a sip of his coffee. His expression didn't change but his tongue moved a little in his mouth and then his lips pursed. "We're going to have to keep digging," he said.

"I've got one left. I've been checking brothers. Belinda Boston had one, Elizabeth Moscineska had two, and Cheryl Nassent had one. John Nassent. So far it's a big nothing."

"Did you contact Madeleine Levy?"

"Yeah. She had her phone number changed but she'll contact us if anybody gets through to her."

"You know the lieutenant told me not to pursue this lead."

"What did he say?"

"He said he didn't give a flying rat's ass whether some nut job wanted to talk to Madeleine Levy. But I know there's something hinkey about this. I know that bastard killed two more girls just last week, and there isn't a man on the force that wants him more than I do, but I want you to follow up on this. Check out John Nassent. It might not seem like much, but there's something going on here and I have a very strong feeling that somebody's going to get hurt."

# 39

The young woman hesitated before opening the door. There was a clink, and one brown eye looked out from under a loop of chain.

"The electrician?"

"Yes, ma'am." And the door opened and he was inside. The woman was nervous. In an instant he knew her life. The kitchen floor was not clean, and the living room table was cluttered with magazines; the woman lived alone. She had stayed home from work today because the electrician was coming. There was a half-full coffee cup on the kitchen counter, another on the table in the living room. As she walked ahead of him he looked at the nape of her neck under the red elastic band in her dark hair.

"It's in here," she said, "that fixture there."

"I'll need a chair or something to stand on."

"Oh. Okay." He watched her bend to lift a chair from the table that stood against the wall of the living room. They were always nervous about having a strange man in the apartment. He did nothing to set them at ease; he watched. The woman put the chair down in front of him, her hand drawn back quickly as his reached out. Behind her he could see the newspaper open on the table. KILLER KEEPS PROMISE AT CONCERT: CLAIMS SIXTH VICTIM. Saturday's papers. None of the papers ever mentioned the one on the Stevens' campus; he wondered why. He was so proud of that one.

The young woman had Sunday's papers too, with practically the same headlines because the media were so pumped up by these killings that they didn't want to let them go in just one day. And today's papers too, with in-depth interviews with psychologists and police experts, analyzing the crimes for the umpteenth time. When he stepped up on the chair, perspective shifted with a bump. Everything looked a little bit smaller. "—gas pipe in the fixture—" the woman was saying. The building was old; the ceiling fixture housed an open gas pipe, from the turn of the century most likely. The woman wanted the gas pipe sealed off and a fan installed. He wondered what she would look like with her head pulled back—but it was idle speculation. He was sated and calm.

He loved what he did. He was still enamored of the stillness of his victims, still enchanted by his anonymity. But something was reaching out now to stay his hand. The vision of the low, dark room? It came more frequently with each fresh kill; since the murder in Cunningham Park it played at the back of his consciousness like a musical riff, faint and changing but ever the same, never getting closer but never entirely forgotten.

Could he be free of the fever need? He could kill for a long time before killing lost its charm, he knew that. And he could bait the press and the whole city with his letters for a long time too, relishing his controlling hand behind every newspaper article, every TV sound bite.

Yet his wife wanted him home. He had frightened her, had driven her away. He had tested her love and found it strong; but he had also made her cry. She was his wife. She was pure—except for that one delirious, uncontrolled moment, the baby screaming in the playpen. But he would expiate that sin. And she would never leave again. He would stay home for awhile.

The woman sat on the sofa and read the paper and didn't look at him. She was wearing sweatpants and a white T-shirt. There was a pair of hunter-green pleated pants slung over the edge of the bed, and a peach silk blouse. There was nothing provocative about the woman's pose on the sofa; she was just sitting there. From where he stood on the chair he could see the top of her bowed head, and the tops of her breasts under the T-shirt.

What would she do if she knew? His hands were busy with the open pipe but he was aware of her. Would she cry? Scream? She sat there and he knew she was thinking about him. The newspaper made a rustling sound as she turned the page. She was still reading about him: there were pictures of the six women. He had Leanore's keys in his pocket. The woman put her hand tentatively over the picture of Cheryl Nassent; Cheryl smiled uncertainly at the camera and the light caught the silver feather at her ear. The woman's finger caressed the earring; it came off soot-gray in her hand. He could still hear the honeyed memory of her voice. Had she told him her name? He never thought of her by name.

There was a time when he had never killed, but that was long ago and he didn't remember it well. A summer day, three or four boys in a guiltless, self-absorbed circle: when you take the right wing off look how he twitches, when you pour the lighter fluid and touch the match to it, look! Taking the legs off flies, if you are an eight-year-old boy, is a perfectly ordinary thing to do. He'd had no sisters to torment. But he could yell, "No girls on the slide!" and push, hard, and mothers would be indulgent. Kiss the girls and make them cry.

He killed a kitten when he was nine. It submitted with slit eyes to the fingers rubbed behind its ears, along the delicate bones of the underjaw. It purred. Its neck vibrated lightly under his hand: sinew and bone. When he tightened his fingers the body pulled abruptly and claws dug into his leg and then he really was angry. He rubbed his thumb against his forefinger with the neck between them, the other hand at the back feet, holding them away from his thigh. He couldn't have said what he was thinking about.

Then the kitten was dead. He didn't remember this now; he remembered it in dreams sometimes, and he always loved the feel of fur. The woman had turned the page and she wasn't thinking about him anymore.

If he continued to kill, would his wife begin to suspect?

He knew she was not a fool. Even with all her reading and all her thinking and all her psychological second-guessing she was blind to what he was doing, as the world was blind—but she was closer than the world. And when she found the panties he had discovered that it was possible for the world to come to him in his most secret places. She would have to be watched.

She did not suspect—he knew that. Even when she held the evidence in her hand she had not known. And he had rendered it innocuous with lies. Always he had the power of his lies. But what if—what if? Gnawing at the certainty of his invincibility. And he could not bear to have her know. To have her innocence destroyed.

Because then he would have to kill her.

"This isn't going to be a very tough job," he said genially, and the woman on the couch lifted her head and smiled a little.

# 40

John couldn't remember whether Eenie Meenie was a gay bar. It had windows—Madeleine had said that most of the gay bars in the Village still didn't have windows. But he didn't see any women in the windows. There were very few women at all on the street here, at the corner of Christopher and Greenwich. It was eleven o'clock on Monday night, June twenty-second, and he really wanted to be with Madeleine. There were a lot of men here, young and muscled and convivial and loud. They all looked the same to John: close-cropped, almost military hair, clean-shaven faces; if there was a mustache it was short and straight. All the men were immaculately groomed. They wore muscle shirts, T-shirts with the collars cut off, skin-tight jeans. Their skin shone with a uniform health-club glow. They called to one another from across the streets.

Quite a few of them had something to say to John. A transvestite in a yellow dress—John would have thought he was a woman anyplace else—called out, "Hey, straight boy, who you think you're fooling? You want a little real action you come right over here to Mama."

"No, thanks, I already have a mama," John said, smiling. Two black men standing in front of an X-rated video store ("Video Rentals, Novelties, Magazines, Rubber Goods") muttered, "He think he like pussy but he hasn't tasted a real piece—" John wondered at their antennae; he would not have taken every one of them for gay; for all the sameness of their uniform he wouldn't have been able to say for certain anyplace else, This one is, or, That one is not. But he was obvious to everybody here.

Eenie Meenie probably was a gay bar. But there was an Off-Broadway theater up the block, and tourist shops—candles, antiques, fancy chocolates—among the X-rated appliance stores and the gay clothing shops. John had been going in and out of bars and restaurants for two hours and he was a little high from the drinks he'd ordered and he hadn't found out anything at all. He was tired of identifying himself as the brother of a murder victim.

He stood for a moment as though contemplating a jump into deep water, and then he shrugged and went into Eenie Meenie. If it was a gay bar he would just leave. "Well, well, Princess, we're proud of you!" somebody shouted at his back.

Inside the door it was so smoky that John could not find his breath. "Don't choke on it, boy," a voice said; an apparition out of the smoke, a pale face with kohl-rimmed eyes and scarlet lips—a boy, maybe eighteen years old.

"I don't intend to," John said affably, heading for the bar. It was a gay bar all right but he was already inside and anyway who knows where hope is?

The long, scarred cherry-wood bar stood like a distant shoreline across the sea of unfamiliar faces, every one of which seemed to be pointed toward him. For a moment they seemed to be moving toward him, like foam on a wave. There were a few catcalls, an overall scrutiny so piercing that John forgot what he was wearing, and then the wave crested, and dissipated into a hundred fragments of bodies—heads, backs, elbows, arms. Every mouth in the place seemed to be moving. Lips smoked and lips talked, and lips opened suggestively or in boredom, and John was still certain everybody was looking at him as he made his way across the floor.

John knew better than to ask the bartender for what he really wanted, which was a screwdriver; he ordered a whiskey and soda. "Sure," said the bartender, blessedly without a smile or even any overt acknowledgment at all. John felt his spine relax a little and he dug in his pocket for a cigarette.

"Need a light?" A chocolate hand, perfect nails. John shook his head, smiling without looking up, but then he couldn't find his matches—how was he going to get out of here without feeling like a fool—and he sat with his cigarette dead between his fingers, and when he looked up the hand was still there.

"Nobody's going to bite you—unless of course that's what you're looking for. Me, I don't like the rough stuff." It was a young black man, perhaps John's age, perhaps younger. He wore a gold muscle shirt that showed his pectorals and biceps to good advantage. His eyes were green. He had a wide, flat nose and the slightly skewed aspect of a fighter. His manner was much younger than John's. He was as amiable as a stray puppy.

"I just need a light," John said, but he smiled in return. "Listen—" he said after one deep nauseating, soul-satisfying pull on his cigarette.

"Felix," the young man said.

"John. Listen—I'm looking for somebody."

"Trying to find a man?"

"Yes and no."

" 'Cause honey, we're *all* trying to find a man."

"That's the no. This is a specific man. I know he wouldn't come in here—"

"What make you think you know? 'Cause he straight? You here—you straight, right?"

John laughed. "Right. But I don't think he would. Women are really his thing. I just came in here by mistake. I'm looking for the Symphony Slasher."

The rap music on the jukebox held a beat and his words fell heavily into sudden silence: "Symphony Slasher." Felix paused in lighting his own cigarette and held the match up like a torch and peered at him under the little flickering light. "That the man you looking for? What make you think he be here?"

"I don't. I didn't know this was a gay bar."

Felix threw back his head. "Hey," he shouted out to the room at large, "Mr. White Bread here say he didn't know this was a gay bar! Now, you want to tell him or should I?" And a wave of faces turned toward him again and a chorus of voices, overlapping, shouted out, "This," with a pause for emphasis, "is a *gay bar!*" The bartender set down John's drink with a flourish; it seemed to John like the ending to a dance routine. "Yeah," he said, "I figured that out."

Felix clinked John's glass against his own. There was a ring of people around them now. Some had heard the words "Symphony Slasher" but most only saw a chance for sport.

"That Slasher guy, he kill women. White women. Don't look like anybody around here be interested in that particular flavor of fish."

"Yeah, man, we don't go for hair pie." There was a chorus of whistles and raucously held noses. The faces went out of focus for a second.

"He murdered my sister," John said quietly.

A hush fell. Glass clinked and voices could suddenly be heard toward the back of the room—"His sister, man." John realized that he was holding his whiskey glass so tightly that his fingers were cramping. He set it down carefully. "Your sister?" Felix said. "I'm sorry. I don't behave very well sometimes. We thought you was here for the experience."

"No. It's not an experience I'm enjoying, particularly." But he felt distracted from his own pain; he would learn nothing here.

"I want to apologize for these ingracious ignoramuses," said Felix. "Unfortunately some people are brought up in barns—"

"I know nobody meant any harm," John said wearily.

"Eddie, get this man another drink. I want to correct the image of inhospitality these cretins have given you of this establishment. I'd like, myself, to—" There was a commotion somewhere in the room, a self-important ripple through the crowd. Whispered voices could be heard: "The Slasher—" "his sister—" and this new noise overlay that; it sounded as if a path were being cleared for royalty.

"Let me through, you silly bitch, I've got something important to tell this guy—Felix—"

Felix, who had stopped talking at the interruption, looked around, leaned over, and asked cheerfully, "Which one was she?"

"Cheryl Nassent." It was the first thing everybody asked. Felix looked blankly at him. "End of April." They never remembered her any other way. But he always said her name.

"Oh," said Felix, "that was a bad one."

"Took her right off the street, in the middle of Bleecker."

"They found her all the way over by the West Side Highway, man."

"I got a cousin lives over there, Horatio and Washington." They were explaining it to themselves. For a moment there was random chatter, static, and then the focus shifted and everybody was looking at the young man shouldering his way through the crowd.

"Let me through, you bleached-out Philistines." The young man was dressed in a black T-shirt ("I'm With the Faggot") and his eyes were heavily made up. His hair was several shades of blond; it was long and a little stringy. "Felix," he said, leaning to kiss the air by Felix's cheek. "Pleased to meet you," to John, with what seemed to be involuntary sexual emphasis. He looked John up and down and John looked him up and down.

"Yeah?" John said in a friendly way. He had finished his drink and he was going home now.

"You know," Felix said with exasperation, "you really could—I swear to God, Em, you've got the manners of a junkyard dog. What do you want? Our visitor is grieving here." John apparently belonged exclusively to him.

"I've got some important information for our visitor, if you don't mind." John found himself wondering if it was really Em, or just M, like the movie.

"What important information, Miss Sissy Pants?"

"You like my pants well enough. Well, Mister White Bread, I really do have news for you. I have a friend, her name is Angel—"

"Is it Em or M?"

"What? Oh, M. Just M."

"Oh."

"Do you want to hear it or don't you?"

John wanted to go home. "Shoot," he said.

"Angel—"

"Oh, no, not that crackheaded little pussy."

"Angel! That girl sure been flying, I tell you—" Again a little ripple went through the crowd. John waited for the eyes to settle back. At least this was more interesting than the MTV over the bar. A woman. He hadn't expected that.

"Yes, Angel. And she looks like one, too. I know she's not the brightest light on Broadway—"

"She sure no gyropsysicist," Felix put in.

"—but she sees what she sees. And she told me she saw the Symphony Slasher a couple of months ago."

Derision leapt from mouth to mouth. Angel was addle-pated, Angel was a druggie and a fool. And a voice saying, "Damn, man, she just different from you all. She got a poet's soul."

"She's something, I tell you," said M. "But I saw her. And she's got a busted cheekbone. Seems she fooled a certain client of hers just a little too well, if you know what I mean, and when he saw the beef he just went apeshit."

John didn't know exactly what he was talking about. Felix leaned over and said, "This dude thought she was a Genny," and John nodded, mystified.

"So, anyway, this guy just beat the living—well, we have ladies present, I won't say. But he kept saying something about who he was or something, and Angel swears this is the guy in the poster."

Once more there was a great deal to be said around the room. Angel wouldn't recognize her mother's tittie. Angel *wishes* she could fool a straight man. And the same voice saying, "You just don't understand her. She different from you all." A lot of things John didn't quite understand. "Where is this Angel?" he asked M.

"She works nights. Up in the meat district." M put an emphasis on "meat"; he seemed equally incapable of not making a joke or of knowing he had made one.

"She's a hustler," Felix leaned over to whisper helpfully.

A prostitute. Of course. "Got it," John whispered back. "How can I find her?" he asked M.

"Just walk up the block, handsome," a voice sang out, "and she be sure to find *you*."

"Felix, get me out of this," John whispered.

"Now, you all lay off the man and just tell him what he need to know." Which they did, eventually, and John had another drink and didn't pay for it, and when he finally found himself alone outside the door he thought that he would miss them all, and that he was glad to be an anecdote in the memory of that bar.

# 41

The concrete island at the middle of the intersection looked like an oasis of light. There were bloodstains in the gutter. There were no trees; there were warehouses and traffic and the dark sky above low roofs. He had passed from the cool, leafy darkness of Madeleine's neighborhood out into the barren meat-packing district.

John had just left Eenie Meenie but already it seemed like a long time ago. He stood hidden in shadow at the corner. The concrete island in front of him was alive with movement, furtive, flamboyant, bizarre. Like a dung heap, or a stage. There was a woman—was it a woman? Tall, dressed in gold lamé, Elvis in stiletto heels. A pair of women who really were, arguing over something on the ground next to them. A purse? A small dead body? They circled like dainty middle-weights. Farther up the block another transvestite talked earnestly with a casting-call drug dealer, all Rolex and Stiff Stuff. John stood in shadow and knew he was the alien here.

A car slowed up the block and a woman leaned into the front window as casually as a housewife leans over a neighbor's wall. The mouth costs so much, the hand this amount. How are the kids getting on at school? You really want to party it'll cost you—this—but no kissing.

The woman opened the door of the car and stepped into oblivion. Tomorrow she might be a rumor—last seen getting into a green Acura sedan, last year's model. Anything strange about the car? No. The driver? Was there a driver? If he had any face at all we didn't notice it.

They open the door to death a dozen times a night and nothing happens; no dark angel rustles overhead, no alien wind disturbs their hair as they bend over their flaccid, sticky bread and butter in the front seat next to the Styrofoam coffee cup, yesterday's paper, and the little pile of change. She would be back in fifteen minutes. She wouldn't even have to rearrange her skirt.

John walked up the dark street toward the hookers under the streetlight. "Want a date?" A voice so young and soft he half expected to see Cheryl's scrubbed face; instead he saw black skin, improbably arched eyebrows, impossibly yellow hair.

"A date," she said patiently.

"Oh," John said stupidly. She stood regarding him from the shadows of a loading dock, her red lips a winking beacon on a rocky shore. "I'm looking for a man," said John.

"No offense taken," she said affably. "Hey, Twinkie, I got a live one for you!"

"No, I—" Once again John stood and let himself be caught up in the comic possibilities of the moment. An enormous transvestite was heading for him. John felt as he watched the transvestite approach that he was the one on display, ripe fruit on a counter in the hot sun; he would be felt and squeezed.

"This more like what you're looking for?" asked the per-
oxide whore agreeably. The transvestite was an Amazon.
Black leather bra, black skirt up to here, a Nile of thigh: all
the semen of every man she'd ever been with could run down
that expanse of thigh with room to spare on both banks. *I
wouldn't even make a mouthful,* John found himself thinking
idiotically.

"I'm sorry," he said, "I'm not really in the market." This
person in false eyelashes and four-inch heels could easily tear
him in two—not even a morsel.

"He said a man," explained the blond whore.

"Yes. I'm sorry. I'm trying to find a man—a specific man—
and I was told somebody here might have seen him. Might
know him. Actually," to the transvestite, barreling through
now as though this were not at all strange to him, these
people, this scene—"I don't think you'd know who I mean."
Two pairs of eyes looked at him but he knew they had already gone on to other things in their minds: that one on the
corner, a shower would feel good, the light in the kitchen as
the sun comes up. The blonde had already forgotten him; she
was digging in her bag for a cigarette.

"He killed my sister," John blurted out, and he saw himself
come to life in their eyes; he saw himself appear. A car pulled
up alongside them, the driver leaning out over the sidewalk;
the transvestite impatiently waved him on. *The Slasher killed
his sister.*

"The Slasher?" the transvestite asked. His lips were wet.
John was wrong, he was no more real than he had been
before he spoke. This was something that was only happening to these people here, *then he said he was looking for the man
who killed his sister and I just* knew *he meant the Slasher.*

"Yes," said John. "Somebody told me somebody here had

maybe seen him." The words were nonsense in his mouth. Cheryl could never have any reality here. John felt himself fading away like the Cheshire Cat, and Cheryl had never lived, not here on these streets where blood ran in the gutters.

"The cops've been up here," said the blonde, "twice. Wanting to know if there've been any weirdos." She laughed; she held a match up to the cigarette while she laughed. "Weirdos. We knew what they meant. Johns who like the rough stuff."

"Hell," said the transvestite. Twinkie. "We got people here *specialize* in the rough stuff."

"And the second time they got this picture and they say anybody around here ever look like that." The blonde took a deep drag on her cigarette and looked at her nails: Dragon Red. *And then I told him all about how the cops come up here rousting us, have we ever seen the Slasher.*

"Did you?" asked John.

"Did—oh, hell, yes. Six or seven guys. And weirdos too. But not what they're looking for. I mean, one guy's got the foxy nose, but he doesn't like blondes. And another one has the eyes but he's too old. One likes blondes but he likes 'em dark like me, you know? The rough ones, we got a Spanish guy's crazy, he likes to choke the girls. Won't none of us get in his car no more. But he's Spanish. And they say they been looking for a dark van, it's got—I forget. They ain't been telling this to the papers or anything, they don't want him to change cars or anything like that. A dark van with something about the front—with paint or something on the front—on the door."

"Tape," said Twinkie.

"Yeah, right, like he was taping over a business name. I remember. But I don't know, we see a lot here, you know?"

Silence for a moment, smoke, and John thought that they would just dissipate like rain—or he would. They would refocus their eyes and he would be gone.

"There was one got hurt bad," Twinkie said, "but's she's not a Genny so the cops didn't care. But she told me she thought it was the Slasher did her. Fuck the cops, they don't think she's woman enough for the Slasher. They didn't even want to talk to her."

"She's not a—?"

"A Genny. A genetic woman. Angel. Says he thought she was a woman and when he found out she wasn't he just went apeshit—you should pardon. Broke her cheekbone."

"That was the name I was told. Angel." Angel was not a woman. It was a waste of time, then. "I don't think I—"

"She's around here somewhere. Listen, I'll show you. It's probably not the guy, I mean Angel isn't even blond. But your sister and all."

"How did your sister die?" asked the blonde. She was wreathed in smoke like the Caterpillar; John half expected her to suddenly point her hookah and say, "But *whooooo* are *yooooou?*" To which he could only reply, like Alice, "Well, you see, I don't rightly know, I've been so many people lately." Angel was not a woman, and he was talking to these people for nothing, and Cheryl wasn't even dead here, she was just a name in a newspaper. The blonde was looking at him.

"I mean, which one was she?"

He had been asked the question so many times just tonight that he had stopped caring. "Cheryl. Cheryl Nassent."

"What month?" Her thoughtlessness was actually invigorating; there was no callousness here, only a healthy animal curiosity; he imagined she was as relentless about nail polish, or lottery numbers. With just the same satisfaction about the mouth.

"Last week of April."

"Last week of April. Oh, that was a bad one." Suddenly she stuck out her hand. "My name's Dixie—really. That's my real name, Dixie. This is Twinkie. We'll do what we can. Scum is scum." John felt a ridiculous urge to cry, and he knew that it would not be considered ridiculous here to give in to it. Twinkie took his arm with taloned fingers.

They walked up the block; Twinkie walked as though he were on a high-fashion runway, and Dixie never lifted her feet off the ground. John could imagine eyes looking at them from every empty window. He had lost control of the night, and he was willing to go anywhere.

At the top of the block, in a pool of shadow, a slim form swayed against a brick wall. Twinkie's heels and Dixie's mules made a loud, uneven clattering noise, like the echo of hoof-beats; the slim form turned a languid neck toward the ap-proaching sound. John's breath caught in his mouth at the sight of the pale face. The figure raised a hand to guard the throat, and Dixie said, "Hey, Angel," softly, as though Angel were a kitten, and John stopped, so as not to frighten her. The boy's eyes were preternaturally bright without giv-ing the impression of seeing anything at all. When Twinkie bent to kiss her cheek his big back obscured the flamelike face.

Twinkie and Dixie spoke among themselves for a moment; when they turned away from Angel his face dissolved into confusion. "Tell this guy what you told us about the Slasher," Dixie said encouragingly; "His sister was one of the girls the bastard got." She tilted her head a little, shrugged her shoul-ders just a little, for John, and leaned forward and said, "She don't know what she's talking about. I mean, she don't lie

but she don't know, either. Good luck." And she unexpectedly kissed John's cheek and was gone. He could hear Twinkie's unself-conscious laughter moving up the street. Then he
turned toward the boy.

Angel stood looking beyond him, toward the unseen river.
He seemed completely unaware of him. "Angel?" John said.
The boy gave no indication of having heard. "Angel, I have
to talk to you. I have to find out about the man you say hurt
you. It's very important to me—"

"I don't exist," Angel said abruptly. He seemed to be
merely continuing a conversation. "These guys in their cars,
they go back to Long Island to their wives and their babies
and I don't exist. I took the test, three weeks ago, you know?
And last week I came back positive. The cops roust us once
in a while, but we don't exist for them either. Like roaches.
You ever really think about the roaches you got in your nice
clean apartment? Even if you never see them. Everybody
dies, baby, right? So some die clean and some don't. I'm
sorry what happened to your sister, all those girls, but nobody asked me, okay? He's kind of like a disease—except you
don't wait around to start dying. I didn't tell because nobody
asked me, okay? Just that one cop, and his partner stopped
him. Because nobody anywhere gives a shit about any of us
down here. I haven't got any get-well cards from the New
York Police Department, you know? But of course you
don't."

One cheekbone hung a little higher than the other; it gave
the boy's face the look of having been grasped improperly
before it dried. John leaned forward to hear him, and Angel
lifted his face toward him. Angel, yes. Great liquid eyes with
something in them a child has, an absence of fear. A siren's
mouth. John forced himself not to lean back, to admit the
power of those eyes and that mouth. Of this boy. John could

not keep his eyes off the mouth, it was like some exotic flower, venomous, voluptuous, ravenous. He watched it the way a woman watches a woman, with equal parts envy, distrust, and empathetic desire.

"You don't get to look forward to very much here," Angel said. "Like—you see these guys?" Gesturing to the empty sidewalk, the street; there was a car at the light, a maggoty form behind the wheel. "They're all like that. Big fat guys. Or little guys like you. You're surprised, huh? Yeah, like you. You're from Queens, right? I can always tell. But you don't have the look. Like ferrets. I had a friend had a ferret, it always looked like it was afraid of you. Like it was going to bite. It never did, but I didn't like to pet it. I like gentle things. They have eyes like that, like, they're guilty and it's your fault. And then they go home to their wives. America's going to die, man, all these guys go home and fuck their wives they still got my spit. This guy, he didn't look like he had nobody to go home to."

"What did he look like?"

"Not really like the picture, unless you've already seen him. But enough like it—but beautiful. He had eyes like—like he could have told you something. He really couldn't tell I'm not a Genny." The boy was proud of that.

"I wouldn't have known, either."

"You wouldn't? That's why they call me Angel. It's not my name, even though I'm a spic. My name is really Jesus. If my mother could see me now." He rolled his eyes.

"Tell me about the man."

"You don't think it's shit, what I do, but I tell you—what's so great about reality? Ain't nobody wouldn't leave it if they could. I was going to be in the movies. I can get a ride out to California anytime. One of my clients, he said I got the bone structure. Before this." He touched his face.

"If you could tell me what happened—"

"He didn't know. He thought I was the real McCoy. Usually they like my act, you know? Where I come on all womanly and after I get a little butch. Show them my balls. You want to see my balls?"

"No."

"Don't worry, I'm just teasing you. He was a beautiful man," Angel went on. "So I opened the door and I got in." He already knew every question John could have asked him, and he knew the things John would never ask. "He looked Asian, like Henry Miller. That's when I wish I'd lived. *Pied-à-terre. Glacé.* All those great words. And all those cafés where you can sit all afternoon for the price of a café au lait. He married a whore, you know. June. After I saw the movie I wanted to call myself June but I was already Angel by then. He had eyes like that. The man. You know I always thought I would know if something was going to happen—and I did. When he looked at me." Angel looked across the street into nothing, into the man's eyes. "But when you know you're going to die anyway. I mean, I've got to live, you know? To make a living. And if it kills me—what was this, anyway?" caressing his Picasso cheek—"a memory, right? 'Cause it sure as hell ain't going to get me off the streets. It didn't change my life. But he was beautiful. So I got in. So what. And I did him—you ever been done by a man?"

"No."

"I didn't think so. You come from Queens, right? Not even any fucking around when you were a kid? So, I got in the car and I did him and he was a pleasure, let me tell you some of these guys stink. And they hold you down so you have to swallow. I spit it back in their faces. They love it. But this guy—I thought maybe he could have been something more. You don't think it ever happens in the front seat of a car? With a whore? It happens. Men love whores. Like Henry Miller. I guess I'm just looking for a way out. I use condoms, I don't want to hurt nobody." He was still looking away; he was talking to himself.

"He looked like the evil prince in a fairy tale. Every girl's dream. So I offered him a little bit more." He stopped talking for so long that John thought he would not come back. "He said, 'Do you know who I am?' That's all. While he was beating me. First I just thought he was turning himself on. I thought it wasn't me he was hitting. And he said—you know what he said? Like God, you know in the Bible, what's he say? 'I am that I am.' Or *what* I am. But that's what he meant. Like God, like I'm supposed to know. And then later I saw the picture and I did know. The same guy that killed all those girls. It would have been a kick if he hadn't hurt me. I'm sorry. But it was—power is such an aphrodisiac—somebody else's. Do you like to feel powerful?"

"I like to feel like I'm not getting a bullshit act."

"I'm sorry. I guess I'm a bad boy."

"We're talking about the man who might have murdered my sister." But he could see it, shining out of the cloudy pools of the boy's eyes: *I aroused his passion, and to me he imparted his secret.*

" 'Do you know who I am,' " Angel said softly. "I'm sorry." He paused again. "And now I know who he is. But what good does it do you?"

"I need for you to tell me if you see him again. You can call me, maybe you can get his license number. And of course I can pay you—"

"I don't want your fucking money"—surprising John—"I don't know if I give a shit—I don't know. It's sad when beauty dies. It'll be sad when I die, won't it? I'll help you. If I don't lose your card or give it to somebody for a joke. John Nassent. Were there a lot of flowers at her funeral?"

"Yes."

"I want a lot of flowers at my funeral. Were there a lot of people there?"

"Yes."

"I got my whole funeral cortege right here," gesturing at the empty street. "He said if he ever saw me again he'd kill me."

"Oh. Well, I couldn't ask you—"

"I'm going to die anyway. I told you—I'm HIV positive. I'm walking around dead right now. It doesn't matter if I don't hurt yet. As soon as I do—first sign—I'm going to kill myself. I'm going to jump off the Brooklyn Bridge. I'll be in all the papers. I was born in Brooklyn, you know that? This way I get to go out big but I don't hurt anybody else. It's going to be cool. I'm going to have all my friends come and watch.

"Don't feel sorry for me, man. I don't want to get old and lose my figure. You think I don't know what this means to you? That guy, somebody should kill him. You are going to kill him, aren't you? Because there's nothing as pretty as a girl—you think it's funny I say that, huh? Well, sometimes you don't get what you want in this life. Your sister, was she pretty? I would give anything to be a girl just for one day, man. Just for twenty minutes. To have a man look at me and—you know, when he hit me I wasn't surprised. He thought he had something else. Well, I got the real thing, but I never met no really nice man that wanted it.

"That car, I got to go." He laughed. "But I will call. If I see him. And if you ever get curious, you don't really get AIDS from spit on your cock. If you need me ask Dixie, she knows." And he was gone. John turned and walked back downtown; he was out of the meat-packing district in five minutes but he carried the boy in his head, the seductive, sepulchral smile and the eyes—the other pair of eyes that had seen the face of the man who murdered his sister.

# 42

"If I hadn't gotten him to take the Pedialyte I don't know what I would have done." Zelly was only half listening to the woman next to her on the bench; hell would freeze over before Mary would take Pedialyte. And now she was trying to eat the wheel of somebody's tricycle. "I used Gatorade when Mary had it," she said absently.

Zelly was looking through a copy of the *Post* while Mary played at her feet. It was Friday, June twenty-sixth, and the Slasher had written the *Post* another letter. WERE THE CHILDREN FRIGHTENED AFTER THEY FOUND HER? She was trying to act, inside herself, as though she weren't thinking about Pat at all. As though she were an audience to herself and had to put on a good performance. *I am not thinking about when Pat could have mailed a letter. I am not thinking about the fact that Pat was out late the night before the concert, that he was gone all during intermission. I have not been thinking about it.*

"Joey threw up again this morning but I think we've gotten through the worst of it," the woman said. Joey cried every time he had apple juice. "So don't give him apple juice," said Zelly shortly, trying to read. Then she looked up from the paper. "But it's not that easy, I know. Mary cries for applesauce and if I don't give her applesauce heaven help me." KELLY WAS HAPPY TO GO WITH ME, TO BE MINE FOR INTERMISSION. It was ridiculous to even think about it. Everything had been entirely normal since the night Pat came to get her and Mary at her mother's house three weeks ago. She must have delayed postpartum syndrome or something. She'd been having bad dreams.

"What's that?" Stacy said, leaning over. "Oh, the Slasher murders. God, this whole thing gives me the creeps."

"Me too," said Zelly. I LOVED THEM ALL. I LOVE THEM ALL.

"You know what I think? I think that Slasher guy comes from around here." Zelly's stomach tightened. "I think so too," she said.

"Did you know Rosalie?" the woman asked. Joey started crying where he sat on the cement, next to the slide; a two-year-old had run right over him. I DO NOT COLLECT CARDS BUT HEARTS, I STOP THEIR FOOLISH BLOODY BEATING. The woman picked him up and murmured in his ear.

"I met her once," Zelly said. "I always wanted to get to know her better."

"Well, she used to take her baby—Brian—to Church Square Park. I used to go to Church Square too, but I haven't been able to go since she died. Just once, and everybody was talking about it." WE WILL MEET AGAIN BUT NOT WHEN THE MOON IS FULL. "You knew her?"

"Rosalie was my best friend in Hoboken. I'm from the Bronx originally. Are you from around here?"

"Born and bred."

"My name's Stacy," she said, and she stuck out her hand but it was sticky so they just laughed and nodded.

"Zelly."

"Rosalie was from Secaucus. When I heard I—I think it was the same guy who's doing it in Manhattan."

"So do I," said Zelly.

"You do?" She paused to disentangle Joey from a piece of plastic beer ring. "This park is filthy," she said.

"I thought Church Square was worse."

"As a matter of fact it is. There's glass, and kids come at night and move the benches around like performance art. You come in the morning and see how far under the monkey bars they moved one today."

"We have the Parks Department guys in the morning, but they don't do much."

"The dogs are the worst. You know, the owners just let them run anywhere. The other day a Labrador came right up to Joey and licked him in the face. Can you imagine? The thing that bothers me is that it's not even legal. The law says you have to have them on a leash at all times."

"Even inside the park?"

"Yeah, that's the law. Joey—not in your mouth. I know it looks like a cookie but it's garbage. I'm sure it's the same guy, though. Rosalie was blond. She dyed it, that's the ironic thing. She just started dyeing it a couple of months before she died."

Stacy was obviously impressed with her own image, of having access to such esoteric knowledge about the victim, as though Rosalie were a celebrity and not a dead person. Zelly could understand that; she herself could only approach the periphery of Rosalie's death. Stacy was a Friend of the Victim. She was obviously not a bad person but she couldn't seem to help herself. Maybe it was the only thing that had ever happened to her, that vicarious death.

"That's the baby," Stacy said, and, "Hi, Brian," to a stocky baby boy wearing a Yankee baseball cap. He was with a pleasant-looking middle-aged Indian woman. "I didn't know his sitter was bringing him up here. I heard he cries a lot more than he used to." He was not crying at that moment. He was looking at his hands. He looked practically supernatural sitting there looking at his hands, once you knew who he was: Baby Found with Blood on His Hands.

"You know," Stacy said, "I'm getting so I'm afraid to walk down the street at night. I just don't go off Washington Street anymore."

"I don't either."

"I'm really getting jumpy. I'll tell you something, the other night—do you ever feel like you get—I don't know—not warnings exactly, but—I don't know—feelings about things? About places? When they look perfectly harmless."

"I guess so. I don't know."

"Well, the other night—actually it was weeks ago—I was walking down Hudson Street—is that a bottle cap your daughter has?"

"Oh—no, it's a piece of something. Honey, don't eat that, I don't even know what it is."

"I was walking down Hudson Street, down by the park? You know, I don't know the name."

"Stevens Park? By Fourth Street?"

"Yeah. Where you can see the Empire State Building across the river. And there was this van. I don't remember if this was before the papers said that the killer might drive a dark van. I didn't get a real good look at it but it was this dark van.

I remember it had lettering on the side, in the front? And it was just sitting there, I didn't even see anything, but I got really freaked out, I couldn't even walk by it. That ever happen to you?"

"No, but I can imagine it."

"I don't know how to explain this but I got such a strong feeling—like if I walked by that van I would never see my home again. It sounds stupid now but it was really scary. It was almost as though I couldn't walk by it—as though there was a wall or something in the way. So I just stood there and listened to the music."

"Music?"

"Yeah. The van didn't even look like there was anybody inside it—I didn't see any light—but it was blaring this classical music, really loud. It's just that they're calling him the Symphony Slasher now—but this was before they were calling him that. Anyway, I got really creeped out and went around the block. And I said to Michael that we really ought to get out of the city altogether. It's time—" And over the gentle blur of her voice Zelly heard her own internal voice like a mantra: *Pat has a dark van. Pat has a dark van and it has writing on the front panel. Pat has a dark van and it has writing on the front panel and he plays classical music all the time, Pat has a dark van.* "—thinking of looking in Chatham," Stacy was saying. WE WILL MEET AGAIN BUT NOT WHEN THE MOON IS FULL. I AM NOT SO SHALLOW WHY A VAN? WE WILL MEET AGAIN.

# 43

They had been drinking wine and he had heard her giggle for the first time. The streets were soft and welcoming and there had never been fear; fear had dissipated on the new summer air. June twenty-sixth. Red wine with dinner, they ordered pasta dishes but didn't eat them. Only once—when Madeleine flinched as the waiter leaned his arm in front of her to put down the bread plate—had the wine reminded him of blood.

Madeleine was jubilant. Now they had a real lead, one even the police didn't have. She hadn't told John that the police had contacted her. She was afraid it would stop him and equally afraid it would intensify his efforts. Now she wondered whether they should call the task force; but the wine dissuaded her. Even to Madeleine events had taken on the quality of a dream. Their shared aim was becoming a hard shell around them, like a cocoon; they were in a cocoon and they were dreaming. They had begun from a point of intimacy many never reach. They shared, in a sense, a past, and they shared the same fantastic hope for the future. And wine and hate and unrelenting hope had made them giddy tonight.

"My boyfriend always wanted to have sex in one of those basement entrances, down the steps," Madeleine said. She was looking at her rape as an objective fact, like weather or a geographical feature of the landscape. From where she was it had no power over her.

"Your boyfriend was an asshole," said John.

"At least I can joke." They were silent a moment; she had taken his arm as they left the restaurant and her hand felt like a piece of fire.

Madeleine was looking up at the gingko trees on St. Luke's Place. They shone with an unearthly inward light, like hundreds of tiny green moons. "Where's the strangest place you ever had sex?" she asked.

"At Kennedy Airport. We found a place—a cul-de-sac at the end of a long corridor past the bathrooms. You could feel the planes taking off through your feet."

"Who's 'we'?"

"My high school girlfriend." The jet engines had roared up his legs and exploded into the darkness of the girl he held in front of him.

"My high school boyfriend and I used to climb through one of the windows of the church down the block. We did it on the altar."

"That's even better."

"He used to be an altar boy." The streetlights reeled slowly and she laughed. They were walking down the gently sloping street and she held his arm tighter so they wouldn't begin to run. Everything was very clear and far away and he knew they were going to make love.

There was no hurry. Her hand was on his arm and he could

see the line of her cheekbone and the flow of her dark gold
hair as she walked beside him. She was really very small.

They came to her building and went up the steps; they
were quiet because they knew they were going to make love.
They were shy with each other and she would not raise her
face toward his. She fumbled with the key and she stumbled
over the familiar threshold.

Madeleine's apartment was small, a space before a window
and a loft bed only. The room was cluttered with books and
papers and clothing strewn across chairs; the kitchen counter
was hidden beneath cups and hand towels and open contain-
ers. John wanted to take her on the floor.

She was standing with her back to him in front of the sink;
she held a yellow china cup in her hand. She held it uncertainly, and her head was bowed. John moved up behind her
and slid his arms in a ring around her waist and buried his face
in her neck. She raised her head back like a cat stretching,
rubbing her head against his face, and she put down the cup
and put her hands on his hands where they lay around her
waist.

Like lightning in his brain he saw her, for an eternal instant, supine, her back against the cement, the man over her.
Then it was gone and she was soft in his arms. He turned her,
gently, and lifted her chin and looked at her eyes. She was
crying. When he kissed her he tasted her salt. She put her
arms around him and he saw it again in an instant's illumi-
nation, legs spread under the man, and felt a swift involuntary pull at the groin and he didn't know if it was the man's
hands on her throat or her tongue in his own mouth.

They kissed across the room and he ran his hand over her
body and it wasn't him it was the man, wherever he touched
her she had been burned. The probing of her tongue excited
him, and he thought of what had been done to her and she

moved her breasts under his hand and her head hit the cement and she was very dear to him, he wanted to protect her, he wanted to take her like a whore. And her kiss was like a sacrament in his mouth.

He pulled her gently away from him and saw that she was still crying. "I'm sorry," she said, and he felt ashamed. He wanted to say something—"I love you"—but he didn't say anything. Even "I love you" would be an insult to her wound. He kissed her forehead. She put her head down against his chest.

"Is that your only bed?" he asked her. She looked surprised but she nodded, still crying soundlessly; her shame was more than he could bear. If he had to he would gladly wait forever.

"It's just as well," he said. "I'm afraid of heights."

# 44

She thought it would be safest just to take the whole key chain: If he were awake when she got back it would be more difficult to slip the single key back on to the ring than it would to put the ring back on top of his dresser. And if he noticed the ring was missing she could just say she hadn't seen it; Pat had put his keys down in exactly the same spot so many times that it wouldn't be hard to shake tonight's memory: the hands reaching out to lay the keys down, the tiny metallic clink, the mind already on dinner and the game and maybe a cold beer. The image the mind replays when asked to remember setting down the keys—is that the most recent image or one of a thousand images overlaid from a thousand days of setting the keys down just so, in exactly the same spot? What other images overlay one another in Pat's mind, each reflexively similar to the last? The mundane tasks of washing up; balling a rag in his hand to wipe the blood from his arms; changing his uniform and tossing it in with the others on Saturdays to take to the Laundromat; washing his face, his hair (or would he drive around a while, rubbing his fingers across his cheek, rubbing the sticky palm of his hand— DID YOU TASTE HER BLOOD?)?

Coins and a hairbrush and a couple of Band-Aids and four stamps. And the key chain coiled like a little cobra in the middle. She picked it up and it weighed a universe in her hand. This was the final betrayal, as real as sweat in a motel room: no matter what she found or didn't find it was the end of her marriage. Maybe it would be better after all just to take the one. She slid the van's key off the ring, working it while she listened to the shower run in the bathroom; Pat was singing. Wordless, low, something she didn't recognize. She was nauseated. She slipped the key into her pocket and it lay along her thigh, the flat cold metal would surely show through her summer shorts, it burned her thigh. He would know she had it. Would he kill her then?

She was in the living room when he came out of the bathroom. He went into the bedroom and she could not move at all. He went over to his dresser; she couldn't see him but she could see his shadow through the doorway; it was a blot, a negative image against the white wall. Zelly looked away, out the living room window, and was surprised to see that it was still light outside.

She had to find out where he parked the van. The shadow wobbled and swayed, and Pat came out of the bedroom. She didn't know how to find out, what to ask. She thought of one thing, too late, the key burning her thigh: "Are you going to have to go out tonight?"

"Not tonight."

"Good, because I told Stacy I'd try to have dinner with her."

"Who's Stacy?"

"Just one of the moms from the park. I've mentioned her."

"I don't remember. I guess so. You're going just like that? Why does it have to be tonight?"

"Stacy said she'd let me know if she could ever get a sitter. It's one of those fluke things. Her next-door neighbor is available tonight. Her husband works late a lot, so he can't watch the baby." She was appalled at how easily she was lying, and she couldn't stop. "Isn't it okay? If you don't have an appointment tonight."

"You're going without the baby?"

"If it's okay with you. Just to the Japanese place up on Washington. It's only a few blocks, and we won't be late."

"I don't mind." He moved up behind her where she was looking out the window instead of at him; he put his arms around her waist. He rubbed her hips and her belly and then he slipped his hands inside the elastic waistband of her shorts. The key burned. She leaned back against his chest and he rested his chin on top of her head. She could smell his skin and his aftershave—those smells were like the smells of her own skin. A memory smelled like that: There had been a summer, and a fight in the summer, a long time ago. Somewhere near the water. And she had cried and he had come up behind her and rested his chin on the top of her head. The wind had whipped around in a frenzy and she had forgiven him. She closed her eyes.

As if on cue the baby began to whimper: she was done with her supper. "I won't go until I clean up after Mary," Zelly said. That had been a long time ago and at the table Mary was painting yam into her hair.

"I'll give her a bath," Pat said. He seemed reluctant to take his hands off her belly. That long-ago summer day came back

again for an instant: the absolute luxury of his arms. She
made her voice empty. "Did you have trouble finding a parking space?"

"Hmm?"

"Were you able to find a parking spot close to the house?"

"It wasn't too bad." Pat relaxed his grip and they both
moved away, she forward and he back.

"Stacy told me they had signs up all over different streets
saying no parking—they're repaving the streets or something."

"No, there weren't any signs on Hudson."

Relief made her dizzy for a minute. She went over to Mary
and began to wipe her sticky face. "No, they're not doing
anything on Hudson. I think it was Bloomfield."

"I have to move the van before ten tomorrow, though,
that's the only reason I got something even remotely close to
the house."

"I wish I could drive the stick, I'd move it for you." Adrenaline was making her weak, she knew she could find it now
but she didn't want to waste time, she wanted him to tell her.
Mary waved her arms frantically to avoid the washcloth and
gurgled delightedly. Pat went into the kitchen with Mary's
dirty dishes. "It's not bad," he said, "it's only by the park at
Fourth Street—" and he said something else but she didn't
hear it because of the sudden ringing in her ears and then a
silence so complete she thought he might have left the apartment. But he was still in the kitchen and he hadn't heard
anything, of course. Hudson and Fourth, her palms were
sweating. She leaned her head into Mary's where it rested
against her shoulder. Her hair was impossibly soft, like kitten's fur.

"You going to get sushi?" Pat came out of the kitchen

toward her and Zelly saw him a thousand times, every time he had ever walked toward her, across a room or a crowd or an empty beach, on their honeymoon in Santo Domingo, with a nimbus around his head from the setting sun; out of the kitchen so many times and the fluorescent light always made a halo; when she was in labor with Mary and he had to go to the bathroom and when she saw him coming back through the delivery-room door she suddenly started crying.

Had they also seen his face?

"You okay? You look like you just saw a ghost." He moved to the stereo and became engrossed in choosing something to hear. Zelly shifted Mary onto the other shoulder and said no, nothing, but he wasn't listening. He didn't suspect anything. Her heart was beating in her ears again. She kissed Mary's head and felt as though if she put her down she might never get to pick her up again. "Here, take the baby," she said; she kept her own head down so that he wouldn't see that she was almost crying.

"You won't be late, right?"

"I won't be."

"Not that it matters. I'm just going to listen to something until the game comes on, and then I'm going to put on the answering machine and watch the game. Yankees versus Philly." Zelly leaned to kiss Mary's head again and Pat ducked his head to find her mouth. "Come back soon," he said. "I want both my girls safe at home," and Zelly reached up and put her palm on his cheek and kissed him unexpectedly, passionately.

"Hey," he said, "your fingers are like ice."

"I love you," she said fiercely.

"I love you, too, honey. And the baby loves you. Whenever you go out you act like it's the end of the world as you

know it. We'll both be here when you get back. I'll be watching the end of the baseball game and Mary will be snug in her
crib. If she wakes up I'll give her a bottle."

"I know I'm silly. It's just hard."

"You moms. You'd think I wasn't fit to take care of her."

"You're not. You'll probably have her up rooting for the
Yankees until eleven o'clock," Zelly said, and she turned and
ran out the door and down the steps and stood out on the
sidewalk in front of the building and cried.

At Hudson and Fourth was Stevens Park, where Zelly sometimes went to walk a little while by herself, if it'd been a
particularly hard day with the baby. Teething, colic, just
nerves sometimes. "Mama," she'd say on the phone, "we're
both teething today. Can you come for a little while?" And
her mother would come and Zelly would walk down to the
park and look at Manhattan across the river. Pat liked to look
across the river at the city too. Right where Stacy had said
she'd seen the van that frightened her.

And it was there, like a big, phony-looking prop in a
movie: the Van. When Zelly slipped the key in the lock and
swung the back door open the noise was enormous on the
empty street. There were kids goofing around on the softball
field across the park; there wasn't any scheduled Little League
game tonight but there were always kids on the field. There
was a big black-and-brown dog running in the dog run and
two people, their heads close together, sitting on a bench
under a tall wrought-iron lamp. The back of the van stank of
Leatherette. The light spilling out onto the sidewalk accused
her, the stale smell accused her. Trespasser, liar. She wanted
violently to be sitting in a curtained booth talking about toilet
training with Stacy while she drank warm saki out of a little
blue-and-white china bottle.

Zelly stepped inside the van and turned the overhead to keep the light on and pulled the door shut behind her and it made that terrible noise again. The interior of the van was not remarkable but it looked remarkable; it was lit from within by possibilities. Gray carpet, with ominous, ordinary splotches here and there; a shoebox in one corner; a bucket; a bundle of sheeny black tarp. A pile of magazines. A sneaker. Of course there was no blood on the walls.

Was the phone ringing in her living room? Stacy had taken her number at the end of their conversation and said that she would call "one night soon." Or had she said, "tomorrow"? Everything she said Zelly remembered as if she had heard it first in just this two-dimensional light, unreal, with a ringing silence in her ears. If Stacy called what would Pat do? There was no way of knowing, because she didn't know who Pat was anymore. She had to move now, and look around this place, and find out who Pat was. *I have to see.*

The magazines were mostly *Popular Mechanics*; there were a few old *TV Guides* and a copy of *Penthouse Letters*: "The Ten Most Beautiful Women in Prime Time." "Wet and Wild, Doggy-Style." The splotches on the carpet were irregularly shaped and spread out over the whole floor. There was a big, dark, moist-looking spot over in one corner: a bloodied head or an overturned coffee cup. The sneaker was a size ten and a half, the walls had not been recently scrubbed.

Zelly knelt in front of the shoebox. She did expect, when she opened it, to see the panties—the purple-pink satin, the insouciant white bow—but what she didn't expect was to see them lying shredded in long uneven strips, as though they had been gripped and pulled between teeth.

Underneath the shredded panties were other things, in a little jumble. There was a ring of keys with a heavy brass tag: Grant Corner Inn. There was a tube of lipstick: Honey Frost.

There was a plain white cotton bra: 34C. Underneath the shoebox was a pile of newspapers, some yellow, some new; wedged down next to them were a pair of scissors and a bottle of Elmer's glue, with its incongruent associations of shiny edible paste drying on sticky illicit palms. The smell of school. There was tape, Number 10 envelopes, Series A stamps. A green spiral notebook with a sticker on it saying $1.99. A red ballpoint pen.

The newspapers on top of the pile appeared at first to be shredded too, but as she fingered them, Zelly saw that they had been cut up in careful columns, with pieces missing, words or whole lines just little holes now. There were fragmented headlines. SLASHER VICTIM LIVES! SYMPHONY SLASHER A POLICE WANNABE? Part of an article, coffee-stained, about the woman who had escaped the Slasher, with only two words missing—her name. WOMAN MURDERED ON SOHO STREET. There were several sheets of heavy oat-tag paper—another reminder of school. Zelly picked up the notebook and it fell open in her hands: DID YOU TASTE HER BLOOD? She leafed back a few pages: UNDER THE MUTILATED MOON.

Zelly was crying and her leg had fallen asleep. She got up suddenly, clumsily, dropping the book and then putting the weight of her hand on a page; she picked it up and flattened the page out as best she could. The book wasn't nearly full. She turned to the last written page: ONE MOTHER DIES, ANOTHER WILL FOLLOW. I WILL CHOOSE THE OR-PHAN AND THE FATE OF THE ORPHAN. THE CRY-ING OF A CHILD AT ITS MOTHER'S SIDE MUST BE STOPPED.

There were clippings from newspapers inserted in the pages of the notebook, long streamers of headlines and carefully cut columns of type. The word "child"; a big *O* and *R* from a headline; the word "will"; the word "stop." Zelly stood holding the notebook as if she had suddenly been struck senile; she leaned back down like a very old person and placed it back in the space next to the newspapers. Each item in the box must be placed just so, the scissors and the glue, the little packet of stamps.

The bucket in the corner stood out against the colorless wall; Zelly's eyes were preternaturally sharp now. The bucket's battered side caught the overhead light and fractured it. *He is he is he is.* Zelly had seen Pat use the bucket when he washed the van, on hot days when the sun made gold tracks in his hair. The bucket was empty, but there was a dark residue at the bottom, a slop of water and something else, and there was a rag in the bucket that was clotted with something else, something dark. Zelly touched it; her hand came away red and she thought for a moment that she was going to scream, but the sound died, just a little snick in her throat; what other voice had spoken inside these walls? Had screamed? The nausea welled up again, so strong it pulled her head back and took her breath and she had to close her eyes. *He is he is he is.*

Zelly looked at the tarp in the corner. There was no place to wipe her red hand. The tarp was lumpy, it was roughly the shape of a body. Zelly held her hand awkwardly away from her side. With her other hand she tugged at the tarp, but it only rolled a little to the side, with a sickening weight, so Zelly just grabbed it with her bloody hand too and jerked it open.

The smell was musty and gagging and somehow sweet at the same time. Zelly felt the metallic taste of the saliva that floods the mouth before you vomit. There was no body inside the tarp. There was just a tiny dark pool at the center, and the smell; the pool was old now, a tarry dark puddle of black against the black material. There was something gleaming in the pool; when Zelly reached over and took it out, she thought she would fall into the black there and never hit bottom. Her fingers were smeared sticky red-black. A feather, a silver tracery on a little hoop: it was made to dangle. Tangled in the hoop was a long strand of honey-blond hair.

Zelly slapped the tarp back together; she remembered that she had some napkins in her fanny pack from when she and Mary went to McDonald's three days ago so she wiped her hands (thinking about Mary in McDonald's proudly smashing french fries on the table) and she wiped the feather earring and put everything back in her fanny pack and looked around the inside of the van. (Had the tarp been folded just that way? Had she screamed for a long time before she died?) The shoebox set atop the papers, had it sat at just that rakish angle? (Had he come to her after, lay in bed next to her, after?) The walls moved in and out, breathing. The bucket moved out of the corner of her eye. In and out, with the overhead light pulsing. She had to get out of there, the door was stuck and the tarp heaved behind her like an animal and the night air hit her like a slap and something glinted in the dark just as she shut the door, *where does he keep the knife,* she leaned over the cracked pavement her stomach heaving her hands still tacky she was leaning over taking in great gulps of air *I will not throw up I will not throw up he is he is he is he is he is.*

# 45

"What do you think of Glemby?"

Blackman snorted into his coffee cup. It was Friday, June twenty-sixth, nighttime, but there were no windows in the room, just a white clock with black hands to tell them the time in the outside world.

"Glemby!" Blackman burst out irritably. "The man has all the charm of a cockroach. And the brains of one, too."

"I don't know, cockroaches are supposed to be pretty smart." Scottie was punching keys on his computer and Blackman was letting the phone ring while two officers with phones already at their ears glared at him from across the squad room.

"Point well taken. But I just don't think Glemby is the one."

Scottie was looking intently at the screen. "I have something to tell you—" he began. "Just a second, I have to get this license plate number in—"

"Damn. Yes. Slasher Task Force." For the next few minutes Easy talked quietly on the phone while Scottie punched in numbers: N2L 110, N2L 145, N2M 127.

Then Blackman hung up the phone. "It was somebody who wanted to know if we were aware of two unsolved murders that took place in Orange, New Jersey, last year," he said disgustedly. "As a matter of fact I was. Two black women, found in a deserted building. What that has to do with—what is it you're doing there? I thought you were still collating."

"I am. I'm also checking out every registration of a gray, black, or blue van purchased in New York City within the last two years. Listen, I finally got a chance to check out John Nassent. Cheryl's brother. And what do you think I find?" He paused.

Sergeant Blackman was pouring from Scottie's coffee cup into a Styrofoam cup that was sitting on the desk from the night before. "You'd better not play games—"

"Sorry, sorry. But this is incredible. It seems Cheryl Nassent's mother died seventeen years ago. She was raped and thrown off a twenty-four-story building."

Sergeant Blackman's hand stopped in the air; he put the cup down and his left fist went to his mouth, tapping. "Why didn't the papers pick this up?"

"It seems the father is dead too. So John Nassent is the only immediate source of information. When somebody writes the book about this case the story of the mother is going to come out, but nobody's dug deep enough yet to tip to it."

"And how did *you* tip to it?"

"Most relatives of victims fantasize about getting the perp. If they happen to find out who it is they sometimes do something. But to try to get to the killer through another victim—that's really kind of weird. So—"

"Actually it's kind of smart. Obviously Madeleine Levy knows more than we're going to release to the press. So assuming John Nassent, if that's who it is, can get to her, he might learn something that would lead him to the killer. That's what we were hoping for when we talked to her, isn't it?"

"Yeah. So I really went into the background on all these guys—husbands, brothers. I thought there'd have to be something else to send our guy over into actually doing something. And when I found out both of Nassent's parents had already died—well, that would make his sister's death even more of a blow. He'd already given us the years of his parents' deaths in his initial statement, so it was easy to go back and check on death announcements. I didn't know what I'd find, but Nassent seemed hinkey to me—his situation was different than any of the other victims' relatives. You know his wife just divorced him last year?"

"Any girlfriends?"

"Not right now."

"So the boy had nobody but his baby sister."

"Chen got the impression Nassent pretty much raised his sister by himself. It's in his report."

"How old is he?"

"Twenty-eight."

"How's he sound?"

"I haven't spoken to him yet. I thought you might like to do the honors."

## 46

He had stayed at home and watched the moon out the window; the baby's crying was like a drill inside his ear. His wife's voice was a squeal. The people going by outside on the street made animal noises and when he was out among them they moved around him with the mindless intensity of chickens. He kept the volume up high on the television set, and he favored baseball games—because somebody used to like baseball a lot, and classical music, and the company of friends. If nobody died he would go mad.

He found a certain comfort in the slow, monotonous, ritualized movements, the brightly colored uniforms, the shush of the crowd, which broke into a long guttural roar every time one of the uniformed men hit or ran or caught a ball. The rhythms were a counterpoint to deeper currents, images that surfaced with a flash, like silver-backed fish, and dove and settled and rose and flashed and dove again. Now he almost knew that low-ceilinged room. A crash, a broken bottle, a cry. A silver flash, and gone. The whores would put it out of his mind.

Last night his wife had gone out, and when she came home and went to bed she had writhed in her sleep next to him. "Pat," she had said, and, "flood," or something like that. He had been home night after night for as long as he could stand it, night after night he had watched the moon through the window and watched her sleeping, her yellow hair splayed out on the pillow. It was mixed up now with other hair, wheat and honey and gold, as she lay on the pillow next to him he thought sometimes of how she would look with her hair all red. The whores would drain the fever like pus, maybe he wouldn't have to do it anymore and his wife could just be his wife and his memories memories only. So tonight he had gone out.

Light and dark, light and dark. NEW JERSEY/NEW YORK. Up familiar streets, tree-shaded, out into the barren light and empty warehouses of the meat-packing district.

John and Madeleine had walked the streets again, but they were no closer to knowing what they were looking for. He had a sharp nose and Asian eyes. A penchant for brunettes, a boundless rage, and a dark van. At first it had seemed that what Angel had told them was an answer; it was not an answer. Nights had come and gone and Angel hadn't called.

John sat in Madeleine's kitchen drinking coffee out of a chipped mug; tonight they had walked over by the river. They went out night after night but they were beginning to know that they would never find him. Bodies lay at irregular intervals, huddled up against walls or sprawled across the sidewalk. The homeless. They could have been dead bodies and no one would notice.

While John and Madeleine were walking a dark van turned

the corner and Madeleine's step faltered. John's breath stopped until the street lamp exposed the driver's flaccid profile; while he was waiting the eternity for the van to pass into the light John thought about how far away his own car was (three blocks), and did he have the keys, was there enough gas, and he felt the blade of his knife, along his thigh, familiar now. And he got to his car in time and he chased and caught and killed the man in an instant in his mind, and then he went back to Madeleine's kitchen and drank coffee. They would never find him.

The nights since they had almost made love had not been uncomfortable. They had reached an unspoken agreement. He and Madeleine barely touched. A hand across her hair, fingers gliding over the small of her back, nothing more. And each time they said good-night he kissed her. John thought about kissing her good-night from the moment of the kiss's end until the moment of its next beginning, investing it with erotic possibilities undreamed of in the simple lay. Her mouth, her hair, her hand, held more than the thighs or breasts of any casual, complete encounter. The memory of kissing her was more real in his mind than any sex he had ever had. Her simple kisses lay tactile on his mouth for a long time. He thought of her at work, at home. Now he sat drinking coffee in her kitchen and thought of her, tangible and fragile across the counter. When they smiled at each other he invested that, too, with possibilities.

The phone rang. Madeleine and John had been sitting in companionable silence. Her kitchen was made more complete by his presence, the space expanded out to meet the walls and the windows through which the outside world leered in. There was no outside world; they smiled, and then the phone rang. Madeleine jumped comically. As she reached for the phone John caught her slopping cup; their arms brushed and she smiled rueful acknowledgment. "Dad," she mouthed. But when she put the phone to her ear and listened she paled and said, "Hang on," and held the receiver out to John, and her face was entirely blank.

Somebody's dead, John thought; the image of another death leapt in his mind. When he put his ear to the receiver he could not at first understand the words. There was a wind in the phone line that disembodied the voice at the other end.

"John?" A tentative, husky whisper, frightened. An invitation. A voice for whom all communication was sexual innuendo. "He's here now. The man. He's with Lucky. You hurry you can get him now."

"Where are you calling from?"

A long pause; wind in the line. "Ah . . . I don't know. It's—it's Little West Twelfth, I think. And—no, it's Gansevoort. Sorry. And Washington. On the corner. There's a phone booth right here. He's here, man. Dark van with tape on the doors. But he won't be long with Lucky. She finishes 'em off fast." A giggle. John realized that Angel was high as a kite; this was just another adventure, another episode in Angel's Life of Angel. "You'd better come before *he* does, Mister Man," the voice whispered excitedly, and Angel laughed again and the phone went dead.

The whore was standing unsteadily under a streetlight, and she had dark hair. He could hear Paganini in the back of his head, very low and fast. The transaction was automatic; he didn't pay any attention to her face. Another whore tried to attract him from across the street, she pulled her skirt up to expose a startling whiteness and blackness. The dark-haired one muttered something and held her hand up absently, in half a gesture; she didn't pause to see if he had changed his mind. Her heel snagged on the step up and then she was next to him; she smelled of sweat and something else; for a moment he was somewhere else, green, and a train was roaring by overhead. My mother used to wear that too, he thought with surprise. He had no memories of his mother. A field, a train, a low-ceilinged room. He became aware of an ache in his left temple.

"You want me to unzip it?" the whore asked nastily. She slurred her words. She was looking at him. He didn't want to see her face. He resented her eyes. *Her eyes had had blood in them.* He unzipped his fly: if she'd had honey hair he would have killed her right there.

She bent her head and with her warm mouth he felt the ordinary, expected stirring. He grasped her hair at the nape of the neck, where the fragile vertebrae gave way to a pocket of soft flesh, just below the medulla oblongata. Beneath his fingers blood flowed and chemical impulses leapt across tiny synapses. The knife lay on the leather seat under his left thigh and with his left hand he caressed the handle: he could stop her breathing with a jerk of his hand.

The whore was sloppy, like a faltering clock. The music inside his head had changed, it was Handel now, a chorus of voices. The wet, dark walls of her mouth moved in uncertain counterpoint; she snagged a tooth against him. He tightened his grip on her hair and looked out the window of the van. All sensation was circumscribed by the four sides of the window. The light on the cobblestoned street, the mouth quickening, hopefully and prematurely. The fair-haired whore was smoking a cigarette across the street, next to a brightly lit telephone booth that he didn't remember having been there a moment ago. A truck drove by and honked as the whore exposed herself again. The woman snagged him on her tooth again, a quick, sharp sensation, and two people walked into the window frame. One was a black whore with long, incongruous blond hair; the mouth became larger, sensation deepened, and he closed his eyes and sank down into it. *And He shall reign forever and ever.* The knife fell through the air and he opened his eyes and suddenly he saw the whore-bastard, the pouting Garbo mouth and the painted mis-matched cheeks; it was standing between the whores across the street and laughing.

Madeleine rose without a word. She turned from John at the door and ran toward the car without a word. He ran, cursing his office-soft muscles and his weak lungs, which began to pulse with burning air after half a block. He had a stitch in his side and the streetlights bobbled ahead of him, out of the trees where the sidewalks were without shadow. Horatio Street, Twelfth Street, Gansevoort veering into view like an oasis in the desert of his cheap, unearned pain.

His breath was ragged and he felt decidedly unheroic. When he turned the corner he could see a crowd of people at Greenwich. He could hear discordant cries, like the cries of seabirds, and he saw two people that looked like birds fight-ing in the sky. They swooped and crouched; a small figure and a large one, sparrow and crow, a high thin keening and a deep-throated bellow of incoherent rage.

It was Angel—Dixie stood to one side, teetering in excite-ment on one heel, and Twinkie was yelling something but he didn't move to help—and a tall man with a sharp nose. The man was dressed in black or blue, and he looked as if he had fallen out of the night: he looked like a piece of the night. Angel was on his knees now and the man was beating him, and nobody else moved.

The mouth was moving frantically, losing the rhythm. He looked out the window and his hand tightened again against the unprotected neck, and the mouth uttered a muffled *humph* of protest he didn't hear. The whore-bastard was gesturing excitedly and holding his hand up to his ear like a telephone.

The whore lifted her head against the pressure of his hand. "Jesus fucking—" she said. He pushed her away from him, hard, against the hard door. "What the fuck—" she said. But he had opened the door and leapt out in one motion—"Where the fuck is my money?" she shouted behind him—and the whore-bastard turned and saw him and his cheekbones were still delicate and sharp, but now they were asymmetrical and his eyes were beautiful and full of fear.

John couldn't hear very well above his own idiot breathing. Even when he stopped, his hands on his knees, gulping for air, he could only hear a sound like the sound inside of a seashell. The man was shouting something—"Lazy, stupid, lazy, stupid." Nobody turned as John walked quickly toward the corner. Dixie's face was transfigured by what was happening to her: *And then he just jumped on poor Angel*—A few other of the hookers and transvestites stood around, and there was a van parked across the street, across from the phone booth, which stood too bright, a prop out of place. A dark car veered theatrically around the corner, lights careening. A red Camry. Madeleine. John was running again now, and Madeleine was getting out of his car across the intersection. At the sound of the car door slamming, the man suddenly stopped beating the boy and looked up and Madeleine froze; her silhouette under the street lamp broke John's heart and he was running faster, Twinkie turned, and Angel kneeling on the pavement broke his heart, and Cheryl lay broken again on the cold sidewalk, and then he threw himself on the man.

*    *    *

Somebody screamed. The man was holding Angel by the hair; his hand had blood on it. The man turned his startled, feral face toward John, and they were as close as lovers. The man's face was suffused with residual anger and new surprise, as though he'd thought he were alone. He looked first beyond John, into the crowd's excited, impassive face. John looked into his eyes while they were looking beyond him and time just stopped: he saw Madeleine frozen beyond them, even though she was behind him and he couldn't possibly see that, and he saw her lying prone on the sidewalk, her pale face averted against intrusive pain, and he saw Cheryl as he had last seen her—had it been at the door or at the kitchen table?—she had been saying good-bye. And in a fraction of a breath the man looked at him, uncomprehending, and John heard his own voice shouting, "Enough! Enough!" and his hand was on the man's hand, his weight against the man's body; there was blood on his hand.

The arm that came down was not his. "Lazy, stupid, lazy, stupid," his uncle was shouting, and another arm came down in another room, and the whore-imposter crouched under the blows, a boy crouched in the corner where they couldn't see him, and under the streetlight a crowd was gathering.

There was a crack of broken bone. There was somebody yelling and the sound of running on pavement and his hand came down again and there were other hands on him, on his back, his neck. He brought his own hands up and turned. A pair of eyes, another echo of something: he had seen those eyes before. He shook the man off and it was like shaking himself awake. He stepped over the whimpering form at his feet and away from the uninvited accusation in the man's eyes. He turned, and he saw a pale face and blond hair, and he thought suddenly of Zelly. It was as if he had come off a drunk to find himself in a strange room; he had to get back to Zelly.

The woman in front of him looked afraid and he didn't know why. She reminded him of someone but he didn't know who. He was separated from all the images by a thin membrane of music in his head: *King of kings, and Lord of lords. Blond hair the color of honey with the sun shining through it, and she had sung him so many songs.* He walked past the woman, and because she seemed to be asking something he said, "Zelly"; he had to get home to Zelly. Was there a baseball game tonight? There was a funny buzzing, the memories getting louder or the crowd—a horn honked and it was like Technicolor on a black-and-white image—and he walked over to his van and got in and closed the door and was surprised that the light didn't go out. The passenger-side door was open—he didn't know why. It looked so strange, and his bloody hand reaching to close it looked strange. With the snick of the door the darkness surrounded him, and it comforted him, and he forgot where he was.

The man's hand fell open and he stepped abruptly back, throwing John off balance. They faced each other like loopy fighters across Angel's stooped body. The man didn't seem to know where he was. Angel's head was down as if in prayer, and as the man stumbled backward he looked down and a spasm of mystified disgust crossed his face; he looked up into John's eyes and started to mouth something—"what"—and paused, almost with recognition, and shrugged, and almost smiled, and turned away.

The man turned toward Madeleine; he walked toward her. John had felt his breath on his face—but he had not killed him. To put the sharp blade against the skin and just push—

Madeleine stood absolutely motionless. John knelt to touch Angel's shoulder; he looked toward Dixie where she stood, her cigarette burned down to a column of ash unnoticed in her hand. When he looked toward Madeleine the man was almost upon her. John leapt forward, but the man veered over toward the van, not noticing Madeleine at all where she stood like a half-hypnotized bird.

"That's him," she said. He moved to take her shoulders but she stiffened and he stood awkwardly, his hands halfway to prayer. They stood for a frozen second watching the man walk toward the van, but as he disappeared inside, Madeleine grabbed John's arm. He tried to pull free but her grip was barbed wire. "I don't think we can do it ourselves," she said. "I can see the license plate." H4J 180 winked under the streetlight. "I'm going to call the police."

They were alone now on the street. There was a little dark spot where Angel's blood was, but he and everybody else had melted into the factory walls and the dark loading docks. John's rage had been knocked away by pure surprise. The man belonged to him, he knew that, in the way that Cheryl belonged now to the man, and would until the man was dead. The man belonged to him but could he kill him? There was a doubt—he had not in fact killed him, although they had been standing with mingled breath and there had been time enough and opportunity to kill him. He wanted the man dead, but he didn't want the police there, with cars and lights and guns and authority. He wanted the man dead. But there was the doubt, and because of the doubt he had done nothing.

"He said something," Madeleine said, walking backward toward the telephone booth, which stood with shining incongruity right behind her. "I think he said, 'Help me.' " There was no sound or movement from the van, which stood poised like high explosives across the street. Help me. Madeleine had a quarter in her pocket. John thought that the image of the van would be fixed forever behind his eyes, he would see that van, and that light across the cobblestones, when he was seventy years old. Madeleine's fingers didn't fumble. She didn't wait for long, and she didn't talk for long. By the time he had reached the car she was done, running on light, silent feet, the van revving its engine as John slammed his door and drove the key into the lock, her feet running around the back of the car as the engine caught, the van sliding silently out from under the streetlight as she flung herself into the front seat and slammed her door, he could hear her loud shallow breathing, and he pressed the gas pedal and the car and the van moved forward in perfect synchronicity and there was nothing but the black van ahead of them and the beating of two hearts in his ears.

Diapers and wipes and talcum powder and zinc ointment. Zelly's eyes were dry. It was ten o'clock at night. For fifteen hours she had been afraid to take a deep breath, because she knew she would cry, and Pat would see her cry.

She hadn't run. She could have run, her heart had been beating like a wing. The police station was six blocks away from the van, she could have gotten there in five minutes. But what about Mary sleeping in her crib? *He is*—yes, undoubtedly so; she had stood gasping for breath to feed her fluttering heart and known there was no more deluding herself. *He is*—but there was no guarantee that the New York police would even believe her. Washcloths and Onesies and Anbesol.

But the talisman of Cheryl Nassent's earring lay cold in her fanny pack: they would believe her.

And the wheels of the justice system would creak and turn and begin to roll; the whole strength of the Slasher Task

Force would roar into action. The policemen would discuss and calculate and aim, and all power would pass from her hands. She could imagine it easily enough: The turn of her key in the lock as twenty policemen stood at firing stance behind her on the stairwell, their weapons drawn. How could Pat fail to hear their footsteps? Or the banal assurances—"Go home and act as though nothing's happened and we'll have a team in there in no time." But how could she not run straight to Mary's crib to protect her from the guns she knew were coming? He was home tonight; no one would die tonight, and she would not put her baby in danger while she knew he was home, his rage quiescent, watching the Yankees lose the baseball game.

When she got home she had met his eyes, and they were unchanged. Fear lay in a film on her vision; a dog would have smelled it on her. The baby was sleeping; she would have known it and cried. Extra sheets for the crib and socks and Mary's stuffed pink poodle. Knowing how thoroughly he'd been able to hide it from her made it easier. The world cannot read your face. The world had not read in his face even the smallest clue.

Until last night Pat had not raped and murdered six women—seven dead in all—and then he had. The worm in the apple had become the apple. Hysteria and strained nerves and unwarranted suspicion had become shrewdness and perspicacity.

Because Pat didn't know she knew, she didn't know. It wasn't that hard, after the first moment. Blankets and eye-makeup remover and underwear. All the baby's dirty clothes out of the hamper, because this time she knew for certain she was never coming back.

She had been forced to wait. The night had been the worst. As she slid toward unexpected sleep he moved over her; she had never refused him; she was afraid to refuse him now. He thrust into her without foreplay, and he didn't touch her neck. It was over soon. When he finished she could taste her own blood on her lip where she had bitten it.

At seven-thirty in the morning Zelly had lain in bed next to Pat, scanning the front page of each section of the *Times*. Pat sat next to her in bed and drank his coffee. Her skin was screaming.

"You want another cup of coffee?" she asked him, calculating how to get out of the house. "Honey—" she said, then she almost said it: I'm going to take Mary out for a walk this morning. But she never took Mary out in the morning, and he knew it. There must be no deviation from ordinary routine.

How he must have enjoyed watching her these past months! How he must have loved listening to her speculate on the characteristics of the Slasher, the likelihood of his making a fatal mistake, all the thousand little details about which she'd had an opinion. She hated him next to her the way a woman would hate any lover who had made a fool of her. As though her mind couldn't accept the full depth of horror offered up to it and had to grab and react to the one aspect of the truth that it could easily understand: he has been laughing at me.

In the middle of the night she had been certain she would call the police the minute Pat left the house. But by morning she knew what would happen if she did that. The police would stake out her apartment, waiting for Pat to come home. She would go to her mother's house ("Just act as though nothing's happened"), but she was pretty sure they would stake that out too, knowing that eventually he would go there. For where else did he go? Home, his mother-in-law's, and out to kill. And Pat would come home and see that the police were staking out his house. And he would know who had told them.

Pat would go to her mother's house. And he would see the stakeout there and then where would he go? How could she put her face outside the door if he were free? She and the baby and her mother would be prisoners in that house. How could she take her baby for a walk, or to the doctor? And her mother—how could she let her mother leave the house if he were out there somewhere? Because he would know who had told the police, and he would kill them all.

Even if he ran she could never feel safe. How long had it taken to catch Ted Bundy after he escaped from jail in Utah? Two years? What would Zelly and her mother do for two years, watching the television to hear the latest news of a killing in Omaha, in Chattahoochee, knowing he could be just around the corner? She could not call the police while Pat was out of the house.

"What are you doing today, honey?" she'd asked behind the movie pages, staring at the grainy newspaper image of a man grabbing a lingerie-clad woman by the arm, the leg—an advertisement for a murder mystery. "She Has to Make the Ultimate Sacrifice," the caption read. Zelly had waited for Pat's reply and wondered what that sacrifice was: was she going to sleep with him or was the man going to kill her? Pat was reading the sports pages.

Her shoes wouldn't fit in the bag. She didn't want to take these shoes anyway. She went to the closet and knelt, and memory rose abruptly. Pat's shoes. She'd had a dream about Pat's shoes.

They stood in a row, inspection-perfect, but in the next instant they would explode into action and fly out of the closet around her head like bats from a cave and she would lose her mind. Zelly reached for a shoe and was surprised when it felt like nothing more than leather.

There was something brown down the outside, possibly dung. Something that had been sticky. Ketchup, or mud. Little flakes fell in a red dust on the floor. Zelly inserted her fingernail under a flake and pulled it away. She touched her thumb to the flake and it disintegrated into a thousand red specks. Suddenly there was a noise outside the door. Zelly turned her head and her whole consciousness was in her ears. She would not be able to move away from the closet in time.

The footsteps halted and then began again. Away from the door and across the landing to the next flight. Zelly stared at the dried blood on her thumb and realized that she had begun to cry.

The letter she left just said, "I can't make it work. I'm sorry. I'm at my mother's. Call me." He would think she was leaving him, but he wouldn't think she was running away from the Symphony Slasher. He would call her mother's, the way he did last time, but now she would put him off. Say anything to keep him there. And the moment he hung up the phone she would call the police.

# 48

"These lights drive me crazy, you know that?"

"I didn't notice," said Blackman. There wasn't a lot of traffic in the tunnel. A few cars had gone by in the opposite direction, and far ahead Blackman could see two sets of lights. One car was red, one was just a dark blur far up ahead. Blackman reached for the Styrofoam cup balanced on the gear shift without taking his eyes off the road. He knew Scottie's hand would reach the cup an instant before his own, knew that Scottie would hand him the cup. "You're better than having a wife."

"You always say that. When are you going to just break down and propose?"

The lights went by for a moment in silence.

Blackman's lips were pushed tightly together. His hands on the steering wheel were drained of blood; it had been pushed away by the force of his grip.

"What do you suppose Levy was doing in the meat-packing district at ten o'clock on a Monday night?" Scottie asked.

"She said she was leaving the scene. Nassent had to be with her. The dispatcher said she was in an awful hurry."

"She'd have to be out of her mind."

"I'd do it. You weren't at Levy's original questioning," Blackman said. "She was the angriest rape victim I've ever seen. And I have seen angry ones. I should have known. Listen," abruptly changing the subject as the car came out of the tunnel into the sudden night, "it adds up that our man would live in New Jersey."

"Patrick Wyche," Scottie said.

"Patrick Wyche. Patrick Wyche. No better or worse than any other name." The highway outside the tunnel was eight lanes wide, with overhead signs and bright streetlights and arrows pointing in different directions.

"I hate New Jersey," Scottie said. There wasn't a lot of traffic, just a pair of taillights on a red Camry swinging around a corner. "The guy the Hoboken Police are sending is supposed to have all the info on Wyche, when we meet him at the house."

"This could be a one-way ticket to where the sun don't shine, going to this man's house."

"Where are we going to look?" Scottie snapped. "They sent Chen down to where Levy said she was calling from. And we got O'Donnell going over to her place to talk to her when she gets in."

"Don't blame yourself. This Nassent thing has been a long shot all along."

"Not anymore."

"No. Not anymore." They were silent as the patrol car passed a sign that read NEW JERSEY TURNPIKE ¼ MILE.

"Shit," said Blackman suddenly, "I think I overshot my mark."

"Second corner by the gas station?"

"Damn, I overshot. *Damn,*" slamming his palm against the steering wheel, "God *fucking* damn. Motherfucking New Jersey highway. We blew it."

# 49

In the tunnel John and Madeleine did not dare say anything. They sat silently and the tunnel lights beat a tattoo across their faces.

John looked furtively at Madeleine and her face was closed. He was shut out—or she was shut in with the memory of the man walking toward her. When she said, "That's him," her voice had been small, like a child's; and now she faced her future with a child's irresolute grace.

Suddenly she turned to him and said, "I love you." Before he could answer she said, "I'm not frightened," and he understood that she didn't want him to answer.

"I am," he said.

The tunnel ended abruptly and the air on their faces felt like hope, cool and dark and sheltering and open to the sky.

"Do you think the cops'll come?"

"I don't know. Do you think they believed you?"

"If you listen to calamity for hours and hours every night, how do you sound? I think I was interesting to them."

"Then maybe they'll send somebody." The street was industrial, fantastic; they were passing train yards, endless shiny-dull tracks in all directions and hulking empty carcasses of trains. The van's taillights shone on the pocked asphalt. They were about five blocks behind the van; when it pulled into the station John slowed his car, but in a few moments, before they reached it, the van pulled away, and when it turned right up ahead of them John noticed Madeleine's hand tense on the door handle. But when they got to where the van had turned they saw that the street ended and there was no place to go but right, and the taillights were still there ahead of them. They were the only two cars on the road.

# 50

He looked into the rearview mirror as the tunnel gave way to cool night air. The mirror had joggled up, and he found himself looking into the shadowy back of the van. There was something lying in the middle of the carpet back there. A little shape, a darker shadow. He pulled the van over into the gas station where he would have made his right turn to go home; what was lying there? It stared with vacant eyes, shark's eyes, button eyes: a tiny brown bear.

Mary's bear. What would Mary's bear be doing in the back of his van? Suddenly an image of Zelly rose, Zelly rooting in her purse for her keys, when was it? Two nights ago, a year ago? For a long time Zelly had carried around a little plastic duck teething ring that Mary no longer found attractive. For luck. In his mind she took things out of her fanny pack and laid them on her dresser: a lipstick, a packet of tissues, a tiny brown bear. For luck. Now it lay next to a dark, triangular stain and looked at the ceiling.

He reached his hand out but did not touch it. Could not. Zelly had been in the back of the van. The chorus from Handel suddenly blasted back into his head—*Hallelujah! Hallelujah!*—and he dug his nails into his palms.

He looked with some surprise at the crescent indentations, which hurt. Zelly had seen the clippings, the unfinished letter. Under the cardboard box the notebook lay undisturbed but he knew she had opened it. The tarp had been moved. She had looked into the bucket. She knew who he was.

His hands as he started the van again were very calm; he felt calm. He had been stopped less than a minute. He was going to have to kill Zelly.

How long had she known? She had had that anticipatory look, like a deer staring down headlights, for some time now. Since she'd run away to her mother's house and then come back. Funny, he'd never truly been able to believe that what he did could have been associated with his other life. Even the panties—they could have come from anywhere. They had slid so easily from her dead body, they lay like a pile of lavender on the gray carpet of the van. Her lifeless eye had stared—he had loved her then. He had moved the panties down over her unresisting thighs and Zelly had held them in her hands.

It was almost a miracle to him that objects did not transmit memory. What had Zelly thought while she was holding the panties? That he was having an affair. She must have done her snooping when she'd said she was going out to dinner with that other mother. Last night.

So last night when he'd made love to her she must have known. He had felt a stirring toward her as she lay in bed with her back to him. She had lain as though asleep, although he knew she wasn't asleep. And in the morning she'd said she had a headache, and he'd noticed that she wouldn't put the baby down at all, but he hadn't thought anything of it. Yet while she stood near the window in the living room (uneasily, he realized now, teetering a little on one foot like an adolescent waiting for a phone call), she had had a memory of the inside of his van. How could he not have known?

As he drove the last blocks, the buildings and the freight yards he was passing began to shudder and buckle in on themselves. Every time he had driven down this road was right here. The silhouette of an abandoned engine doubled in on itself; the lights in the tenement across the street were on and off and on again, pale against the lightening sky or a bright yellow beacon in the dead of night. The empty train cars gleamed with every shade and nuance of light he had ever seen move across their hulls. He had seen a man once, coming out of the mouth of an abandoned railroad car; the man was there now, forever descending, looking down, one foot held irresolute.

As he turned the corner Manhattan swung into view, in shadow, in bright sunlight, dim with rain. One had screamed, and three had struggled. One had never seen his face at all. One had smiled at him. Two had spoken. They were all the same woman, and in the dark front seat of the van he began to hear her voice. *Hushabye, don't you cry, go to sleepy little baby*. She used to sing him that. His house was half a block away. He could see a light in the living room window. She had not called the police. Behind the shifting memories his senses were clear. There were no unmarked vehicles, no snipers hiding behind parked cars. There was no foreign presence in the apartment; the bland welcoming light was no subterfuge. On the porch next door an old Italian woman sat with her deaf husband; her placidity was unfeigned. Along the length of the street no leaf stirred. *When you wake, you shall have all the pretty little horses*. He would say hello to the old woman and her husband and he would go upstairs and kill his wife's lying eyes. *Blacks and bays, dapples and grays, all the pretty little horses.*

What did she used to say? When you're bigger we'll go to London to visit the Queen. That's what she used to say. Just like in another of her many nursery rhymes. And he had believed her. The other he could not remember at all. Even with the rush of memory, the sudden availability of memory, he could not remember him. An arm, a hand. The arm would be raised forever, and it would be forever falling.

After he killed her he would have to do something with the baby. He couldn't just leave it there. The baby sitting next to its dead mother had not cried. In the closed low room where he crouched watching he did not cry.

When he opened the door to the apartment he did not know for a moment what he would see. That other room was suddenly so real that he almost forgot what he was going to do, and he hesitated against the blank wall of fluorescent light that came out of the kitchen. Where was she?

Something was wrong—the absence of monotone chatter from the television set. He could see it standing dark in the corner through the living room door. He knew it was no trap. There was no one waiting here, no drawn sweaty guns.

The apartment was empty. She was gone. As he stood in the kitchen the kitchen disappeared and he didn't feel anger or relief or regret or fear. Somewhere a wall melted and he was aware of only one thing: She was gone.

The boy sat uncomfortably in the little space under the stairs. He was five years old. His father's raw voice sometimes took on the cadence of repetitive ritual; his mother's retorts, her whimpers and her screams, were part of an ancient call and response. From where he was crouched under the stairs they couldn't see him. And when they could see him it didn't matter. Their entire lives were lived out in this illegal basement studio apartment. In the dark, from his mattress in the corner, he heard love and he heard hate, and when he heard love he thought it was hate, because he heard so much hate.

The only real love he recognized was in his mother's voice when she spoke only to him, in the lullabies she sang and the stories she told. When his father wasn't home the single room took on the rareified aspect of a bell jar, in which he and his mother existed unmolested and only for each other. Then the door opened and the familiar litany began again.

This time it was very bad. He was a small boy, brown-haired, with deep brown eyes that had little folds at the inner corners. He looked like his mother. His mother's hair was honey blond, and he could see her now across the room, with the light on her hair where his father held it clenched in his fist. Schubert was on the stereo—he knew that because his mother loved that music, she always played it. "Ave Maria" and the *Lieder* and the Quartetsatz. She used to play classical music all the time, especially when his father was out of the house: "The Flight of the Bumblebee" and "Jesu, Joy of Man's Desiring" and "Peter and the Wolf." Her favorite was Schubert, who had died young. Her name was Emily. His father's rage was inexplicable. His father never spoke his name. His mother did: "Patrick." Never Pat, always Patrick. "Patrick, when you're a bigger boy we'll go to London to visit the Queen." In her mouth his name was a caress.

"You're a fucking whore," his father was saying softly. Patrick where he was hiding caught his mother's supplicating eye. Do not, she said with her eye, do not move. Do not breathe if you can help it. She had showed him once how a little animal will freeze when a bigger animal wants to eat it.

He had been the bobcat and she had been the squirrel and they had laughed.

His father held a liquor bottle up in his right hand. The top slopped over with amber liquid; there was a puddle on the linoleum. The violin swelled. "This is the music the universe moves to, Patrick," she had told him. Beneath the stairs Patrick held his breath, his nails clenched against his palm in crescents of pain, and then the bottle was flying, her head was wrenched back—he loved her—and the bottle hit the wall across the room, leaving a big wet spot and a smell. Now there was something else in his father's hand. He held his breath—it was a hot pain in his chest—and his father's arm went up and the knife came down and for a moment Patrick was afraid of his mother, because he was afraid of blood.

If his father saw him now he would kill him, he knew that. His father stood over his mother as she looked at the ceiling with her mouth open and his breathing filled the room; it was the room, the walls pulsed raggedly in and out to the beat of his father's breathing. The violin had become romantic, yearning. His own breath was too big for his chest, and it frightened him too. He couldn't stop it, and his father would hear him. In the darkness under the stairs Patrick crouched into a little ball and lay on his side waiting to die.

Some time later he became aware that his father was gone. The music had ended and the needle rasped against the empty record. He had lain for a long time and then become aware that he was awake. He didn't know if he'd slept. The high small windows were black. His mother had not moved. One eye stared unblinking at the gray ceiling. The blue iris was flecked with red. Her mouth was open as though she were about to speak.

Patrick crawled out from under the stairwell: Then he was next to his mother. He couldn't hear anything from outside on the street; he wasn't aware of any street. There was nobody in the apartment above this one, nobody in the world except for him and his mother.

Patrick didn't know how long he sat there—he became aware, after a long time, of a strange sweet awful smell—and he didn't notice how many times the window went from black to gray to bright to black again. He loved her and he couldn't make her move. This is what "dead" was. The unwearying eye, the cold rigid fingers, the rancid smell. If she would not move he could not.

First there were voices, then pounding. Then silence, and Patrick was relieved, because he knew that they were going to take his mother away from him. The windows were light then. There was a violin playing all the time in his head now. When the windows went black again the voices came back, then pounding. He held her head in his lap—he was covered with blood—and held his breath, and for a moment he heard nothing but the needle, which was still rasping against the record.

Then there was the sound of wood groaning and splitting, and unfamiliar outdoor light, and horrified, self-righteous cries. Patrick hated them; it was as if he were to blame for the blood. He heard them talking but he didn't understand it—he heard "four days"—and when they tried to pry him away from her he fought them. And when they carried him out he fought and flung himself backward and looked at her one more time and promised himself he would find her again.

## 51

The lighted window got brighter and brighter the longer he looked at it, and everything around it, the street and the trees and the other houses and windows, receded into haze and blackness. The yellow-white square of light seemed almost to pulse. Then he shook his head slightly and the window swam back into focus. It was the third-floor window of an old brownstone two blocks off Washington Street, in Hoboken. He didn't know what this street was called; there were no signs.

The van was parked on a leafy street in front of a dark porch where an old man sat in silence next to an old woman. John could just see the man's tall form disappearing into the building next door. To see him again was shocking. After a long moment the man's silhouette appeared at the third-floor window.

He was dark against the window, a monstrous shadow thrown across the pale ceiling. He moved across the room, stopped, and moved again. For some reason John had assumed that the man lived in a house. What now? Would he and Madeleine saunter up the steps, with a nod to the couple next door? Ring the bell, go up the stairs, introduce themselves, and kill him? John turned his head to find Madeleine looking at him; when their eyes met she laughed. Her laughter was bitter and rueful and genuinely amused.

"Any ideas?" she asked; and then she gasped.

"Wh—" said John. The figure at the window, which had been standing like stone, suddenly sank out of sight. John and Madeleine looked at the empty space, and after awhile it started to get brighter and brighter.

"Is this wrong?" John asked once, and Madeleine didn't answer him; she said, "I don't hear sirens, do you?"

"I don't think you're going to hear any. Even if they come, they won't come with sirens."

"But I told them—"

"And a thousand other people told them today, too. How many tips do you suppose they've got, just today, from people who think they saw the Slasher? Or know the Slasher, or sleep with the Slasher, or are married to the Slasher?"

"But the police have to come. I don't want you to kill him."

"What do you think we've been *doing* for the last four weeks? You do want me to kill him. You *asked* me to kill him, remember? God, I'm doing this for you. For Cheryl, yes—but for you, now."

Madeleine's face was turned away. "I don't want you to kill him. I want him dead. I just don't want you to be the one to do it. I know I'll be ready soon, and when I am I don't want to touch palms through a plate of glass three inches thick, you know?"

"Madeleine," he said, "I have to. I didn't do it, back there.

I wasn't sure, back there. And I can't bear to think about the consequences. But if the police take him they'll put him behind bars—and he'll still be alive. He'll be *alive*. Cheryl isn't alive. It's a miracle you're alive. Madeleine," and she turned her head and her eyes were full of tears, "I have to kill him. Even you can't stop me, and I love you."

Above them the man reappeared, rising like a swimmer out of deep water. John started his motor and backed catty-corner across the street away from the van. There seemed nothing to do but to wait for him to leave the apartment. The old woman watched his car from her porch.

When the man walked out of the building he stopped and looked up. John could see the thick wafer of the half-full moon; "I don't know what we're doing," he said to Madeleine. The man began walking toward the van.

"We're giving up the future for the sake of the past," she said. "Follow that bastard."

# 52

The street was quiet. An old woman sat unmoving on the porch in front of the patrol car. An old man dozed next to her. There was a light on in the third-floor apartment of the row house next door.

"We have to wait for the Hoboken guy before we go up there," said Scottie.

"I knew he wouldn't be waiting for us!" Blackman fumed. "Damn hick police." Down the block two pairs of taillights turned the corner. "What was that?" he barked.

"The one in front looked like a van."

"Follow it."

"The lieutenant gave us specific orders to wait in front of the house."

"I don't give a shit. Follow it."

"If it was—"

"Go."

The old woman watched the police with impassive eyes from where she sat on her porch in the dark. When the patrol car got around the corner the street was empty.

## 53

The needle scratched syncopation against the record: *ch ch, ch ch, ch ch.* Zelly lifted it, and she could suddenly hear sounds from outside her mother's house: the voices of people passing by on the street, as if from very far away, the whine of a siren far away. Even the leaves right outside the window seemed far away. The ordinariness of this room, this light, in her mother's house, insulated her from the terrible reality outside.

She had been waiting all evening for the phone to ring. This time her mother had not questioned her, seeing enough, perhaps, in her daughter's red-veined eyes to preclude interrogation. Zelly knew she couldn't tell her mother. Let her find out from the newspapers, from the journalists who'd bang on their doors and call on their phone as soon as the news broke. Let her find in their explanations, extrapolations, their guesses and innuendoes, what her own daughter could not bring herself to tell her now.

How could she convey to her mother the inside of the van: the stale air, the muted light, the dark spot glistening on the open tarp? She kept her fingers wrapped around the feather earring in her pocket almost the whole time she sat with her mother in the artificial brightness of the kitchen. Would her mother believe her if she saw that earring, if she saw the picture of Cheryl Nassent wearing that earring dangling in her honey hair?

Zelly's sister Linda had told her a story once about a woman in the Bronx. One day the woman's husband said to her, "Don't open the closet door." After awhile the smell coming from the closet was horrific. And a young woman from the neighborhood was known to be missing. Linda's friend knew her, too. The husband squirted disinfectant under the closet door. "Don't open the closet." The woman became pregnant and eventually the smell subsided to a musty staleness. "Don't open the closet door."

After the woman had her baby she took it to her mother's for the night and went back to her apartment alone, and alone she opened the closet door. Inside was the missing woman. She took what was left of the body out of the closet and dragged it down the hall and into the elevator and out the back of the building and left it on the trash heap. It left a trail. When the police came to the apartment and asked her why she had finally opened the closet door, she said, "I couldn't bring the baby home with that in the house."

Was that woman mad? Easy to say yes. But Zelly knew now that reality is what we tell ourselves to believe. If we don't open the closet door there is nothing in the closet. It was inconceivable to her mother that her son-in-law be the

Symphony Slasher—so he wasn't. And no amount of evidence to the contrary would make it be so, if it could not be so. No earring, note, no bloody tarp could make it be so, if it could not be so. Her mother had waited a year to open her father's stamp book. What had her mother believed for a year? Zelly went to her mother's house dry-eyed, and made up the bed in her old room and said only, "It'll never work, Mama." And her mother made tea, and hovered around her youngest child and her granddaughter, offering food. Sandwiches and soup and ice cream and nut-bread and fruit. Tea and soda, and milk for Mary. Zelly's jaw hurt from not crying. Her eyes hurt. The baby was strangely lethargic, as though she sensed her mother's effort and it drained her, too.

Zelly tried to be normal but she no longer knew what "normal" was. She was able to laugh. Her mother told her stories about her nieces and nephews and she laughed. Then Mary snuggled into her neck or Zelly noticed the way the sun shone on the tablecloth and for a moment her eyes filled with tears.

Mrs. Thuringen didn't ask any questions at all. She made only one astrological observation: Pluto was conjunct Uranus, which meant violence and strange power. "That means you must not be drawn into an argument if Pat calls." And then there was more fruit, and hot chocolate, and gingersnaps for Mary.

Just before her mother went up to her room for the night she took Zelly by her shoulders and said. "If you really mean to leave Pat I'll back you one thousand percent. You always have a home here, you know that. You and the baby just stay here as long as you like.

"But if you do change your mind again, you mustn't be

afraid to let yourself do what your heart says is right. If you wake up tomorrow morning and discover you really just want to go home, I don't want you to be afraid to tell me."

The needle scratched against the record. The silence contained within the walls grated like a jagged nail against the skin of her nerves. And yet she missed him. He was already in the past tense, in prison blues behind a high electrified gate, a photograph in a newspaper. And she missed him. Not what he was, and maybe not anything he had ever actually been, but the idea of him as she had always held it, hers, private and unseen by anyone; curiously, now, inviolable.

She hesitated above the old red portable record player, covered on the sides and around the edges with torn stickers: Fleetwood Mac, Bruce Springsteen, the Police. Pat was always telling her she had no taste in music. Remembering that hurt. They had stayed here last Christmas—before he had killed—and he couldn't listen to the records she'd left here, "The Eagles for Christ's sake?" so he'd brought something of his own; it was still there: Schubert's Quartetsatz. The record lay next to the record player; it was dusty. He must have forgotten it and then bought another copy, because he hadn't stopped playing it at home. He played it when the moon was full. Zelly surprised herself by knowing that—but she could see it, the moon fat through the window; she could hear the music now.

It was stupid; she was crying. It was worse than if he were dead. Bruce Springsteen—*The Wild, the Innocent, and the E Street Shuffle*. Her hand reached out but picked up the Schubert instead. She moved the needle over the record. The single strand of music soared up and away, plaintive and exhausted. There was no future outside the black squares of the windows. No tomorrow. No past, even. Zelly leaned back against the pillow and closed her eyes.

\* \* \*

A door slammed downstairs. Zelly froze. The door slammed again and again in her brain, until, in an endless fraction of a second, she recognized the sound: a branch hitting against glass. When it came again she was ready for it.

# 54

Washington Street was crowded, with cars and people and movement and light. Madeleine's heart was racing; John could feel it. At a light they pulled up three cars behind the van and her hand found his across the cold awkward shift knob and the paper-cup holder. Third Street, Fourth, all the way up to Eighth. There was a stoplight at every corner. John made sure he kept two or three cars behind the van. The car in front of them was beating out a rhythm of rap music and drums that shook their bodies through their seats. The sound echoed off the four- and five-story buildings that lined the avenue, and every face turned toward it. The sidewalks were crowded with white metal tables; every other storefront seemed to be a restaurant, Tex-Mex, Italian, Thai. Every table outside every restaurant was full. The van slunk among the traffic on the busy street, it sucked up light and vibrated with threat. Of course it looked like any other van and nobody noticed it.

"I've never been to Hoboken before," Madeleine said. "I didn't know it was such a happening place. I wonder why he said, 'Help me.' "

"If he said it."

"If. This looks kind of like Bleecker Street on a good night. I thought this place was supposed to be dead." The word "dead" sounded like an obscenity.

There were groups of people crossing everywhere along the crowded blocks; nobody paid much attention to lights or corners. Six or seven college students walked right in front of John's car. They were walking backward, looking at a girl walking backward away from them and saying something: "Cigarettes? I need to get cigarettes. Do you—" John became aware again of the knife at his side.

"This place reminds me a little of Bleecker Street, too," he said. Where Cheryl had disappeared.

A horn blared right on their tail and John lifted his foot from where he had unthinkingly pressed it against the brake pedal. Suddenly other horns blared too, like dogs taking up a cry, and John looked up the street and slammed the brake again, and brakes around them squealed and crunched and for a second horns and voices reached a cacophonous pitch. But John didn't hear any of it. Ahead of them, half a block, a whole block, two, there were cars, and the lights were turning red.

The black van had disappeared.

# 55

Poor Zelly. Mrs. Thuringen lay in bed looking at the patterns the leaf shadows made against the ceiling. Zelly was so fragile now, so brittle, like a chrysalis with something terrible inside waiting to take wing. Mrs. Thuringen had been wrong to send Zelly back to him, she knew that now. Something had obviously happened since then—Zelly would tell her in time—but she was at a loss to know what it might be. She could hear music from down the hall in Zelly's room. She recognized the piece, it was one of the only ones she knew the name of: the Quartetsatz. Pat was always playing that. Mrs. Thuringen felt a moment's irritation: Don't play that. That was music to wallow in, and Mrs. Thuringen would have no wallowing in her house.

He had humiliated her daughter in some way. Mrs. Thuringen was aware of the inadequacies of her imagination, which was not modern. Had Zelly found incontrovertible proof of infidelity? Had Pat done something that could not be explained or forgiven? She herself had not quite gotten over the panties-in-the-mail idea. Did he appear by the side of the bed one night *wearing* the panties? Mrs. Thuringen smiled to herself involuntarily, with a pang of guilt, and the back door closed.

All of her mind became a laser point of concentration. She saw the leaves moving in shadow shapes with preternatural clarity. Each leaf was serrated, like a knife. They intermingled in a meaningless slow-motion pavane on the ceiling above the bed. The back door had just closed. A little snick, a sound as familiar, after thirty years, as the sound of her own intake of breath. The door had been opened; somebody had just come in.

Mrs. Thuringen counted the seconds. On the seventh step the floor would creak. All of her ten children had come in late as teenagers and been caught out by that guilty seventh step. Five, six—and a small squeak. Somebody was walking across the kitchen floor.

John and Madeleine drove in controlled hysteria up and down the streets off Washington. Down one block, up another, John hastily scanning the parked vehicles and feeling his pulse race when he thought—but it was a gray one. Eighth Street, up to Ninth, past row houses and the occasional bar, keeping count in his head because there weren't any street signs. Madeleine looked out the window; he knew she was crying.

It was over. The police had the tip, let the police find the killer. But he would think, in years to come, whenever he looked at Madeleine over the breakfast table or over the heads of their children, that the man was still alive somewhere. The man would have a name and they would know where he was being kept, on some death row or in some hospital—but he would be alive. And Cheryl would turn to liquid and dust, and the man would be alive.

"There," Madeleine said; it had all happened already in his head and so for a moment he didn't know what she was talking about. But the van was there, sliding silently into a long driveway at the side of a house with a tall green hedge.

Mrs. Thuringen lay absolutely still. The leaves intertwined obscenely. It was Pat, of course. Indignation welled in her breast and shot down her arms into her fingers. She clenched her fists and unclenched them, like a fighter limbering up for a bout, and got out of bed. Her feet found her slippers immediately, from long habit.

There was no sound now. Why didn't he just ring the doorbell? She had no doubt it was Pat. She wanted to ask him: What did you do to her? To make her look as if she had seen something. Mrs. Thuringen didn't know what Zelly had seen, but whatever it was had taken all the trust out of her eyes.

It had been so hard not to say anything. Her daughter had hardly put the baby down all day. Her eyes kept seeing something else; the living room wasn't there for her, the sun room where she used to play with her brothers wasn't there. "I can feel autumn already," she'd said once, looking out the sunroom window. But her mother knew that the chill was only inside her.

Mrs. Thuringen's feet did not falter: The rug was threadbare, if you didn't know it you would trip. The bannister squeaked just at the top of the stairs; Mrs. Thuringen put her hand just ahead of the spot. This time she wouldn't send her daughter back. There was no one at the bottom of the stairs.

"Pat?" Mrs. Thuringen spoke softly; no point in waking

Zelly yet. A swift creak and then nothing. She could envision the foot poised to come down. Besides, she wanted to have a word with Pat herself.

"Pat, come here right this minute. I want to talk to you." After ten children she could be anybody's mother, and almost anybody would find himself doing her bidding like a child. There was a moment's hesitation and then the foot came down. And footsteps could be heard, in measured pace, coming toward the living room.

Going up the dark path next to the house was the hardest part. The van's motor settled eerily in the driveway, next to a big stone house with a high box hedge surrounding it. A dark figure had disappeared up a narrow path. Following him was very hard. When he wasn't there, crouched and waiting with a knife, it got easier.

John motioned for Madeleine to stay in the car but he didn't know if she would. He couldn't hear her behind him; he couldn't hear anything but his own breathing.

A pane of glass was broken on the back door. There was a deep long yard that faded to nothing, and the houses on either side were dark. The imperfect moon lit the leaves of a bush silver—it was a creeping yew, and John surprised himself by noticing that. In a few months it would have little orange poison berries all over it.

The glass door was ajar. John's hand went where the man's hand had gone, grasping the handle (he half-expected it to move under his fingers), and he was inside. A kitchen, with a black-and-white linoleum floor. Step on a crack, break your mother's back. If he stepped on that floor, would it hold his weight?

He crossed the kitchen but he could hear nothing. There was a hallway and a lot of doors. There was a noise somewhere—a footstep? But he couldn't tell where. There was music, maybe classical, very faint. He started toward the sound. He was aware of every hair on his body and he was aware of nothing at all—the doors, closed, on either side of the hallway, the brown carpeting on the floor.

He stopped beside the first door and put his ear to the wood and listened. The wood made a seashell sound against his ear. Had there been a voice? He opened the door—the single bravest action of his life—and he couldn't see anything at all. Books, a desk, a vase full of leaves or a mass of spiders—there was a noise behind him. A voice? Not behind him, but the other way down the hall.

He didn't close the door. He backed out of the room and turned but the doors all looked the same this way too. Like Alice he chose one.

Mrs. Thuringen took two steps down the stairs and then she saw his face. His face was completely calm. He was saying something. It wasn't the knife he held in his right hand that frightened her, it was his face. *He is,* she thought, stepping backward up the stairs, her foot for the first time in thirty years unsure. Zelly had said it, they had laughed about it, the absurdity of it, *he is, he is, he is,* and he sprang up the steps and her arm went up and the first cut didn't even hurt she was so surprised—*he is*—and she found her voice to scream but could not find her daughter's name, or even, "He is," but only a wordless howl like a dog or a cat.

In the dark in the kitchen Madeleine found the telephone where it hung on the wall, and with difficulty her fingers found the right buttons: 911. The phone rang once. "Jersey City Police, three-five-six?" A woman's voice.

"I'm in a house in Hoboken with the Symphony Slasher," she whispered into the receiver.

"Did you say Hoboken, miss? The number for the Hoboken Police Department is five-five-five, two-one-hundred."

"But I'm with the *Slasher*. Can't you send somebody? I think the house is—"

"I can't hear you, miss," the voice said placidly. "Can you speak up?" Madeleine hung up the phone. This could not be happening. Breathe, she told herself. Two-one-hundred. She punched the buttons (with the little musical beep loud in her ear) and waited. Just breathe; they'll come.

There was a violin playing, and for a moment Zelly didn't know where she was. She was going to get new curtains for her room. She thought she heard her mother calling her. Then she snapped awake and all the particulars of her life fell back into place. The baby—that was the first thought, and then all the rest followed. Had there been a sound?

"Maybe he won't call until tomorrow," she said to the stuffed bear next to the head of the bed where she'd been lying, against the wall. Mr. Brown. One of his eyes had come off once a long time ago and her mother had sewn it back on with blue thread. Zelly's fingers traced the button eye absently, lovingly. Mr. Brown. She reached down into her fanny pack where it hung around her waist. She missed Mary for a moment, fiercely, even though she was in the next room. She rooted through the fanny pack for Mary's little button-eyed bear to hold. It was a talisman, as her baby was a talisman, a guarantee that there would be a future.

The bear was gone. At least she couldn't find it—a pen, tissues, rosy lipstick, coins—anywhere in the pack. Not at the bottom either. There was the silver feather earring, wrapped in a pink tissue. It lay on the tissue like a tear. But where was the bear? When had she—the van. Last night in the van.

She'd thought she heard her mother calling. She couldn't hear anything now except the Quartetsatz. She couldn't have been asleep for more than a moment. No door slammed, no floorboard creaked. But there had been something, like a cry, while she'd been sleeping. Zelly got out of bed and walked out into the hall.

The kitchen, the hallway, doors. John had never seen so many doors. Every room seemed to have three or four. He was in what looked to be a sewing room. He had heard the scream—whose house was this?—and he had run toward the sound and hit his shin soundly on a box or a stack of something and he'd shoved open a door, his leg throbbing—he hadn't made a sound but he thought for an idiotic minute that somebody must have heard the pain screaming up his leg—and found himself in another empty room. He was furious with his leg. This room had three doors; he had heard a scream and the stomach-clenching sound of a short fall, a thud like a body falling down steps.

He headed through the door nearest the direction of the noise and found himself in the hall just outside the kitchen again. There was the very faint sound of music. The noises had been maddeningly close. Where was Madeleine? He realized he had never been afraid before. Really afraid. He kept forgetting to breathe. He had his knife in his hand and it didn't make him feel anything except more afraid. He could only hope with a sick feeling that Madeleine had stayed in the car.

The phone rang once, loud in her ear. "Hoboken Police Department, may I help you?"

Madeleine spoke low and fast. "I'm in a house with the Symphony Slasher."

"Can you give me the address, please?" A man's voice now.

"I don't know the address. The house has a high hedge around it."

"We'll need more information than that. Can you tell me the telephone number?"

Madeleine's eyes locked on the strip where the number should be. It was blank. She forced herself to breathe: in and out. "No," she said. "Please. Can't you trace my call?"

"Well," the man said evenly, "not if we pick up on the first or second ring. It doesn't get into the system." Madeleine was holding the receiver so hard it hurt her hand.

"Do you know what section of town you're in?"

"No." She couldn't breathe; she was going to cry, or scream. She forced herself to speak normally. "There aren't any street signs."

"Listen, I'm going to put you through to somebody who can help you. You just hold on."

There was a noise outside the room. Were those footsteps she heard, coming down the hall outside the kitchen door?

"Lieutenant Viscotti, may I help you?" The man's voice was loud. "Shh," Madeleine said without thinking.

"Miss, you say you're in a house with the Symphony Slasher?"

"Yes!"

"May I ask who you are?"

"I'm Madeleine Levy. Call the Slasher Task Force, they know. Madeleine Levy. This is not a joke. I'm somewhere in Hoboken with the Slasher, he's in the house. I don't know whose house it is—"

"What are you doing there?"

"It doesn't matter. The *Slasher* is here. Can't you just trace the goddamn call?"

"It isn't that simple, Miss Levy. Just stay calm. We're checking our indicator system right now. If the phone rings more than twice over here—"

"The phone rang one goddamn time. Don't you have any equipment over there to trace calls?"

"If your number is not listed with our indicator system we will contact New Jersey Bell and have them trace the call. They will get back to us with the number—"

There was a noise outside the door. Madeleine heard it clearly. A noise, like footsteps, right outside. If he heard her she was dead. "Hurry," she whispered into the receiver before soundlessly placing it back in its cradle. And then she was gone.

There was something lying at the bottom of the steps. Her mother was lying at the bottom of the steps. Zelly went down the steps as if she were just going down the steps, not as if her mother were lying at the bottom of them, probably dead. Her mother lay twisted, like a thing that had happened to break, and there was a stain and a bad smell. Zelly stopped before she got to the bottom, one foot poised in midair; then she turned and in one motion was running back up the steps.

She was thinking and she wasn't thinking. "Dead" had registered without content or emotional weight. Dead and "the baby," and she was running, taking the steps two at a time, while her brain was still processing the information that if the bowels had voided the body was certainly dead.

The baby's room was at the end of the upstairs hall. Could he have passed her room before she came out? There was a light on in the baby's room; not the night-light. The hall was endless and she wasn't thinking but she had an image in her head: her mother's sewing scissors. Were they in the sewing room downstairs or had her mother left them in the living room or were they in the basket next to her bed on the second floor? The rooms on either side of the hallway jerked by at the periphery of her vision; would she see the gleam of her mother's scissors? The mirror of a bathroom cabinet glistened as she went by. The heavy books in her father's library, the hairbrushes on dresser tops, the ornate patterned rug in her sister Molly's room—and then she saw the gleam. It was only for an instant. The scissors were there, innocent and sharp, and Zelly ran over to the basket fast but carefully, quietly, and as she bent over the basket the baby began to cry. Everything froze for a fraction of a heartbeat and Zelly's hand was on cold, reassuring metal (*Mama's scissors, Mama's dead now*) and she had already turned toward the sound of her daughter crying, the scissors wedged between her fanny pack and her waist underneath her light summer sweater (*Mama's dead the baby's crying*) and she was at the door to the baby's room.

Pat was standing in the middle of the room holding Mary. He was holding her in one hand, and in the other he held a knife. There was blood on the knife. Mary hadn't liked being woken up, that's why she was crying. Mary loved her daddy, he never made her cry. She didn't know it was her grandma's blood.

"Give me the baby," Zelly said. Her voice was calm.

"Hello, Zelly." Pat's voice was calm and gentle. "In the park that time, I don't remember, was it a girl baby or a boy baby?"

"It was a boy baby." Mary was working herself up into a

fury. Her little face was beet-red. "Pat, the baby's crying. Please give her to me."

"You know who I am." Pat was smiling at her across the room. She was freezing and her palms were hot and wet. The metal of the scissors was freezing against her skin.

"Yes," she said, "I know who you are."

They looked at each other. "I have to kill you now," Pat said.

"Put the baby down."

"It's not because you know. Even though," his voice rising suddenly, his arm where he cradled Mary tensing, his fist tensing, "you shouldn't have done what you did. You should not have gone into my van you know that don't you?" He was yelling and the baby was yelling and then he got quiet all of a sudden. "I would have anyway. I know now. Do you remember what I said?" Zelly stared into his eyes above Mary's crying face. "The greatest love—" he prompted.

"The moment of death is the moment of greatest love."

"Yes. The greatest love." He looked down and smiled. "I wish," he spat out, raising his head, "that this brat would shut up."

"Give her to me. I can shut her up."

"Of course you can. You're her mother." The word sounded like an obscenity and it sounded so sad. Zelly felt a bolt of anger like electricity. "Yes," she said. "Give her to me." Pat was halfway across the room. He had raped, and he had murdered. And he had murdered her mother.

"Come get her," he said, and he smiled a little.

Zelly took one step toward him. "You don't want to hurt the baby, Pat. Just put her down."

"Put her down? Don't you want her? Come here." One step more. If he reached for her now he would probably miss. She stood. "Put the baby down, Pat."

"You're beginning to get on my nerves, hon." His voice was rising again. Mary wailed.

"If you put her down I can get her to go to sleep."

"You shouldn't have gone into the van," he said quietly. "I never wanted to kill you. But now—well," smiling a little, the arm holding the knife slackening, lowering, "now that I have no choice I find it isn't really such a hard decision. Is it, Zelly? Not really so hard at all."

"Pat," Zelly said softly, "put the baby back in the crib." Her husband continued to look past her. "I didn't think you'd ever find out," he said. "But now that you have . . . well. But maybe not the baby, huh, hon? Maybe." He turned and bent a little, lowering Mary into her crib. Zelly tried to keep her face impassive. "That's right, Pat. Put her in her crib," and his eyes snapped back toward hers and his arms snapped back up and the baby wailed again.

"You think I'm stupid, bitch?" he screamed, and then suddenly he did bend down, and he gently put Mary back into the Port-O-Crib. For a moment his head was down—the crib was on the floor—and he wasn't looking at Zelly but she didn't move.

Pat rooted around a second and found a bottle under the blankets and put it gently in his daughter's mouth and smiled down at her. Then he straightened up and smiled at his wife. He raised the knife a little, showing it to her, and took a step toward her across the room. "And maybe yes," he said, "after."

There was nothing else in the world but the baby, not even the knife. Already Mary had almost stopped crying, the way babies do; she was sucking the bottle even though her breathing was still snaggled every third or fourth breath by strangling sobs. When Pat took his hands away from her (holding the knife awkwardly away from her body as he used both hands to put her into the crib) Zelly felt a cold thrill on her own body just where Pat's hands had touched her daughter's. Pat took another step. If he went after her the baby would be safe. Another step. Cold just above the knees, as though she had been lifted out of cold water. The baby would be safe. When Zelly turned and ran, the cold chill raced up over her whole body and out the top of her head.

There was a light at the top of the stairs. The stairs were across a dark room; the darker bulk of a sofa crouched in one corner like an animal. There were chairs, a patterned rug. The room was bigger than the ones John had already gone through, and it was airier. The living room. The man was upstairs, John was certain of that. He had heard something—running feet—just before he came through the door. There were two other doors, but the sound had been going up.

There was faint light coming in through the windows. There was a body at the bottom of the stairs. John hadn't seen it at first as being apart from the other large, dark forms of tables and chairs. It lay sprawled where it had fallen, probably down the stairs.

John walked toward the body, forgetting caution. It was a middle-aged woman in a flowered nightgown. One thigh was obscenely exposed. He could see the woman's face; it was devoid of expression, as though death were boring.

Who was the woman? What was the man doing here? There was a baby crying. The sound was so incongruous that it had not even registered. John's ears had been tuned to the faintest whisper of a footstep, the faraway closing of a door. There was music playing and a baby crying.

There were voices coming from upstairs but all he could hear were the cadences. Then silence, and then a man's angry reply. And the baby's crying.

John ran up the stairs with no thought of caution or his own safety anymore: a baby. The voices were coming from the left. John ran down the hall toward them, but when he came to a room it was empty. He could hear music playing from beyond a door on the far wall. Then there was another hall, and another room, and the music was coming from beyond that door. And John wrenched the door open, his heart a living thing in his throat.

Someone had just come down the stairs. Madeleine didn't know where the stairs were. The moon shown in a lopsided circle outside the window. The footsteps were coming toward her; they were running. She was in a large dark room that was crowded with furniture; she was afraid that if she moved she would bump into something and make a noise.

In the darkness she could see his face. He might be anywhere. She looked at his face inside her head. The lip pulled back in private ecstasy while he hurt her. She looked around for a weapon. If he came through the door she could kill him, but she could not survive looking into his face.

The room was brightly lit. Books lined the walls, and there was a big roll-top desk in one corner. There was a stuffed pink poodle on the floor. There was a playpen in the middle of the floor. John moved over toward the crib, feeling faint—the baby made no sound—but she was only sleeping. She wore a little pink gown with a ruffle and elephants and she was sucking her bottle in her sleep; her lips pulsed beneath her closed eyes. There were tears on her face and her skin was red and mottled. There was a noise behind him. Footsteps, maybe voices, out there in the dark outside the bright door. John turned and followed the sound.

\*    \*    \*

At the bottom of the steps she had to jump over her mother's body. For one sick second in the air she was afraid she would land on it. It was rage that fueled the jump, rage that sent her surefooted across the living room into the sun room beyond. To lay herself down by that body would be a luxury—never to get up. Her mother, her baby. Her baby—she had to keep going. Anything else he'd done didn't even matter. He had killed her mother. If she even allowed her brain to complete the thought she would be paralyzed. But she had to move. If he found her he would kill her too, and who would there be between him and the baby? Her brother Daniel used to hide under the drop of the long tablecloth on the big wooden table over by the far wall. Joey used to just open a door and hide behind it and when you came to get him he jumped out and scared you and ran away: he said it didn't count unless you tagged him.

Zelly slipped behind the dark red brocade curtains that covered the window seat. There were curtains on the inside as well, against the glass, keeping out the night. She felt her mother's scissors, useless inside her sweater. The seat was small, a child's size. Zelly pulled her knees up against her body and hugged them. She could hardly breathe; a cough caught in her throat. She could hear Pat walking deliberately toward this room. It had been a stupid place to go. He would know she was in here.

"Zelly," his voice came, gentle as a snake, "I know you're in there. I have so much to tell you. Come home with me." Zelly knew she had gotten to the point where she almost literally couldn't think anymore. The images welled up without words—her mother, her mother dead, her baby, newsprint pictures of dead girls, a blackened spot on a crumpled tarp, an earring, a tiny brown bear, a knife. If she put words to the images she would begin to scream. The scream was there already.

"Zelly," Pat was saying; he had moved past the sun-room door, into the room. "I could kill the brat now, Zelly. I could go back upstairs—" He stood in the doorway now. Zelly could see him in her mind, in the pitch blackness of the window seat she could see him. She put her hand under her sweater and touched cold metal.

Lieutenant Viscotti: tapped the cradle of the telephone until he heard a dial tone. "Get me the Slasher Task Force," he said. "Kirby!" he yelled to an officer passing his door. "Get ready to put out an all-points. House with a hedge. Black van in driveway. Sirens on."

"What've we got?"

"Looks like we've got the Symphony Slasher in our backyard. I'm running this past the Slasher Task Force now. Concentrate on the area around Stevens—where the old houses are. There are hedges there repeat, sirens on. Get the car closest to Castle Point Terrace—" He paused, raised his hand, then motioned to Kirby. "Yes," he said into the phone. "This is Lieutenant Vincent Viscotti of the Hoboken Police Department—"

The door was already open, and maybe that saved his life. If he had opened the door the man would have seen him. The man was standing in a doorway across this dark room. He was a shadow only, a big outline of a man, almost invisible in the dark.

The shadow figure was bulkier at one side, halfway down; an arm held a little bit out from the body, a thickening. John stood stock still; he was holding a knife and the man was holding a knife.

The man moved into the room. "Zelly," he said—John thought it was "Zelly"—"I want to go home now, don't you? Where did you hide from those bastard brothers of yours?" The voice was calm and mocking. The man was moving toward where John stood half-hidden behind the open door. When the man started yelling John became acutely aware of how cool the metal doorknob was against his hand. "Where the fuck are you, you bitch? I'll stick you like a chicken, you dirty cunt! You never, never, never—" and each "never" was punctuated by the man's fist slamming against a tipsy end table, smashing something made of china, upending a lamp onto the floor—"*never* knew who I was! With all your stupid reading and all your stupid theories and fucking prognostications"—books and another lamp and a pillow went now—"you never knew! So—" and the voice dropped suddenly—"let's go home. The baby's crying, Zelly." And it was, again, a thin keening. This time John was sure the man said, "Zelly."

"The baby's crying and I know you're in here and it's time to go now." The voice was consoling. A child might have come. John wondered where Zelly could be hiding. Was the baby the man's baby? The man moved to one of the windows and pulled back the shade with a single sweep of his hand. Pale light from the street poured in and made a big puddle of light in the middle of the floor. The rug was blue, John noticed, with flowers on it. The man walked to another window; John could see now that the room was circular on one side, with four curtained windows in an arc along one wall. The man stood thoughtfully in front of another window, his hand on the curtain. There was a wedding ring on his hand. John wanted to call out, to tell Zelly that someone else was here with her and that the baby was okay. But if John moved at all the man would see him; he would turn. And when he turned it was by no means certain that Zelly, whoever she was, would be any safer than she was right now.

"Zelly," the man said with exaggerated patience, "come out now and I won't kill the baby." He jerked the second curtain open. The room got still lighter. There was no rustle, no hint of anyone else in the room. "Okay, bitch," the man said conversationally, "I'll be going back upstairs now. If you don't think I'll kill Mary, just think again. Am I capable of it? Will I kill her? You know. You decide."

Suddenly there was a rustling from one of the floor-length curtains that covered the bay windows, and a woman stepped out and into the light. She looked very young.

"Good choice, Zelly," the man said.

"Pat," she said. The simplicity with which she spoke was shocking. The man had a name and this woman knew his name. She was his wife. She was wearing a wedding ring too; John had not thought that the man could have a wife. A wife, a baby. A life. The woman just stood, simply and without defense, and looked at the man.

"Pat," she said again. The man looked at her and John thought he was crying but it was only a trick of the light.

"Blackman here." He held the radio mike in a clenched fist. "We're in front of Wyche's house. The Jersey guy never showed. Request to proceed with interro—damn it, I know. I know." He paused, listening. "What?" he asked. "You just—what? An all-points bulletin? What's that—house with a hedge," signaling to Scottie, who immediately started the car's engine. "Yes. Got it. Sirens. Out."

The car was halfway down the block before Blackman spoke again. "The Hoboken Police just put out an all-points on the Slasher," he said. "Madeleine Levy called, said she was in a house with him. They don't know where. Turn the goddamn siren on and drive. I'm not going to sit on my ass waiting for news of the next murder."

From where John stood behind the door, the man was only about ten feet away. The woman was lovely—what an odd thing to notice. Her hair was paler than Madeleine's or Cheryl's, and the sadness in her face was beyond anything John had ever seen. She stood as though she were being held up by a wire at the top of her spine. The man stood before her. He was big. Much bigger than the woman, than Madeleine, than Cheryl.

The man's name was Pat. It was Pat that had killed John's sister. Pat that had raped and tried to kill Madeleine. Pat's wife, if that's what she was, simply stood before him. There was no pleading in her eyes. One hand hung down, one rested at her belt.

"Don't you want to go home?" Pat asked her. John did not dare move.

"I do," said the woman. Zelly. Light from the windows silhouetted them both, and she stood in a nimbus of light. Now her face was beyond sorrow or fear or anything John could name. Her face could have been carved out of rock. She didn't move, and John waited, watching her magnificent resignation, and then she sprang straight toward her husband.

Zelly sprang, and John saw the flash of something silver in her hand, and he did not hesitate: he ran toward the man, his knife firm in his own.

Pat wasn't ready for Zelly to come at him, and neither of them was ready for someone else to be in the room. Pat was caught completely off guard.

When he turned from his wife's attack he turned straight into John. John moved, and the knife went into Pat (which is what John was idiotically thinking, *The knife is going into Pat now*) and John felt it all the way up his arms, it felt the way it feels to hold a knife when it goes into a piece of cake; there was that same spongy resistance.

The man—Pat—was down. The woman—Zelly—was standing directly in front of him with her hand held up—protecting, supplicating—and there was blood on the front of her shirt. He saw what she was holding—scissors—saw that the scissors were covered with blood and her arm was bloody too and her eyes were enormous. John's eyes met them for an instant and then he was bent over the body, stabbing, stabbing, and with each terrified thrust all he thought was, *Don't get up, Don't get up,* and he might have been saying it, and it seemed like he'd never be sure, could never be sure, the man would get up—Pat would get up—he couldn't be dead it was too easy, and the feeling, creeping like a numbness up his pumping arm *he's dead he's dead he's dead* the image of Madeleine the image of Cheryl—dead—he was pumping his arm up and down and he couldn't stop and then there was a hand on his arm and he dropped the knife and it was Madeleine but his hand was shaking, the woman was just looking at him and his hand was shaking.

Zelly's face was very calm. She could have been looking at what was in front of her or she could have been looking at something far away. There was some sort of odd light over everything, odd shining light—and every line and every hair was clear. Pat's face where he lay on the carpet was very clear in that light; one eye was visible, it looked at the carpet and there was blood at his nose, and along his cheek there was a long, thin line of blood. The blood seemed to eat up the light.

John was panting, and he felt nothing. He turned to face Madeleine. Somewhere, incongruously, a baby was crying. The sound mingled in his head with another, high-pitched, keening sound, and both seemed to be coming from a long way away, and coming closer, and he looked at Madeleine with his bloody hand held out, and listened without comprehension to the sound of the baby crying and the approaching sirens.

*Acknowledgments*

I would like to thank my dear friend Jane Cushman; I will always be glad I sent it to Jane. Also my friend and editor Susan Kamil, whom I fought every step of the way: I'm happy you won. And my husband, David Bayer, without whom I would not have this life. Also David Doty, for his invaluable help with research. And, finally, Kobe Japanese restaurant and Le Royal de Paris, where much of this book was written.

*About the Author*

JESSIE PRICHARD HUNTER lives in Hoboken, New Jersey, with her husband and daughter. *Blood Music* is her first book.